More praise for
an hour in paradise

D0106216

"Leegant reveals herself to be an empathic, gifted creator of people and worlds."   —*Publishers Weekly*

"Leegant's provocative and memorable stories, suffused with Jewish lore and wisdom, are not just terrific Jewish short stories . . . Leegant's characters are unforgettable."   —Susan Miron, *The Forward*

"A collection [that] dazzles with humanity and other-worldliness."
—Sara K. Eisen, *Jerusalem Report*

"Leegant demonstrates talent and flexibility. . . . Ten debut stories explore the challenges and meaning of modern Judaism."
—*Kirkus Reviews*

"Wonderfully nuanced stories . . . one wants to shout out the word that a new, very talented Jewish-American writer has arrived. . . . *An Hour in Paradise* is, in short, the real goods."
—*New Jersey Jewish News*

"A stunning debut. . . . Rich and soul-satisfying stories that linger long after the tales have ended."
—Fran Heller, *Cleveland Jewish News*

"[A] splendid debut collection. . . . Displaying a generous spirit and a sense of humour, Leegant offers up parables about ordinary miracles granted to those who seek love, or forgiveness, or even a glimpse of the . . . divine." —K. Gordon Neufeld, *Calgary Herald*

"[Leegant's] characters throb with life and humanity. . . . Compassion for the Jewish condition in all its quirky manifestations rings through every line of these fast-paced tales."
—Shoshana London Sappir, *Hadassah*

"At once magical and down-to-earth, Leegant's memorable stories reflect on the spiritual nature of the human quest for self-understanding." —Bonny V. Fetterman, *Reform Judaism*

"Absorbing tales, with writing that's full of verve and wit."
—Sandee Brawarsky, *Jewish Woman*

"Young and old, men and women, all are authentic in Leegant's creative hands. . . . These stories are a pleasure to read."
—Gila Wertheimer, *Chicago Jewish Star*

"Each [story] is a gem."
—Vicki Cabot, *Jewish News of Greater Phoenix*

"With a narrative voice that is part Gabriel Garcia Marquez, part Philip Roth, and part Jonathan Safran Foer, [Leegant] traverses the spectrum of modern Jewish identities."
—Emily Klein, *J: The Jewish News Weekly of Northern California*

"*An Hour in Paradise* surprises, satisfies."
—Stuart Lewis, *Kansas City Jewish Chronicle*

"Leegant has a gift for catching moments of truth and pain in lives that did not unfold as planned." —Sylvia Rothchild, *Jewish Advocate*

"Leegant moves with ease from one fictional voice to another. . . . [Her] scenarios . . . play out with humor, grace and a sense of divine mystery hovering just beyond their horizons." —*Lilith*

"Move over, Nathan Englander. This collection is a dream of a read, its lovable characters drawn with wit and warmth. Each story is a gift, a guided tour of a perfect small calamity of the heart and soul." —Elinor Lipman, author of *The Inn at Lake Devine*

"Joan Leegant writes stories that last, stories that take root in the soul. The worlds she creates are all rendered with care, with love, and with a steel-eyed resolve to give us the truth of ourselves. This collection marks the beginning of what I am certain will be a long and important literary career." —Bret Lott, author of *Jewel*

"Joan Leegant is a gifted storyteller, blessed with the insight and wisdom to highlight those moments that change and define whole lives. These characters—wildly different in voice and situation, yet all craving a sense of self—all but leap from the page. Their stories are compelling and memorable." —Jill McCorkle, author of *Creatures of Habit*

an hour in paradise

an hour in paradise

stories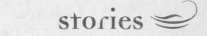

joan leegant

w. w. norton & company
new york london

OUACHITA TECHNICAL COLLEGE

Some of the stories in this collection were originally published, in slightly different form, as follows: "The Tenth" in *Nimrod International Journal* (Fall/Winter 1998) and in *With Signs & Wonders: An International Anthology of Jewish Fabulist Fiction,* Daniel M. Jaffe, editor, Invisible Cities Press, Montpelier, 2001; "Lucky in Love" in *Columbia: A Journal of Literature and Art* (Winter 2001); "How to Comfort the Sick and Dying" in *Bellingham Review* (Spring 2001); "The Lament of the Rabbi's Daughters" (as "The Four Daughters") in *New England Review* (Fall 2002); "The Seventh Year" in *Prairie Schooner* (Summer 2002); "Henny's Wedding" in *American Literary Review* (Fall 2000); "Accounting" in *Crazyhorse* (Fall 2002); "The Diviners of Desire: A Modern Fable" (as "The Diviners of Desire") in *Pakn Treger* (Summmer 2002).

Copyright © 2003 by Joan Leegant

All rights reserved
Printed in the United States of America
First published as a Norton paperback 2004

For information about permission to reproduce selections from this book, write to Permissions, W. W. Norton & Company, Inc. 500 Fifth Avenue, New York, NY 10110

Manufacturing by Quebecor World, Fairfield
Book design by Blue Shoe Studio
Production manager: Amanda Morrison

Library of Congress Cataloging-in-Publication Data
Leegant, Joan.
An hour in paradise : stories / Joan Leegant.
p. cm.
ISBN 0-393-05439-X (hardcover)
I. Title.
PS3612.E3495H68 2003
813'.54—dc21

2003005445

ISBN 0-393-32584-9 pbk.

W. W. Norton & Company, Inc.
500 Fifth Avenue, New York, N.Y. 10110
www.wwnorton.com

W. W. Norton & Company Ltd.
Castle House, 75/76 Wells Street, London W1T 3QT

1 2 3 4 5 6 7 8 9 0

PS
3612
E3495
H68
2003

FOR ALLEN

EVEN AN HOUR IN PARADISE IS WORTHWHILE.

—Yiddish proverb

CONTENTS

ACKNOWLEDGMENTS

For support during the writing of this book, my sincere thanks to the Massachusetts Cultural Council and the MacDowell Colony, where several of these stories were written. I am indebted to Elaine Markson, my agent, and her assistant, Gary Johnson, for their unflagging enthusiasm, and to Jill Bialosky and Deirdre O'Dwyer at W. W. Norton for their exceptional care and expertise. My appreciation to the editors of the journals and anthologies in which many of these stories first appeared, with special thanks to Paul Zakrzewski and Dan Jaffe. For their encouragement all along the way, I thank Art Edelstein, Bret Lott, Sharon Sheehe Stark, Chris Noel, Ellen Lesser, and Sena Jeter Naslund. Special thanks to Nathan Ehrlich, Peretz Rodman, and my mother, Selma Leegant, for help with factual details ranging from Talmudic tractates to the geography of the Bronx. Finally, my inexpressible thanks to the three who make it possible for me to write at all, my sons, Eli and Nathie, and my husband, Allen Katzoff. Their love and support are beyond measure.

an hour in paradise

THE TENTH

AFTER FIFTY-ONE YEARS as a rabbi, Samuel Steele had believed until that morning that when it came to the often elusive tenth man needed to complete a minyan, he had seen everything. Drag queens. Blond farm boys with names like Swenson, Nordstrom. A former monk who sometimes wore his robes. He gazed out the big window of the study in what he was sure would be his last shul—small, sparsely attended, and like almost all of its members, dying—and watched Beaconswood Avenue come to life. He had been wrong.

The steady flow of pedestrians had already absorbed all but one of the handful who'd made up that morning's quorum, conducting them like a gentle stream into the everyday world. It was a beautiful day, one of the first of real spring, the season always late getting to Boston, as if it had to stop somewhere else along the way. Birds, green leaves, a blue sky, like a postcard. The trolley stopped on the corner with a loud clang, the car Nathan Lefkowitz should have been on. Instead, Lefkowitz, at eighty-six the oldest of Samuel's congregants, lay sleeping on the couch behind him, recovering. It was Lefkowitz who had been charged that morning, as he had for the past forty years of mornings, as far as Samuel could tell, with finding the tenth man. They could pray without a full quorum but most of the men, some weeks all of them, were saying the Kaddish, which could only be said with the requisite ten. And what else could they do for their dead now but pray?

The door of the trolley flew shut, and the car lumbered on. Samuel glanced over at Lefkowitz, who was covered with a thick blue banquet cloth, the only thing Samuel could find in the closet, left from the days when the shul still put on functions. At six forty-five that morning Lefkowitz had posted himself outside the shul, standing by the door, as was his custom, counting. By ten to seven there were eight of them, including Samuel; by five minutes of the hour, they had nine.

Taking no chances, Lefkowitz had immediately begun to make the rounds, starting with the trolley stop. There, he would have politely inquired of any of the men if they were Jewish and, if so, could they help form a minyan. Samuel had watched him from the study window, as he did every time the older man ventured out, his small and ancient form draped in a gray raincoat. He admired Lefkowitz's style. He had been privy to a variety of techniques in his day, from strong-arm tactics laying the guilt on reticent Jews to the ultimate in discretion that verged on code, so much so that it was sometimes impossible to know what religion was involved, or even that it was religion at all. He appreciated Lefkowitz's straightforward manner.

Having no luck at the trolley stop, Lefkowitz had turned around and begun walking to the other end of the block. He passed Samuel at the window but didn't look up. At the other end, they both knew, was a less promising source, an apartment building heavily populated with college students. Samuel had never actually seen Lefkowitz at work there—the building was out of view—nor had he ever approached it himself. But he had heard enough to imagine. To guess that the handful of rumpled students who emerged at that hour probably didn't live there and had instead spent the night in someone else's apartment having too much to drink, or smoking marijuana, or being in love or something simulating it. It was hard to know. The two or three souls Lefkowitz had managed to pick up there in the year since Samuel had arrived invariably fled before the singing of *Adon Olam*, at the first sign of anyone removing a tallis and preparing to conclude lest, God forbid, they might have to face anyone, talk about themselves.

The street was perking up, more trolley clangs, more traffic. That morning, however, astonishingly, shockingly, Lefkowitz had been successful at the student apartment building: a set of Siamese twins.

Recruitment hadn't been involved. According to Lefkowitz's account after the service, he hadn't even opened his mouth when they stepped out of the doorway and said, *You're from the synagogue up the street, aren't you?* Lefkowitz was in the middle of telling this to Samuel when suddenly his face turned ashen and he began to tremble. Samuel helped get him onto the couch, then went to the kitchen for a cup of orange juice. By the time he got back, Lefkowitz was asleep. That was over an hour ago.

Now Lefkowitz was coughing himself awake. Samuel went to the couch, handed him the juice. "Did I tell you what they said to me as they came out of the doorway?" Lefkowitz said, as if he were dreaming, not an hour, not even a minute, having passed.

Samuel sat on the edge of the couch. Of course Lefkowitz was shaken up, they had all been shaken up. Not given to talk, especially not to anything resembling hysteria or gossip, the other men had left quickly, keeping their words brief, hushed, covert. *Poor fellows, God help them, see you tomorrow.*

But Lefkowitz was taking it the hardest. And why not? He was the one who'd first seen them, the one they talked to. " 'You're from the synagogue up the street, aren't you?'" Lefkowitz said. "That's what they said, Samuel."

"And then what happened?"

"I couldn't utter a word. Though they seemed nonplussed, like they were used to it." Lefkowitz paused. "I don't know how they live."

Samuel nodded. Who could imagine such a life, forever side by side with another? Where the line between where one began and the other ended disappeared halfway down? Or had never even existed?

Lefkowitz went on. "Finally, I began to recover my senses. But before I could think of what to say, they asked if they could come to the minyan." Lefkowitz's eyes, a faded gray that thirty years before might have been pale blue, seemed to be pleading with Samuel, as if Lefkowitz were afraid he'd made some terrible mistake. "So I asked if they were Jewish."

"And?"

"They said yes. But I couldn't tell who was talking. One of them or both. It was like one voice coming from two people, or two voices speaking at once. Or maybe one was speaking and the other gesturing. I couldn't tell, it was so confusing."

Samuel put his hand over Lefkowitz's. More than anything, they all feared confusion: the tricks the mind played, the lapses that happened without them knowing. But who wouldn't have been confused, the two of them standing in a doorway chatting with poor Lefkowitz as if coming upon such a tenth were the most natural thing in the world?

"The walk back is a blur," Lefkowitz said. "I don't know how we got here." He waved his free hand aimlessly. "All through the davening I'm thinking: I never saw them walk, how did they walk, one pair of legs, two half bodies on top, two arms?" The hand came down, limp, onto his chest. "But they must have walked in front of me. They were holding the door when I got here."

Samuel pressed Lefkowitz's hand. "Maybe you kept your eyes down, Nathan. Maybe you looked away, not to make them feel like a pariah." Lefkowitz turned, shook his head. "When in your life did you ever stare at the misfit, the cripple, the crazy person?" Samuel insisted. "You were fed it with your mother's milk like the rest of us: don't make a mockery of the stranger, a spectacle of the infirm."

Lefkowitz made a sad smile. "Paganism, that's what my father called it. The side shows at the circus, the veterans without legs that we looked at in the street." He paused, remembering. "By him, one look made it into a freak show, one glance and we were as bad as the barbarians who made midgets dance on tables. Always, we were one step away from idolatry."

"You're not losing your mind, Nathan. I'm telling you, you looked away. Wild horses couldn't have made you watch those two unfortunates."

AFTER POURING LEFKOWITZ another cup of juice and making him nibble on half a tuna sandwich that Samuel's wife, Ellie, had packed for lunch, Samuel put Lefkowitz in a cab with instructions not to even think about returning at dusk for mincha.

"We'll miss you but we'll manage, you have to rest," Samuel said at the door of the taxi. His disorientation, his near-faint, and, most distressing of all, his certainty that the fright he'd had was somehow his own doing, that he should not have engaged in conversation with the two young men: this, Samuel knew, was what Lefkowitz was thinking as the cab pulled away, Lefkowitz looking at him from the window, imploring, as the car melted into the traffic. Because at eighty-six one did not gloss over such disturbances of the ordinary. Nothing was chance.

Back inside, Samuel went into the sanctuary, the lights still on, the room just as he had left it when the service had concluded. He walked to the bima at the front, climbed its single step, stacked up the prayerbooks scattered along the table next to the wooden ark holding the shul's two Torahs, picked up someone's gloves, a box of cough drops. He glanced around the room. Except for the makeshift ones he'd managed to pull together in the military—an unused supply tent in Korea, a storeroom on an Air Force base on Cape Cod—this was the smallest shul he'd presided over, and the one he liked best. The whole place had a cluttered feel, a kind of intimate disorder he'd found himself craving after years of sterile spaciousness in his suburban posts. When the job came up, it made sense. They were moving to Brookline anyway, where Ellie had family and where they could tell themselves they were retiring so they wouldn't have to think about retiring somewhere else.

He put the gloves and cough drops on a little table that looked like a castoff from someone's redecorated living room, edging the gloves up against a pile of loosely folded tallises. Extras, for guests. The topmost one slid to the floor, one of the slippery types, smallish, for bar mitzvah boys. Had the visitors worn any? He didn't know. He picked it up, folded it, the silky fringes slipping out of the neat square as soon as he placed it back on the pile. With no sexton to keep things in order, things accumulated: unclaimed gloves, a menorah left standing until Pesach, more and more volumes scattered about. After a while he and Ellie would come in on a Sunday and spend the day putting away, organizing, dusting the bookcases in the study that had surely once been stately but, like everything else, were now chipped and marked, the shelves sagging.

He picked up a paper that had fallen between the lectern and the wall, a flyer for a lecture somewhere. *Kabbalah: Lessons for Today.* But he had no complaints, didn't need a custodian, new bookcases. That could wait for the next rabbi, if there was one. A young fellow, or maybe a girl nowadays, straight from the seminary and hungry for a job, whose task it would be to revive the place, bring in young people, maybe the Russians who were filling out the neighborhood.

He nudged the lectern back. Meanwhile, his congregants had no interest. The business of a Hebrew school, bulletin boards with colorful pictures of Queen Esther in the spring and Noah's Ark in the fall, fundraisers and budget meetings and politics: who wanted that anymore? They'd had enough in their time. That's why they'd hired him, their last old rabbi: to run a quiet place, services three times a day, the latter two at dusk—one before dark, one immediately after—a little drasha in between if he had something to say, a page of text together if he didn't. It was as though all of them, himself included, had stumbled upon a precious secret: that a dying shul, rather than being a depressing last gasp, the hollow-eyed harbinger of the disappearance of some little pocket of Jewish life the way it was so somberly and miserably described in the magazines and newspapers, was, actually, a rich reward. A place, even, of spiritual peace, where they could utter comforting and well-worn recitations without the distraction of worrying about the future. Any future.

He walked to the ark and carefully opened the doors. The Torahs, ancient sisters, rested side by side undisturbed. They had not been removed that morning, there had been no reading, but he had never relinquished the habit of checking. No one's eyesight was as good as it used to be, and the last thing anyone wanted was to be responsible for a Torah slipping out of its perch and landing on the floor. A sacrilege that carried with it the penance of a forty-day fast. Not that he'd ever heard of such a thing being enforced.

He checked each Torah's footing, the ends of the spindles snug in their well-worn grooves. What if the visitors returned the next day when there was a reading? When the young man he'd hired to chant it came in? Avi, from Brandeis.

He ran his hand along the first one, over the faded brocade cover that looked like a nightgown worn by a newborn baby, the kind that slipped softly over the head and tied just below the feet. It had been a great relief to find at the shul not only one but two Torahs so dressed, the uncomplicated cloth a welcome relief from the silver-plated armor that had encased the Torahs in his more prosperous congregations, suits of mail that had made them not only terribly heavy to lift but like objects of war, things to be shielded and guarded against. As if the silver casings were meant not to protect the sacred scrolls from without, but to keep anyone from penetrating within.

He moved his hand to the second Torah, over the soft brown cloth that was probably velvet but had been worn so thin it was impossible to be sure. A baby's nightdress, yes, but also a shroud, for these were old men's Torahs, vessels draped the way they would all be draped in the end: in plain, worn cloth—their own tallises—with no need for fine jackets or ties or properly shined shoes.

A siren sounded in the distance, and he closed the doors of the ark, stepped off the bima, and walked along the rows of benches, three to a row, like park benches with wooden seats and straight backs, armrests on the ends. For these, too, he was grateful. He hated those long fixed pews, the ones with the pockets in front. Like church, they were to him, and a shul was not a church. The older he got, the less tolerant he was of such imitation. Predictably, like all old men, he was stretching himself backward in time, back to his childhood shul, cramped, dusty, books piled up in every corner like this one and where, next to his father, he had absorbed the rhythms of how and where and when to pray, if not necessarily always why. Praying became to him as involuntary as taking in air and letting it out, as much a part of him as talking, seeing, tasting. Eat. Sleep. Breathe. Pray.

Slowly he walked the rows, checking for fallen eyeglass cases, a stray wallet, a set of dropped keys, until he came to the third row, the last bench on the right, closest to the door. He stopped, looked on the floor, the seat, the arms.

This was the place reserved for guests, where that morning they had sat. He let himself down onto the bench and studied the seat as if a sign were about to appear, carved in the wood. When had he noticed them? Unlike Lefkowitz, who had seen too much, he had had only a glimpse.

He looked up at the bima. He hadn't seen them during the service, his back to the congregation as he hunched over the lectern, no need on the days when there was no reading for him to turn around. Instead, he would concentrate on the sounds behind him, focus on the contents of the eastern wall in front of him.

He squinted up at the wall's decorations. A pair of copper plates etched with shepherd scenes, a cheap painting of dancing Hasidim, an out-of-date poster of ruby-cheeked kibbutzniks happily loading bushels of oranges, an inset of Jerusalem bathed in a sentimental golden glow. He never really looked at these when he was davening, fixating instead on random details—the flying black coat of a Hasid, the garish glow of the Dome of the Rock—isolated images that would get themselves insinuated into his prayer. He stared at the oranges, bright, like crayons. He had looked at them all through the morning prayers. Now, from his place on the bench, it surprised him to see them inside their own picture, part of a whole scene, as if they had some other life to go home to when he wasn't up there with them.

He turned to the doorway. Could he have seen them before the service? When Lefkowitz disappeared from view on his way to the student apartments, he left the study window and began to put on his tefillin, as he did every morning, privately. It was his moment alone with the memory of his father on whom he had first seen the black leather straps and little boxes containing, he'd believed then, a little boy of two or three, a piece of God. Each morning now he would try to dwell with his father, conjure his face, summon his voice, an expression, a few words; try to feel him, the looming presence he'd stood beside every morning of his early life, his father's huge tallis sweeping over him and sheltering him like a great white sail.

He turned back to the bima. Before and during the service he had not yet seen them. But he had sensed them. Felt, at the start, hunching over the lectern, that someone was there. For a fleeting moment he'd thought it was his father. Then the sensation vanished, and he was alone.

He got up, walked back up the bima, looked out into the row where he had just been sitting. It wasn't until the very end, then, when they'd finished singing *Adon Olam* and he'd turned around and begun the casual ritual of removing his tallis and unwinding his tefillin, that he finally saw them.

Saw them standing and smiling, dark hair, clean-shaven, pale shirts, white maybe. They were looking straight at him, the backs of the benches in front of them only partially obscuring their lower half. In the next instant, they were moving in perfect unison toward the door. And then, in a single swift motion, a pivot, like a great bird preparing for flight, they were gone.

A horn blared outside, a trolley jangled its bell. A collision averted. He knew what he had to do.

He stepped off the bima, strode out of the sanctuary. There were a hundred questions. Who were they? Why had they come there? Would they come back? But there were other questions, too, terrible questions, brutal questions he had not allowed himself to think before. How should they be counted? Were they one man, or two? The tenth, or a ninth as well? Were they even a man at all?

He stood before the bookcases in his study, questions parading across his brain like an occupying army and defying his desire to give a simple, compassionate response—of course they should count, of course they should participate, what does it matter!—rude guests that arrived unbidden, filing in one after another: Could they stand on the bima for an honor? Could they come up to the Torah the next day and make a blessing? What if they traced themselves to the Cohanim, the priestly class who were permitted no deformities, whose descendants were bound by special rules?

And as for how many they were, did the soul of a man reside in his heart, of which each of these young men, thankfully, possessed his own, or the brain, of which, likewise, there were two?

Or was it instead at the site of his procreational and most primitive power, the locus of the covenant of Abraham, whose exquisite and excruciating bloodletting seal took place simultaneous to the bestowal of his name? A site at which these most blameless young men had been granted only a single shared strength.

Slowly, he pulled out a thick text. He had no choice. If nothing else, he had learned in his seventy-six years that there was never a simple answer to anything, that even compassion was a layered thing. That a pair of Siamese twins were not necessarily two, or even one, when it came to counting in a minyan, or when it came to formulating any rules by which to live. And that their appearance that morning could not be passed over or forgotten, that it carried with it a host of deliberations, arguments, even fears, trailing it like a small but insistent wake.

THE TWINS WERE not in shul the next morning. Nor did anyone need to find a tenth, a full quorum having assembled outside Samuel's study well before starting time. No one mentioned the young men, asking instead after Lefkowitz, who hadn't made it in.

At seven sharp, Samuel took his place at the lectern, told himself to call Lefkowitz after the service, opened his prayerbook, and began. He stared at a dancing Hasid. Behind him the men murmured and chanted, loosely linked singing, a string of bells in a breeze.

He turned a page. A vague cloud hovered over him, something tugging at the back of his awareness. Disappointment. He was disappointed that the young men hadn't come back. Although he'd worried how Lefkowitz would take it, and about everyone's capacities for restraint, for the ability not to stare, he'd hoped they would return. He had done his homework and found enough to bring them fully into the ritual. They could count in the minyan as two, be given honors at the Torah, participate in all ways. He was going to welcome them, embrace them, fold them into the circle of old men who, themselves, were already moving toward the peripheries of life. What better place for such guests than among those for whom even the most extreme oddities hardly mattered anymore? Among them, they could be ordinary Jews, ordinary human beings, their strangeness lifted, removed.

Instead, that morning they had Avi, the Brandeis student, who'd brought a friend: Jeff? Josh? He couldn't remember. He closed his eyes to the Hasid, trying to concentrate. A sound rose up behind him, they were singing the *Sh'ma*. Recently he had estimated he'd said the *Sh'ma* ninety-six thousand times in his life, three services a day, once more at night before falling asleep, and countless times of fear when, in his fright, he called out God's name. Never, of course, would he expect an answer. Though lately he'd discovered in himself a shameful desire, a wish to have, just once, a glimmer. A sign.

He put his hand over his eyes and murmured. The disappointment cloud lowered itself over him, dragging on his shoulders like a cloak. Of course the strangers hadn't returned, he had been foolish to expect them. Just as he had been foolish to think he could somehow contain them by resolving his legalistic puzzles. He had sat in his study the day before proving to himself the compassion of the tradition, even with its dogged insistence on the law. What did it mean, he'd asked himself, a thick volume of Talmud open before him, that a two-headed man had appeared before Solomon demanding to inherit doubly from his parents and that Solomon had ruled against him? That the man was decidedly one?

He had pulled from the bookshelves Rashi, Ibn Ezra, Maimonides, stacking the yellowed texts on his desk until he found an answer: the application of the law should amplify the store of good in the world.

And so he concluded: by declaring the two-headed man, driven by greed, to be one, Solomon had reduced the sum of evil in the world; declaring the visitors to be two, each to count toward making a minyan, doubled the store of good.

He found more. Three hours later, the afternoon sun diffuse and tired, he read in the crisp white pages of a loose-leaf binder the painful modern precedent: a pair of mortally ill Siamese twin babies. Was it permissible to perform a surgical separation that meant certain death for one in order to give the other a chance for life? The answer was riddled with doubt but on one issue was certain: two lives, two persons. Then, a postscript. Despite heroic medical efforts, four weeks later, two burials.

Exhausted, he had closed the binder and called Ellie to pick him up, watched for her from the study window. Fifteen minutes later she drove up.

He gave her a light kiss on the cheek. She smiled, looking into the rearview mirror. What would he do without her?

"How was your day?" she said, watching the mirror.

More than ever, he wanted to tell her everything. About the visitors, Lefkowitz's fright, the terrible medical case. She was a compassionate listener, plus, a Talmudist's daughter, she had a fine mind, a first-rate education.

But he would refrain. In all his years, through half a dozen pulpits and hundreds of personal encounters, he had been scrupulous about guarding his tongue, vigilant for the dangers that came of too much talk. Even if the hearer was his most beloved wife.

"Fine," he said as she pulled out into the traffic. "And yours?"

She smiled, watched the road. "Okay. Thelma Greenspan called, they're back from Florida. I said we'd come by this evening."

He nodded. After so many years they both knew the rules. Respecting the boundaries was by then second nature. Though he never failed to remember that keeping a marriage alive under such conditions was no small thing.

BEHIND HIM IT had become quiet. Avi and his friend were on the bima, opening the doors of the ark. He stepped away from the lectern and positioned himself behind Avi, who took out a Torah and led them off the platform in a little procession.

The men reached into the aisle with their tallis fringes to touch the scroll. He'd been a fool the day before, poring over his books, contorting himself over precedents. Did he think the strangers had come to the shul to demonstrate the inclusiveness of the tradition? He had used the law thinking he was welcoming them, but really he was trying to dismiss them. Dismiss their strangeness, their power.

They were winding around the back, passing Lefkowitz's customary seat. He glanced at the empty row, Lefkowitz's blue velvet tallis bag still on the bench from the day before.

Lefkowitz. Now he knew what Lefkowitz had been worried about. The shul had no sign out front, nothing to identify it but a faded Jewish star carved in the stone over the door, so worn it barely signaled anything. Set back from the street, indistinguishable from the rest of the block, it would hardly be noticeable to a stranger.

Then how was it those particular strangers seemed to know before Lefkowitz even spoke that he was from the synagogue up the street?

Of course: Lefkowitz had been thinking of Elijah. Elijah, who was said to come regularly down to earth to perform miracles. There had to be a thousand stories, a thousand tales. Elijah in the forest, Elijah on a train, Elijah as a beggar, a child, a woman, intervening to rescue from poverty, heal disease, arrange a marriage, avert a stillbirth.

And complete a minyan. If he wanted to look it up, go to the fancy computerized system at Brandeis and type in *Elijah,* and next to it *minyan,* he would get a hundred entries, five hundred entries. And why not? The imagination was unlimited and, as Ellie would say, so was the misery of the peasants in Europe who made all those stories up, the products of wishful and magical thinking, fodder for old men and little children. Not that it did those peasants a lot of good, she would add, Elijah's miracles miraculously absent in 1939.

He followed Avi down the middle aisle, past the third row and the empty bench by the door. The guests were absent, Lefkowitz was absent, even his father seemed absent. Putting on his tefillin in the study earlier, the men rustling just outside his door, he'd found it difficult to summon his father—his face, the color of his hair, whether he'd always worn eyeglasses—as if the sensation of the day before, his father in the sanctuary with him, had scared his father's spirit away. As if his father, like Lefkowitz, had had a shock and needed to rest.

The processional over, he took a seat in the first row while Avi continued up the step to where Bernie Freedman, a regular, at sixty-seven the baby of the shul, waited with Avi's friend. Gently, they removed the Torah's cloth covering and slowly unrolled it to the right place, took their places by the table, and Avi began.

He closed his eyes, listened to the street sounds, the trolleys still intermittent. Unlike Ellie, he wasn't so sure. Who said Elijah was absent in 1939, hiding, as some claimed, like God? Who was to say that every one of those who lived wasn't a miracle? Life and death, poverty and riches, might there not be otherworldly guides to help conduct humanity back and forth between opposite worlds?

A cluster of birds had converged at the window as though to investigate Avi's chanting. He opened his eyes. A streak of color flew off a branch. Was it so outlandish? If Elijah could come to Bavaria, to Kraców, to Minsk, why not also to Brookline, among old men grateful for a quorum, not likely to flinch?

Avi's friend was taking a turn, his chanting surprisingly smooth for such a young man, as if he were seeing not words on the parchment but pictures. The sea, waves, clouds. Anyway, it didn't matter if he or Ellie or Lefkowitz or anyone else believed whether such figures roamed the earth. You couldn't identify them and, even if you could, there was nothing you could do about it.

They stood. The Torah reading was over. Bernie Freedman held up the scroll for all to see, then, with Avi's help, rolled it up, slipped on its faded dress. They opened the ark, placed it next to its silent companion, and closed the wooden doors.

Slowly, Samuel walked up the single step for the concluding prayers. No, he knew what really lay behind Ellie's fierce refusal, her vigorous denial of such otherworldly possibilities. It was fear, raw fear. The same fear that had caused Lefkowitz to tremble and he, himself, to bore like a beetle into his dense books until his eyes burned. Terror at ever having to see unwittingly such figures at work, acknowledge the finger of God so close at hand.

THE SERVICE OVER, Samuel went out onto Beaconswood with the others, shook their hands, and waited for them to blend into the pedestrian traffic. Then he walked up the street to the student apartments.

He stood in front of the red brick building, a few scrawny blades of grass forcing themselves out of the little patch of dirt, competing with candy wrappers and Coke cans. What was he doing there? He looked at the glass door. He could try to open it but even if he succeeded, what would he do? Stand in the tiny vestibule on top of old newspapers and magazines, sandwiched between two doors, looking like a loiterer, a thief, someone coming to steal their packages and mail?

Packages and mail. The door opened easily and he stepped inside, a row of tarnished gold buttons on the wall. Evans. Iannino. Winter. Katz. What was he looking for, two names written side by side broadcasting the presence of Jewish Siamese twins? Steven-Stuart Schwartz? Was he crazy?

A noise, a knob rattling: the inside door opened with a whine. A girl with a backpack, Miss Evans or Miss Iannino, thinking he was a Peeping Tom, an intruder, a pervert, who'd call the police and have him arrested immediately.

"Need some help getting in?" She was holding the door open for him, smiling. Reckless girl, letting him in like that. He could be a criminal or, at the very least, a suspicious-looking old man with a beard. Clean-shaven all his life, recently he'd grown an unruly feathery sort of thing that Ellie said made him look wild-eyed, like the aging Albert Einstein, or Heschel. Now a sweet-looking girl was letting him in as if he were some legitimate resident who simply had forgotten his key.

In a second, she was out the door and he was inside, in a drafty-looking stairway, the building hushed, as though asleep. He squinted at the name by the door nearest him, *Nestor, J.* typed in the little slot over the buzzer. What did he think he would learn at these doorways at eight o'clock on a Thursday morning?

The door opposite Nestor, J. opened. He turned, waiting to be scrutinized, evicted. Instead, a young man, twenty, twenty-one, softly closed the door behind him and smiled. Sweatshirt, jeans, sunglasses in his hand, he was heading for the front door and the street.

"Excuse me," Samuel said, and heard his voice echoing loud in the foyer. "I'm looking for someone, maybe you can help me? Twins, they were here yesterday."

The young man thought for a second and shook his head. "Don't think so. You're sure they live here?"

"I don't know, just that someone met them here, walked with them down the street."

The young man paused, pointed with his sunglasses to the stairs. "A couple of brothers live on the second floor, maybe it was them. They look kind of alike." He shrugged. "That's all I can think of. Good luck." He put on the glasses and was out the door.

Samuel stood alone in the hall. Of course they didn't live there, otherwise the young man would have noticed. And if they were visiting, he would have to interview everyone in the building. And then what? Explain why he was looking for them?

Why was he?

The outer door opened and a man tossed a stack of newspapers into the vestibule. He had to leave, he didn't belong there. He pulled open the heavy doors and went out onto the walk.

The street had come to life, the air like a newly opened box of ladies' dusting powder. He looked all the way down Beaconswood, the trolleys out in full force, young people with backpacks and light jackets waiting at the stop. The whole city, the whole world, it seemed, had awakened to a fresh new day while he had been inside looking for—what? Was he an old man whose grip on reality was slipping?

He walked up the path to the sidewalk, trying to take in the freshness, a scent maybe of flowers somewhere, then abruptly turned and looked back at the student apartments.

The doorway. There was something wrong with it. It was the doorway from which Lefkowitz said they had stepped just as he'd walked up. It was too narrow, a railing on either side, barely wide enough for one. And it was shallow, not deep enough to hold anyone comfortably for more than half a minute. Even he, a small man, would have had a hard time balancing himself on the little step, feeling himself tipping forward, the door urging him from behind. It didn't seem possible they would have been standing in the doorway, waiting. Could they have waited outside?

He stared at the glass. Why would they be waiting at all? Waiting for what?

Lefkowitz. Lefkowitz! He had forgotten to call! Lefkowitz, who the day before had had the fright of his life. Where was Lefkowitz? He had never missed a day at shul without calling, without making sure someone knew where to go for the tenth man. Samuel had told him to stay home for mincha last evening but not for the morning service today. It had to mean only one thing. That Lefkowitz was sick, or dying.

And that they were not Elijah at all but the Angel of Death, who had come for the one person who was certain to appear on that day, in that time, in that place. Lefkowitz. Was it so impossible? Who was to say? Who knew except the dead, and the dead never talked to the living. Only the living talked to the dead, and got no answers. Or so he had thought.

He turned and hurried down Beaconswood. If it was a beautiful day, which it was, he must not take the time to notice. If the birds were out in record number, as they seemed to be, and if it looked as though the bluest sky and the softest air had settled, finally, around him, he mustn't stop to appreciate it. Neither the strange young men nor Lefkowitz had returned to the shul that morning, and such unexplained coincidence, such disturbance, such a sign, must be registered and not forgotten or overlooked or sidetracked, regardless of the weather. Or life.

He pulled open the door of the shul, got to his study, fumbled with the desk phone. Shaky, he found Lefkowitz's number on a sheet in the top drawer and dialed, listened to three rings, four, five, then began mumbling the *Sh'ma*. If Lefkowitz didn't answer, he would call Bernie Freedman, who still worked, went to an office where someone would have to answer the phone. After that, he would call Ellie, wait for her outside, and watch for her in the humming spring air he would force himself to ignore.

LUCKY IN LOVE

SIX PEOPLE ATTENDED my mother's wedding. Her mother Mae, my aunt Rose who was carrying twins though no one suspected at the time, Rose's husband Lou, my mother's best friend Peshy who lived upstairs in 6D, Rabbi Wax, and, of course, the groom.

My father was not among them.

Solly Birnbaum—Solomon on paper but the royal association didn't take—was around the corner outside Fishman's Pharmacy pacing and smoking cigarettes and wondering how he was going to make it through life with Blanche Levine married to someone else. The fact that Solly was himself already married didn't enter into it: he was prepared, so the story went, to leave Estelle at the drop of a hat, just the drop of a hat, if Blanche would only give him the word. But Blanche hadn't, so on an overcast Sunday in March of 1959, Solly Birnbaum stared at the gray Bronx sky from the corner of Gun Hill and Jerome and shuddered at the thought of his beautiful Blanche, his adorable Begonia Blanche, sleeping with someone else.

"So what do you think he does?" my mother says to me, winking a little and gently poking Solly with her elbow, the two of them perched on the sofa like careful miniatures. It's eighty-five outside, seventy-five in here with the air-conditioning, and both of them are wearing sweaters. I've flown down to Sarasota because, though my mother won't say what it is, I know Solly's not well; I hear it in her voice.

"I don't know, Mom, what does he do?" I say. Solly's got his eyes closed like he's dozing but I know he's listening because right then he smiles.

"Well," my mother says, settling in, her hands clasped in her lap. This is her favorite part. "He went to the phone booth in Fishman's and called us up." She leans toward me. "Imagine that? He goes right in and calls the apartment, interrupts the whole wedding."

"And?" I say. I like this part, too, though lately the facts have been beginning to change, the truth as slippery as a fish. Each time my mother tries to catch it, it slides away and something different pops up, biting the bait.

"And he asks to speak to Rabbi Wax!"

"Rabbi Wax," I say. Last time it was my grandmother, and before that, Rose. It doesn't matter, though, because Solly always says the same thing.

"'This can't go on!' he yelled into the receiver," my mother says, a stage whisper so as not to wake Solly, who's now really asleep. "'She doesn't love him! He doesn't love her! *I* love her! She loves *me*!'" My mother sits back. Solly lets out a little snore. "'Too late,'" my mother says in a ponderous baritone, imitating the rabbi, like God enunciating the Ten Commandments. "'Whoever you are, young man, you're calling too late.'"

IT'S NEVER TOO late, my mother has told me with pride and conviction many times, and after a brief interlude of forty years, she and Solly did get married. That was last September. By then Estelle had been dead two years and Bertram Katz, the original groom, also my father, had long since flown the coop. Now Bert's in Sunnydale, my

next stop after leaving here; his latest woman, one Ina Katz, no rela-
tion, has left him, he says, for younger prey—his words. He's lonely
and wondering if he's made too many mistakes in life. Fortunately,
I'm not one of them, so I don't worry that he's referring to me.

The buzzer sounds and I get up and let in Yvonne, the visiting
nurse. She's here to check Solly's sugar again, the levels all out of
whack, something not right and it's not the insulin. Blanche says it's
only that Solly's not doing a good job monitoring, is sneaking sucking
candies when she's not looking.

"Wake up, Mr. Birnbaum," Yvonne says, tapping Solly briskly on
the shoulder, no time for pampering, appointments the next hour
with probably half the building. My mother, meanwhile, has been
softly stroking Solly's hand.

Solly opens his eyes, quickly sits upright. "Just a little snooze,"
he says, blinking himself awake. "Heard every word you said."

"Let's go," Yvonne says, almost shouting, though neither Solly
nor my mother is hard of hearing. Solly pulls himself off the sofa
with effort and shuffles with Yvonne to the dinette, where a little
army of paraphernalia awaits: needles in cellophane, little glass
insulin bottles, a stack of alcohol preps, a magnifying glass, his flip-
top glucose meter. He looks bad, aged ten years since I saw him last
fall doing the Kazatzka at Leonard's, looking like a real pistol.

"I picked up the most adorable pocketbook," my mother says,
practically springing off the couch, trying not to watch them. She
strides toward the back of the apartment. I follow. "Maybe you need
a new bag?" she calls out. She's like one of those little tornadoes in
the cleanser commercials on TV, whipping purposefully down the
hall. "Great selection, all discounted, five minutes from here, I'll give
you directions."

"Why don't we both go out for a little while," I say when we're inside the bedroom. She's already in the walk-in closet. The closets here, she's told me on the phone, are even better than the ones in Queens, cleverly fitted out with movable white shelving, finally enough space for all her shoes and pocketbooks, a special section at the end for the garment bags that hold her cocktail dresses. She's brought every one of them, all her stylish off-price New York clothes, every stitch, for her new life with, finally, the right man.

"Nah, nah, you go, you'll enjoy it," she says on her tiptoes, reaching up. She's got a pocketbook in every color, three or four for every season. Bert was a lousy husband, unfaithful and unreliable, but they had a great social life, once upon a time.

"It'll do you good to get out," I venture. My mother hasn't left the apartment in a week, according to Yvonne, who let it slip during the first visit of the day, seven-thirty this morning. Even the groceries were delivered. "Solly'll be okay for a few hours," I say. "Yvonne said she'll set out his lunch when they're done and check back on him before she leaves the building."

My mother turns to me, a neat row of thick pullovers directly behind her that she'll never wear in Florida. Pink, yellow, baby blue, pastels to set off her honey-brown hair because sixty-eight is too young, she says, to throw in the towel and go gray. She's holding a square box that says Leather Mart on the side, and for a second I think she's going to let down her veneer of cheerful bravado and stop pretending nothing's wrong. "You've got to get out, Mom," I whisper. "Even for an hour. For your own sanity."

She inches toward me, starts to open the box. Then her face hardens, a look of resentment crossing it like a wave, and all of a sudden she's looking at me as though it's my fault she's been cooped up, my fault Solly's sick and that her long-awaited shot at happiness isn't turning out as planned. She leaves the closet, tosses the box onto the chenille bedspread, snatches up her old white patent-leather purse with the fake gold clasp and cracking sides, and marches out of the bedroom.

"Elise and I are going out," she barks at the front door and is immediately out in the hall. I give Yvonne a little wave—Solly has his back to us at the dinette—and Yvonne shoos me out. *Go, he'll be fine, go.* I pause a second, waiting for Solly to say something, but nothing comes so I pick up my bag and go out. My mother is already halfway down the corridor.

LAST YEAR, WHEN Blanche was still in Queens, she told me at the Empire Deli that she and Solly Birnbaum were getting married.

"That's really great, Mom," I said, folding my hands, forcing myself not to take another pickle. We had a standing date: I'd drive into Queens from Long Island once a week straight from work to meet her for supper, just the two of us, without Steven and the kids. She got a break from playing Grandma and I got to inhale the aromas of the Empire: pastrami, half sours, steamed franks. It was as if there were a nasal barrier at the Great Neck exit of the Expressway: no real deli smells allowed into Nassau County. "When did this come about?" I said.

She tipped her head and made a small smile. Solly and Estelle Birnbaum had been family friends for as long as I could remember, and after Estelle died I saw a few sparks, some flickers between my mother and Solly. I was glad. Bert had taken off while I was a teenager, and though my mother never seemed to harbor the sort of bitterness I saw in my friends' mothers who'd been abandoned by the once-man-of-their-dreams, she was entitled to her share of happiness. "Oh, we've been thinking about it," she said, evasive.

I nodded therapeutically as if she were one of my clients. "So you've been seeing each other for a while? I mean, not just friends?"

She tipped her head again, both of us watching the waitress make her no-nonsense delivery of our meal. The wedding news had to be the explanation for my mother's food choice. Who ordered salad at the Empire? A hunk of iceberg, a sliced egg, and an unripe tomato quarter. It could only be the excitement, living on love. A waste of a great culinary opportunity, as far as I was concerned.

I picked up my corned beef on a bulky and smiled at my mother, waiting for the answer.

She reached across the table and laid her thin hand on mine. "I think I can finally tell you the truth, honey. You're not Bert's child. You're Solly's."

I held the sandwich in midair. Was she talking metaphorically? "What do you mean?"

"Just that. Solly's your real father."

"Real father?"

She nodded.

"You mean—?"

Another nod.

"You slept with Solly Birnbaum? Before I was born?"

My mother made a weak smile, sheepish, as if expecting someone to finally give her a good scolding.

"I can't believe this," I said, putting the airborne roll on my plate. "After forty years I'm supposed to believe that Bert is not my biological father?" This did not make sense. I had talked to my father last week, heard all about his trip sightseeing for alligators. How could he suddenly not be related to me? I lowered my voice. "Who knows about this? Are you sure you're not making this up? Some magical wish after years of unhappiness that your true family be constituted once and for all?"

She shook her head. "I'm not making it up."

"What about Jeffrey?" It was a stupid question. My brother was five years younger than me, Bert firmly in the picture by then.

"No, just you," she said. "I told everyone you were a few weeks early. But you weren't. I was pregnant at the wedding."

"And no one knew?"

"Solly knew. And Rose, I think. She was mad at me for a long time and I never found out why." She picked up her coffee. "I think she suspected."

I glanced around. The place had filled up, people in every booth. Across the aisle two men were bent over their menus, studying them like they were gastronomic Talmuds, running their fingers along the plastic and reverently repeating the words to each other. *The Madison: turkey and chopped liver with cole slaw and Russian dressing. The Jefferson: . . .* I turned back to my mother. "And all these years," I whispered, "with Estelle and Dad and the four of you together so much, nothing ever happened? Nothing between you and Solly?"

My mother stiffened. "Of course not. It wouldn't have been right. He was married, I was married."

"And Dad?" I said, leaning across the table as far as I could go, my plastic pearls threatening to drag in her Italian dressing. "Does Dad know?"

"Your father? Bertram?"

"My father, my father, the guy I've been calling Dad my whole life."

She looked up, chin raised, defensive. "No." She looked away, then back at me. The defense had evaporated. "Maybe. I don't know. Maybe that's why he was such a philanderer all those years. Maybe he was paying me back."

NOW, IN MISS Daisy's Pancake House on Ocean Drive where everything, including the pancakes, has the consistency of mashed potatoes, my mother has gone off to the ladies' room, allegedly to wash but I know it's to primp. I sip burnt coffee and watch the dishes that are being delivered to the other tables, wonder why in the world my mother has picked this place. Is she feeling old? Has she lost her sense of taste since moving to Florida?

A tray with three plates of waffles goes by. They look like the frozen kind, deep airy squares that taste like cotton and function mostly to hold in the whipped cream and runny strawberries. In her day Blanche Levine was a knockout. Hair done up in a French twist or a fifties pageboy, perfect makeup, a taste for clothes. I've seen the pictures, she and Rose posed on the roof of their building like a couple of red-lipped models, someone's sheets flapping in the background. For her first wedding, despite the fact that she and my grandmother had been living on air, subsisting for years on a nothing insurance policy left by my grandfather who'd delivered milk for a living, plus whatever Blanche brought home working six days a week at the accessories counter at Stern's, she managed to appear in a snazzy knee-length lavender silk dress with tucking down the front, a choker of real pearls, and a matching lilac hat like a perfect half shell. For her second wedding she did no less, and on not much more money: a white linen suit with black piping, white sandals with heels too high for even me to manage in, and a single red rose pinned on her lapel, her one concession to her matronly status.

From the other end of the restaurant she makes her way toward me. I give a little wave. She looks haggard; the primping has been ineffectual. She arrives, slides into the booth, pulls her old-lady cardigan around her. One quick glance at the menu, and she puts it aside.

"What'll you have?" I say, smiling, trying for upbeat.

"I'm not hungry," she says. "I'll stick with coffee."

"Mom, you've got to eat. When did you last eat—breakfast? It's one o'clock." I eyeball the menu, pump up the enthusiasm. "The omelettes look good. Western, cheese, tomato. Choice of toast or English muffin."

I look up, hopeful. Her feeble attempt at makeup has failed, and black smudges have formed under her eyes so that she looks ghostly under the fluorescents. She seems to be daydreaming. "Did I ever tell you what Solly did on the day you were born?" she says.

I give up and close the menu, shake my head.

"He ran out to get you the biggest stuffed animal he could find," she says, her eyes suddenly brighter. "Absolutely the biggest." She leans forward. "And where do you think he went?"

I shake my head. Where?

"FAO Schwarz," my mother says, triumphant, giving the table a little tap. "Only the best. You know what it was?"

"No."

"A giraffe! You remember the giraffe? It was huge, as big as me."

She sits back, smiling. I have no idea if this is the truth. Or if there really was a giraffe and it came from someone else. Or if Solly bought not a giraffe but a baby teddy bear or the cheapest wind-up toy in Woolworth's because how could he justify such an extravagance to Estelle?

"You loved that giraffe," my mother says wistfully. "It was right next to your crib. Don't you remember?"

"Not really, Mom, I'm sorry. Did we have it long?"

She sighs, looks up at the ceiling. "Did we have it long," she repeats to the ceiling tiles, then looks back at me. "I don't know. I only know when you got it."

I nod. A waitress in a pink-checked apron is heading our way. She's got a ponytail and those pointy-shaped glasses from the fifties. I want to ask her if maybe she remembers the giraffe.

"Good afternoon, ladies," she drawls pleasantly. "You need a little more time?" She knows the clientele, is overly patient, overly kind, and I long for the gruff waitresses from Queens and the old impatient Blanche who got antsy if no one appeared to take her order within twenty seconds of sitting down.

"I'll have the Swiss cheese omelette," I say.

"All right," the waitress says, writing it down slowly, mouthing the words. *Swiss. Cheese. Omelette.* "And what about you, ma'am?" she says to Blanche.

"Just coffee," Blanche says, drawing her cup and saucer closer.

"That's all?" the waitress says. "No waffles, flapjacks?"

Blanche shakes her head. I'm not sure she knows what a flapjack is.

"All right, then," the waitress says, collecting our menus. "I'll be back to freshen your coffees."

We smile and she leaves us. Blanche has slipped back into pale melancholy, whatever had flickered with the giraffe now gone. "Don't make mistakes, Elise," she says, picking up her cup and staring at what's inside. "Don't have regrets."

AFTER EXACTLY TWO hours, with Blanche checking her watch every twenty minutes, we're back at the apartment. Blanche doesn't have a key.

"What are we going to do?" she says, panicked. The white patent-leather pocketbook hangs open like a mouth, a mountain of crushed tissues and a lipstick threatening to spill out. "I forgot the key, I never forget the key! I'm always with Solly so we lock up behind us, or I take the car so I have a key! But we took your car, the rental car, so I don't have a key!"

"It's okay, Mom," I say, and reach for the buzzer. "We'll just ring the bell, Solly'll get it."

"No!" She clamps an icy hand on mine. "We can't!"

"What do you mean, we can't?"

"Solly's not supposed to walk," she blurts out. "He's not supposed to get up by himself."

"What are you talking about? What's the matter with him?"

She looks away, stares at the door that seems posted there like an armed guard. The pocketbook is still gaping, mute. "Nothing," she says, stoic. "Nothing's the matter."

"Mom, obviously something's wrong if Solly isn't supposed to walk. You can't hide it from me forever. What is it?"

She watches the door, says nothing.

I glance down the corridor. I feel like we're a couple of intruders. "Does someone else have a key?"

"No."

"No one? No neighbor? What about Yvonne?"

Silence.

"Is there a super in the building?"

She turns to me. "This isn't Queens, Elise. They don't have supers here."

"Well, they have property managers, someone or some company. They have to be able to get into an apartment." I put down our shopping bags—a pocketbook for Jessie that I know isn't weird enough for her fifteen-year-old taste and which she'll end up insisting I keep, and some bath towels Blanche has picked up, as if she and Solly didn't already own thirty between them. "I'm going to the lobby to see who's listed as the manager and what their phone number is," I say. "Every building has that information posted somewhere."

"It's Rain Country Management," Blanche says, not taking her gaze off the door. "Next building over. Ask for Sheila."

"You've done this before? Locked yourself out?"

"Once or twice."

"You or Solly?"

She turns to me, seems to crumble. "They're the ones who found him."

"Found him?" The elevator dings at the end of the corridor. We can't stand here and have this conversation. I snap her pocketbook shut, pick up the shopping bags, and steer her by the elbow to the elevator, then down into the lobby. We sit in matching upholstered chairs next to a fake fern.

"Solly fell," Blanche says, looking tiny in the big chair, her voice even tinier. "I wasn't here. I was out, I don't remember where, shopping or something."

"What kind of fall? Did he trip?"

"He got up from a chair too suddenly. He was five minutes away from a coma, his blood sugar had dipped so low. Ten, fifteen minutes more until anyone found him, he would've been dead."

I start to pull my chair closer. The fern is in the way; I push it with my foot. It's light as cardboard. "So someone came in, revived him?"

"It was luck, dumb luck. Next door was a man fixing the dishwasher. He heard a thump and called the management quick. They came right away, dialed 911 before they even left their office." She looks away. "Ten years he has diabetes and now, all of a sudden, it's doing this. Like it was waiting for him to finally be happy."

I reach across, squeeze my mother's hand. What is there to say? I turn professional. "Of course you're upset, of course you're anxious." She keeps looking at the wall. I sound shallow and useless, canned blather coming out of my mouth. "Naturally you're feeling protective, afraid to let him be by himself in the apartment."

She whips back at me. "And what should I do—leave him to fall again? This wasn't a simple fall, Elise." She pulls her hand away. "He was in the emergency room for hours, all night I waited there before they stabilized him. He has a hematoma on his hip the size of Manhattan."

"What's a hematoma?"

"A bruise," she says, irritable, as if I should know. "But no ordinary bruise. A bruise that isn't healing."

"You have a doctor you trust?"

She waves my question away. "You know what these doctors are like. They come here to make money. You think they're interested in a long-term relationship like Dr. Benvenito at home? They see Solly come in like this, they write us off immediately. Treat us like morons who don't understand anything."

"But you've never let anyone treat you like that, let a doctor patronize you."

"It's different now," she says. "They have all the cards. They scare you with all the terrible things it could be."

Behind us the elevator dings; I hear the flip-flop of beach shoes. My mother looks at her hands. A couple about her age, dressed for the pool, matching towels neatly folded over their arms, watch us on their way to the door. I smile politely, wait for them to pass, which they seem to do reluctantly, almost warily, and it occurs to me it's not us they're concerned about, it's the chairs and the plant: they don't like the fact that they've been moved. "Busybodies," Blanche murmurs when they're gone.

I inch closer to her. "You have to fight the doctors, Mom. Take charge, like you always did."

She shakes her head, looks again at the wall. "It's harder now, with Solly."

"What do you mean? If anything I'd think you'd be stronger, even more determined."

"Sometimes love makes you strong, Elise," she says. "But sometimes"—she looks at me—"sometimes love makes you weak."

THE DAY AFTER our news-breaking dinner at the Empire last year, I called my mother. It was six in the morning; I'd waited four hours to dial.

"What am I supposed to do with this information?" I said, revved, three cups of coffee pulsing through me. I picked at an

English muffin, meant to absorb some of the acid. It wasn't working. Darts of pain were playing ping-pong in my abdomen.

"I don't know, honey," she said, sounding tired. I hadn't woken her—she was an early riser, at work by eight, preparing for a day of having to say no to welfare cheats. Every week at least a few dozen situations broke her heart. "Can you ask a colleague for advice? They would help you."

I tapped the tabletop. That's what Steven had said. *Make sure you get a courtesy discount.* Not that he hadn't tried to be supportive when I gave him the news, rolling in at nine o'clock just when he was prying Jessie off the phone and getting the boys to bed. *Solly instead of fly-by-night Bert?* he said to me in the bathroom where I'd herded him, the only place we could get a minute of privacy. *I should think you'd be glad.* "Therapy doesn't help with this, Mom," I said, frustrated.

"It doesn't? What does it help with, then?"

"It helps people with neuroses and lousy adjustments, with things they can change or control." I waved a hand, irritable. "It doesn't help with a suddenly revised ancestry, a totally new genetic makeup."

"I don't know about that, Elise," she said. I could hear her at the stove, putting on her old percolator. "What about all those people who suddenly find out their grandparents are Jewish? Or the boy in last week's *Times* who went to meet his father, the lady who'd had a sex change? Don't you think therapy would help them?"

I tapped faster, annoyed. Of course she was right. I should look on the bright side. At least my father was Solly, not Estelle. "I know it's a shock," she said. "I don't blame you for being upset."

Outside, it was getting light. Inside, the coffee was declaring victory over my digestive system. "I'm not upset. Just confused."

Silence. She was thinking. I stretched my neck, suddenly

exhausted. I had four clients before lunch. "Did I ever tell you what Solly did on the day Jeffrey was born?" she said.

"What?"

"Yes. When Jeffrey was born."

I stared out the window. A cardinal landed on a branch. "No."

"Ah, well, then." I heard her pulling her chair up to the old speckled table, probably glancing at the yellow clock that was supposed to look like the sun, pointy rays sticking out like Medusa's snakes, waiting for her half bagel to finish toasting, a slice of Muenster and one of tomato ready on the plate, her grapefruit juice already poured. An orderly woman with a disorderly past. "First we brought you over to their place when I went to the hospital."

"Their place? Not Aunt Rose's?"

"Nope. It was Solly and Estelle who took care of you. All day, well into the night."

This didn't sound right. I was five. Wouldn't I have gone to Rose's to be with the twins, or to Grandma Mae's? Was Blanche embroidering the past here, trying to make whole cloth out of a few questionable threads? "They took you to the zoo," she said. "Out for ice cream, popcorn, the works."

"The zoo? It was open?"

"Of course it was open, it was always open. Solly took the day off from work to be with you." She paused. The cardinal flew off, impatient. "It was also to help Estelle, of course. Remember, she had Philip and Howard by then, two boys, and wild, too."

I took a pointless nibble at the English muffin. "But that wasn't all," Blanche said. "When it came time for dinner Solly took you for a special treat." She stopped, waiting for me to ask.

"And what was that?"

"Your first dinner out at a restaurant. Patricia Murphy's, on Sixty-first Street. Or maybe it was Sixtieth."

"We went to Manhattan for dinner?"

"Absolutely. What was the rush? I wasn't coming home, and God knows where Bertram was."

Upstairs, the water was running. Steven. In ten minutes he'd wake the kids. They'd come stumbling down for breakfast looking for Froot Loops and clean socks, oblivious to my exhaustion, my vigil, the fact that the day before I'd found out our gene pool had changed. "You had a wonderful time," my mother said. "You told me all about it when I came home from the hospital. The fancy tablecloths, the tall glasses, the popover girl."

I tossed the English muffin into the trash. The pipes banged: Steven in the shower. Around midnight last night he'd offered to take off from work today if I needed him, I was probably feeling a little stunned. I'd rolled off of him, then rolled my eyes: And abandon my seven scheduled appointments? Their mental health would have to come first.

"They were good to you," Blanche said.

"Who?"

"Solly and Estelle." There was a catch in her voice. "She was a good friend, Estelle." Blanche sniffled, probably digging around in the pocket of her robe for a tissue. "I miss her."

SHEILA AT RAIN Country Management gives me a spare key. I thank her profusely, more for saving Solly's life than for the key, but she looks at me blankly, doesn't know what I'm talking about. Maybe it was Cindy or Ruthanne in the office that day, she says. I nod awkwardly, promise to return the key, then go back to Blanche and take her upstairs.

I open the door with dread; now that I know Solly shouldn't walk alone, I'm terrified of what we might find: Solly sprawled, comatose, on the floor, or groping desperately for the phone, or, worst of all, bleeding from the head after crashing against a piece of furniture on the way down.

Instead, Solly's on the couch reading the newspaper. I quickly survey the room, see that he can make the dinette-couch-easy-chair circuit without having to let go. Next to the couch, neatly folded, is a walker I haven't seen before. I'm guessing Yvonne has put it there and that my mother had hidden it for my arrival.

"Have a nice time, girls?" Solly says, putting down the paper.

Blanche goes to the couch, leans down to kiss him. I hold up the shopping bags like I used to do with Bert when my mother and I returned from whatever compensatory outing we'd been on, trying to make up for Bert's missing attention with a new blouse or a pair of slippers. It seems the way to act with fathers. Though neither Solly nor I have acknowledged this fact. It seems too personal, too private, too soon. "Yep," I say, feeling fourteen, pulling out a yellow towel. "Some new towels, a great deal, seven-fifty each." I lift up the brown shoulder bag for Jess. In the full light I have no doubt she'll hate it. "And a new pocketbook for a lovely granddaughter."

"Excellent," Solly says. His voice is hoarse, thin. It's an effort to speak. "Did you have lunch?"

"Oh yes," Blanche says from the little galley kitchen. She's directly behind the couch, separated from us by a half wall. Solly can't see her without turning around but I can. She's putting up hot water for coffee, instant. She's probably up to ten cups a day. Immediately I suspect she's smoking again.

"Yes? Where?" Solly calls out over his shoulder.

"Oh, a great deli on Atlantic," I say, perching on the arm of the couch so I can see them both. "Roast beef, pickles like you shouldn't know from, salami sliced thin, strudel for dessert." Solly smiles. It's easier having diabetes in Florida than in Queens, he says. The food is so lousy, he's not even tempted. "Okay, we went to a pancake place," I say.

"Pancakes. For people without teeth," Solly says. My mother coughs in the kitchen. Smoker's cough. "You couldn't take her to Romanov's, Blanche?" Solly calls. "You couldn't show Elise something nicer than eggs and maple syrup?"

"Who eats at Romanov's in the middle of the day?" my mother says. She's taking down cups and saucers from the cabinet, white porcelain with a rose border, from her good set. "It's a dinner place. The only people in there at one o'clock in the afternoon are old cockers, retirees with nothing else to do but eat."

"And what are we?" Solly says, talking to the middle of the room. "Upper management?" He looks at me, winks. "We're retired, too, Blanche, remember? That's why we moved here."

"I thought we moved here to enjoy the good weather. To have fun, go swimming, learn to snorkel. Get a good tan." Something in her voice makes me turn to watch her. Bitterness. She fills two cups with hot water before the lid of the teapot clatters into the third, splattering onto the counter and scalding her. She pulls back her hand, and I start off the couch to rush over but she holds up the other hand, furious, adamant—*I'm all right!*—so I sit back down.

"There you go, I rest my case," Solly says, cheerful, winking at me again. He's seen nothing of the kitchen. "That's what retirement is. Vacationing in the sun all day, every day."

I cautiously glance back at my mother. She's dumping in spoonfuls of coffee in each cup. It's going to taste like mud. No one will be able to drink it. "And we were supposed to start a new life, too, Solly," she says, the spoon banging against the porcelain. In a second she'll start saying things she'll regret. "We came to make new friends just as if we were a couple like everyone else, married forty, fifty years, starting a new phase together." The stirring is fierce, and if she doesn't break the cup she's going to knock it over and burn herself.

"And we are starting a new phase, Blanche," Solly says softly over his shoulder. "Just like any other couple, together for forty years. If not always married, at least always together."

I get up, go to the kitchen. Tears are sliding down my mother's face. I take the spoon out of her hand, lead her to the couch, where she sits down and puts her head on Solly's shoulder. Back in the kitchen I empty the cups, pour the coffee down the drain.

AT YVONNE'S INSISTENCE Solly and Blanche have gone to the doctor. The hematoma looks bad, and there are other signs, Yvonne catalogued them for me in the corridor after her evening visit while Blanche pretended to be busy cleaning up the frozen fish squares. Jaundice, something suspicious around the eye, and, most worrisome, gangrene in a toe. The toe will have to be removed, not today but soon, then maybe a second and a third because these things spread and you want to catch them early. He can be fitted with special shoes, maybe he'll need a cane, but the alternative is worse.

I sit on the couch and page through the wedding album. The dishwasher hums; Blanche picked at her salad and baked potato; Solly ate for both of them. Shots of the required hora, Solly lifted up in a chair, me and Steven and the kids at our table, Blanche and

Peshy, who came all the way from California, friends for sixty years, grinning together over a centerpiece. A couple of weeks after Blanche told me she was marrying Solly, I called Peshy, fishing. What did she know about that first wedding, about Blanche marrying Bert?

I knew she was in love with someone else. But it couldn't be.

Why not?

I don't know, she never said. But maybe—Peshy's voice dropped to a whisper, as if someone might hear—*maybe he wasn't Jewish.*

You never found out?

No. What was done, was done. A pause, Peshy sighing. *Now she's finding happiness with an old friend. What could be more wonderful?*

I turn the thick plastic pages. Rose, unsmiling. My mother's buddies, most of them half her age, from the Welfare Department. Howard and Philip, Solly's sons. I move closer to the light, scrutinize them flanking their father in their dark suits, Howard just like Solly, fair and compact, Philip the spitting image of Estelle, jet-black hair and blue eyes, a real looker, on his third wife. Now she's leaving him, too, Blanche has told me, poor Philip, not lucky in love. I search for a resemblance, something of either of them in me, something of Solly. But there's nothing. I am Blanche's girl, and always have been. Yet even if I did find something, a taste for Turkish taffy, a fondness for pistachio ice cream, I don't think Solly would want me to mention it. Not because of me or him or Howard or Philip but because of Bert. A kind of unspoken pact. Loyalty to a fellow father, who, although not much of a husband, did a respectable job with me.

There's noise in the hall, a key in the lock. In an instant I know it's not good news. Blanche walks Solly to the bedroom to lie down; back in the living room she sums it up: the doctor wants him admitted this evening, compromised kidney functioning, infection, unstable blood pressure. They won't keep him long, IV antibiotics, tests, but when he comes home there'll be follow-ups, more appointments, more medication, Yvonne or someone else coming in. They'll take it one day at a time, but this is how it's going to be.

I offer to go with them to the hospital, and Blanche accepts. In the den where I'm sleeping I change into something presentable. When I come out the smell of cigarette smoke is hanging in the kitchen. Blanche has packed Solly's bag, has put on lipstick and a smart blazer, its hanger still in plastic from the move, determined, she says, to walk in there like his rightful wife and demand complete information.

I follow her down the hall to the bedroom. Midway she stops, turns around.

"Surgery in two weeks if the infection's gone," she says. "Three toes. Two on one foot, one on the other. Ten days in rehab, three months of physical therapy." I nod. We go wake up Solly. Special shoes, a cane. No more Kazatzka.

BLANCHE AND I are on the balcony sipping iced tea. It's the first time since I got here that we sit outside. A breeze comes in off the water and we hear the ocean in the distance, see palm trees and pastel stucco buildings by the light of the full moon.

My mother has told me that Solly waited at Fishman's that day another three hours. They had had a plan. Even if she went through with the wedding, even if she married Bertram Katz under Rose's watchful eye, did the respectable thing rather than shame herself and poor Mae and the memory of her dead father with an out-of-wedlock pregnancy, he would be there for her. All day he'd wait at Fishman's, and after that he'd wait at home, ready to leave Estelle whenever Blanche wanted. Just say the word, Blanche, my Begonia Blanche.

Blanche didn't come to Fishman's. It got dark and began to rain and Solly went home. Philip was two, the apple of his mother's eye, mother and son alone, suffering with a preoccupied, lovesick Solly. Three years later, when Blanche had given no sign of changing her mind, Estelle became pregnant with Howard, and Solly turned his attention to his family.

"Why didn't you ever leave Bert and go to Solly?" I ask. It's so bright out it feels early, though it must be close to midnight. It took hours to settle Solly; to get all the paperwork, see that the IV got started, wait for the doctor, pin him down to specifics. *You're a lucky man, Mr. Birnbaum. Your wife's watching out for you.* "There must have been opportunities," I say.

My mother watches the sky. "I couldn't do that," she says. "There were too many people involved. What about Estelle? She was my friend. She'd suffered already." She turns to me. "And what about you and Jeffrey? What kind of mother changes husbands in midstream?"

"But weren't you ever tempted? After Bert left, when you were alone?"

She turns back, studies the moon. "Once, we came close. It was at Howard's bar mitzvah. Bert was gone a year—you remember? It had been such a mess, him coming and going, then finally gone. You were sixteen."

I remember. I had scrutinized my mother then, looking for flaws, for what it was about her that would make him leave.

"It was at that party they had," she says. "An inn or something on Long Island Sound. June, like now." She gestures with her chin. "A big moon like this. Some place with a veranda."

The Viking, I want to tell her. A romantic place. A boy I'd never met before tried to kiss me on that porch.

"I must have been standing outside by myself," she says. "Solly came out, and it was all we could do not to embrace right there—the stars, the moon, the breeze, the sound of the lapping waves. He was always a romantic, a pushover for that sort of thing."

I try to picture them, Blanche forty, forty-one, my age, Solly a little older. "He took my hand right there," my mother says. "Held it up to his cheek, not concerned about who might see, and said, 'One day, Blanche. One day it'll be our turn.'"

We're silent a moment. A plane, a moving white light, glides soundlessly overhead. "That's a nice memory, Mom," I say, though, really, it sounds like one of those overdone movies from the forties— a big veranda, tinkling glasses, elegant clothes. All that's missing is the swelling violins. The moon seems to sink a little, as if on cue. Immediately I feel guilty for thinking this.

"There's more."

I turn to her. There's something funny in her voice. I can't tell if she's smiling.

"We snuck off that night."

"Really?"

"Yep."

"Where'd you go?"

"My car."

"Your car?"

"Yep. That crummy Ford Pinto."

I want to laugh. Me, sixteen, on that porch, worrying that Blanche might see a strange boy kissing me, while all along Blanche is in the backseat of the Pinto doing it with the host. I can see her in one of those cocktail dresses, a black sheath maybe, with a beaded front, a low V, a drape of flimsy chiffon in the back. It's probably in one of her garment bags right now, twenty feet away, having a good laugh. How did she manage in that cramped car with all those dress parts, a cloth-covered belt, the zillions of hooks and eyes, the silky lining you had to be so careful with?

"Didn't you worry about your dress?" I ask.

"As a matter of fact, I did. It was silk, a pastel. Turquoise. Wrinkles easily. And stains."

I try to call it up, a color like the sea. I don't remember a dress like that. "And Solly, was he wearing a tux?"

"No, it wasn't that fancy. Still, he had to be careful, the host and all."

The breeze picks up. Blanche's sweater rustles on the back of her chair. I reach across and drape it over her shoulders, see the Viking, the big French doors to the porch, Blanche and Solly sneaking past Howard and his thirteen-year-old friends, who themselves are sneaking off to smoke or feel up girls, and me, sneaking off with that boy, everyone trying to grab a little passion, a little love. Did I tiptoe away, go somewhere in the dark and kiss that boy? I don't remember. If I didn't, I should have.

"Did you look at the album?" Blanche says.

"Yes."

"It was a great wedding, wasn't it?"

"It was."

"Worth every penny. Solly had the time of his life. It's important to celebrate. Days like today, you're glad you did, glad you blew the bank for once."

I nod, pick up my watery tea. The moon is a golden dome, a

giant coin. Somewhere a foghorn blows. Tomorrow we'll visit Solly in the hospital, take turns playing gin with him. Now a warm wind is coming in from the Gulf, stirring the palms and gently mussing my mother's hair. She lifts a hand and smoothes whatever she can back into place.

HOW TO COMFORT
THE SICK AND DYING

THE FIGURE IN the bed seemed so shrunken under the sheets it would have been easy for a visitor to think he'd stumbled onto the pediatric ward.

Of course he had not. Reuven Schweller—bearded, tzitzit fringes threatening to slip out of the waistband of his pants, a black yarmulke pinned to the top of his head making him look, he knew, like a caricature of something even without an artist's rendering— knew exactly where he was and why. He'd been sent by the Rebbe to make a sick visit to a man he didn't know. A dying man who surely wouldn't want Reuven there any more than Reuven wanted to be there. Why would he, Reuven coming in unasked, intruding on the man's potentially peaceful departure from the world and advertising a piousness which, if the dying man knew anything about it at all, positively shrieked the man's existence as an abomination. This was, after all, AIDS, and it wasn't from faulty blood. Whatever Reuven might try to do or say, the rules he was making himself live by, the backbone of his desperately rebuilt life taken on in hopes of lifting him out of his own drug-hazed despair not all that long ago, practically spat at the man's way of life. If rules could spit.

Reuven moved softly from the doorway to the chair at the foot of the bed, clutching his raincoat. This was his first sick visit; the Rebbe thought he was ready. Reuven wasn't so sure. Maybe if he was lucky the man wouldn't wake up, and he could leave. Though of course there was no such possibility. *One who leaves the bedside of the dying is worse than a father who denies his own child bread.*

A sigh flurried like a feather through the waifish form, stirring the sheet. It was only enough air for a bird. It was not enough for a man, even one so reduced—and disappearing.

The man opened his eyes. Two sunken windows. If ever the body receded so far that the soul was near enough to the surface to be clamoring to go free, it was now. "May I help you?" he said.

Reuven blinked himself out of his stare. Help him? He must look preposterous and hopelessly out of place, a full burst of health on his face, no yeshiva-boy pallor for him, a high school wrestling star once, getting back his old strength with vitamins, a strict vegetarian diet. What did he know about suffering? "I'm Reuven Schweller. I hope you won't mind a visit."

Nothing moved, only a small smile on the dust-dry lips. Did the body finally forget thirst? In order to simplify things, crumble more readily into the earth? "A rabbi," the man murmured. "Things must be bad."

"Oh no, no, you misunderstand." Reuven waved a hand. "I'm not a rabbi."

The eyes closed, the man's face so pale it was blending into the pillowcase. He looked all of seventy pounds, his hands lying on the sheet like two still fish. Was this dying, real dying? Not the dying to oneself that Reuven in his short life had tried two or three times already, this latest an attempt to make himself over out of some impossible need for atonement. And which, he was certain, wasn't working. "Not a rabbi?" the man said. "You just look that way because . . . ?"

Reuven looked down at his suit, dark and heavy, formal. He was twenty-nine years old. He hadn't worn a pair of jeans in three months.

"Doesn't matter," the man said. Reuven looked up. The man had opened his eyes again, pale green, or maybe it was gray or a distant blue, and pointed with one of the fish hands to his own chest, at the flimsy hospital gown that hung off his shoulders like a shroud. "Who'd call this dressing?"

Reuven tried to smile. What could he say? *I could have been you? What was it—freebasing? The downtown baths? The hollow-eyed girls on Fourth Street?*

The faded eyes closed, cheekbones suddenly too prominent, coming to the fore of the parchment skin as if announcing themselves: *Soon this is all there will be.* The cracked lips moved. "So, you've been assigned to cheer me up?"

Cheer? The Rebbe didn't say anything about cheer. *Bring a glass of water, smooth the blankets, whatever they ask. Small acts of kindness, like what a child would do.* And if not that, Reuven had thought, maybe a need for talk, expiation, unburdening the guilt over a wasted life. About this, he knew something. He fidgeted with the raincoat, looked at the bedside table, a plastic water glass. "Look, can I get you something? A ginger ale? The newspaper?" There'd be a vending machine, a gift shop. He could kill some time, bring back whatever it was, then go.

No answer. Maybe the man had fallen asleep. Reuven glanced at the window, the blinds so tightly closed it would have been impossible to tell if it was day or night. And nothing on the walls, no posters, no pictures, only a bolted TV perched like a huge intrusive eye.

"Why don't you tell me a story?"

Reuven turned back to the bed. A story? He was no storyteller.

The last story he'd told was the one he gave his parents years ago about his supposed respectable life. A made-up job description, social whirl, even a nicely furnished apartment which, from a distance of a thousand miles, they had no reason not to believe.

"So?" said the man. "You've got a beard and one of those little hats. You're supposed to know stories."

A hot flush rushed to Reuven's cheeks, he felt the old response heating up. *Fuck you, wise-ass.* He took a breath. Could the man see through him? Was the new persona melting away, Cinderella's footman reverting to a rodent at midnight? *I'm not really Reuven, you know. I used to be Robert. I was a small-time dealer, grew up in a split-level suburb. I'm not what you think.*

"So?" the man said.

"Right, okay. All right." Reuven ran his palms along his pants and glanced around the airless room trying to free-associate. He could imitate the style of the Rebbe, who could give a simple parable that illuminated the world. He stared at the blinds, a yellowish tinge to the slats. "Once there was a farmer. He had twelve daughters and twelve sons. He sent the daughters to get married and the sons to learn a trade. He gave them each ten rubles and told them not to come back until they had each doubled their money and accomplished their tasks.

"Years passed. Then one day the offspring began to trickle back to the farm. Each had doubled their money and accomplished their task. The boys had become traders and the girls had all married. The problem was, the brothers and sisters had all married each other. Seeing the holy bonds of matrimony used for such abominable unions, the father took a look at the last of the returning couples and dropped dead on the spot."

He stopped. It was as if a spell had overtaken him, a complete story rolling off his tongue, unbidden. And what was it? The worst depravity: an incest story. And on top of that, an insult to the dying man whose own unions had probably not been all that kosher either.

His raincoat was a humiliated heap on his lap. He made himself look away from the blinds and turn to the bed. Mercifully, the man was asleep. Reuven gathered up his coat and hurried out of the room.

HE HAD NEVER told his parents the truth. The dealing, conniving and lying, ripping off, one way or another, everyone he came into contact with. His cashing in on every meager friendship, every well-meaning gesture. He had never told anyone.

He stared out the grimy window of the Q-13 bus onto Bell Boulevard and watched the trails of belching exhaust on the other side. Nor had he told the Rebbe, though he suspected the Rebbe might have guessed. How could he not, the Rebbe a worldly man, glassy-eyed Robert Smith—like he was fooling anyone, Smith—arriving desperate and skinny, still shaking off the coke dream, bottomed out the day before in a filthy room over a girlie parlor on Tenth Street. It was not something the Rebbe had never seen before. The place they put Reuven, a young men's dormitory in the middle of the yeshiva grounds, was probably filled with guys like himself, though no one ever said. Reuven was not in a position to ask. It was his last chance, word of the Rebbe's willingness to take in strays, no questions asked, somehow having filtered through the fog that passed for Reuven's brain, taking hold long enough for him to get his stuff together, get in a cab, and ring the bell. Come to the study sessions, don't cause trouble, and he could stay. He sat in the Rebbe's dark study, grateful for the lack of good light, and rummaged for his checkbook. *We don't want your money*, the Rebbe said, waving his hand, dismissive, as if the money, like Reuven, had come up from the sewer.

The bus jolted and stopped. An aroma of perfume. He shut his eyes. Someone sat down next to him, a woman, he was sure of it. The perfume, or maybe it was soap or shampoo, freshly washed hair. He turned to the window, breathed in deep, trying for the bracing sharpness of glass, something to cut into him. The Rebbe was no fanatic. *We live in the modern world, it's no sin to look at a woman.* But for Reuven it was sin. One look and he'd lose it all, any restraint, the capacity to stop himself. He'd be talking this one up, whoever she was, twenty years old or forty, it didn't matter, first laying on the charm like he used to, acting respectful, interested in their work, though most of the time he never even heard what it was. He'd ease her into a bar, nodding to this or that with pretend interest, his face operating under separate instructions—*now smile, now look concerned, now say, Wow, that's amazing*—a glass of wine, a few hits, his desperation rising, then to her place where finally he could screw her a couple of times, spew out his own particular brand of poison, then leave. They had all been the same to him, faceless women and girls: strangers he picked up in laundromats or on the street, his friends' girlfriends or wives, his cousins, Sheila and Mindy, at their brother's wedding, telling them in the bridal room during the reception that it was okay, they weren't really blood relatives. He had screwed them all. It didn't matter who they were or how he knew them. If he'd had a sister he'd have screwed her, too.

And now, how far had he come? Telling incest tales to the dying.

The woman shifted her position, he heard the crunch of shopping bags by her feet. Maybe a dress, a pair of pretty shoes, a gauzy blouse. The shampoo smell was everywhere, and it was coursing through him, the old urge. He could do it right now, this minute. Slip off the yarmulke, hide the fringes, or maybe none of that would matter, maybe she'd like it, kinky, weird. *Hey, I fucked this really religious guy today.* He squeezed his eyes tighter, leaned his face on the cold glass. *He who climbs up from sin stands higher than the righteous of the righteous.* Someone hit the buzzer. He opened his eyes. They were thirty blocks from his stop. Groping like a blind man, he stumbled past her out of his seat—dark hair, a tan collar of a tan coat—and as soon as the doors opened, he fled the bus.

DEATH DOES NOT take a vacation. He was expected to visit the man again, to go every day, Booth Memorial the Rebbe's beat. All the Queens hospitals were divvied up, one rebbe per hospital, so if one of the Rebbe's students failed to show, if Reuven didn't go back, Booth Memorial risked being assigned elsewhere, and this would not sit well with the yeshiva. Not that there was any shortage of places in Queens where one could go to comfort the sick and dying, starting with under the overpass to the Expressway a few blocks from them, where at least a dozen wasted alcoholics could reliably be found each night slowly killing themselves.

The last one out of the morning minyan, waiting for everyone else to leave, Reuven finished unwrapping his tefillin from his arm. He fumbled with the straps, tefillin a new thing for him, a couple of weeks, the leather leaving indentations in his skin, distorting the tiny needle marks. He'd gotten off easy with the needle business: he was still alive. Some vestige of restraint, a muted impulse for life, had kept him from going further. Somewhere along the line he was forced to take notice: a Lubavich Hasid on the street told him he, too, was holy, that a spark of the Divine lived in the dark sea of his soul. Reuven laughed in his face. Two days later he sold a deadly dose of something to one of the girls downstairs. The next day he packed his things and took a cab to Queens.

He worked on the straps, rolling them clumsily, twice, three times, finally getting them into the velvet pouch, nervous, always nervous, with the little black boxes. What if the boxes were two-way? What if the one he wore on his forehead didn't just whisper its parchment contents to him—*You shall love your God with all your heart, with all your soul, and with all your might*—but sitting up there, next to his brain, was drawing his thoughts out, too, recording them in some ancient invisible script? What then? One more week of this, and the box would be bursting. And then one day it would explode, his treacherous questions exposed, hanging like a bloodied sheet in front of everyone in the morning minyan: What am I doing here? How can this ever make me holy? How can anything ever make me holy?

In the yeshiva cafeteria he pushed his breakfast tray along the metal counter, the choices paralyzing from behind the glass: French toast, English muffins, bagels, cold cereal. Should he take one of the breads? If he took bread he had to wash; had to go to the little sink by the wall for ritual handwashing, say a blessing, and utter yet a longer one at the end of the meal. But who was he kidding, pretending to piety when he couldn't even tell a simple story to a dying man or sit next to a woman on a bus like a human being?

He put his tray down at a crowded table, pulled up a chair. Next to him Meir, his six-foot-five Talmud teacher, a onetime forward for YU, glanced over, took in the cup of black coffee, the skimpy bowl of Frosted Flakes. "Not hungry, Reuven? What—you don't like Mrs. Ostervitz's cooking today?"

Reuven made a weak smile, took a cold spoonful.

Meir's large hand came down onto Reuven's free one. "Listen, my friend. Don't expect miracles overnight. Or even in three months. It's a long haul, you'll see if it's for you." The hand lifted and Meir's chair scraped the linoleum. Reuven kept his eyes on his bowl. "There are no easy answers," Meir said, standing, his tray a ceiling over Reuven's head. "But you already know that."

IT IS BETTER to perform a good deed than to light a candle before God. The blinds had been opened. The man was awake. "Nice to see you, Rabbi."

Reuven moved quickly to the chair, his raincoat over his arm. *Rabbi.* The man was mocking him. He willed himself not to react. Besides, he knew the man's name now, had checked the little slot by the door, the Rebbe's anonymous instructions from the day before— *Room 210, B-Wing*—no longer sufficient. Now there was a face, a voice, a person.

And a name. Ash. A. J. Ash. The sound made Reuven shiver. Was the man Death itself? The Angel of Death warning Reuven that his own time was up? He shifted the raincoat on his lap and forced himself to start, say something. "Hey, how you feeling today, Mr. Ash?"

Ash nodded, pale hairs from the back of his head pushed up on the pillowcase, the room brighter, for the open blinds, than the day before. It didn't seem to matter that Reuven knew his name. Or that yesterday he hadn't. A beam of light stretched across the linoleum from the window all the way to Reuven's chair, spring not far off, a blue sky and a warming sun. Ash would never again be outside to feel it.

"So," Reuven said, "where you from?"

"North Carolina." Ash put on a thick falsetto, exaggerated southern boy. "Ah'm from No'th Ca'linah, y'all." He wheezed badly, once, twice. It was an effort to speak, even without the theatrics. "But I'm no good-ole boy."

Reuven nodded. He had never been to North Carolina but he'd been to New Orleans. Mardis Gras, prostitutes, crab claws, lines of powder. He folded his hands, kneaded one of his fingers. He could use something like that right now. "So how come you don't have a southern accent?"

"How come you don't sound like *Fiddler on the Roof*?"

A cough, then another wheeze. Ash, the color of his name, wasn't interested in an answer. He tried to moisten his lips with his tongue. "You here to save my soul?"

"Oh no. Nothing like that." Fidgety, Reuven pulled the raincoat toward him in case any stray fringes had escaped, the white threads meant to direct the mind to heaven. Did people think he could possibly save anyone's soul?

"You don't do that? Only the Christians?"

"I can't speak for the Christians," Reuven said, and thought, *I can't speak for the Jews, either.* He glanced around: no plants, no futile boxes of candy. Did Ash have no friends, no other visitors? "Look, can I get you a drink? Tea? Orange juice?"

Ash ignored the question. "Had a Jewish boyfriend once. Jeff. Jeff Shulman." He closed his eyes. "Great cook."

The raincoat was slipping off Reuven's lap, obstinate, as if it didn't want to be there. Reuven pushed it to the side, stuffed it into the seat. "Oh? You like to cook?" Ash coughed again, deep and phlegmy, foamy yellow spittle seeping from the corners of his mouth. It was like a bad trip. Very bad. Reuven scanned the little bedside table—the plastic water glass, an untouched cup of green Jell-O. "You want me to get a washcloth or something?"

Ash took a shallow breath, then coughed again. The room seemed to smell of eggs, a sulfurous odor coming from Ash's body as though he were decaying, decomposing, before Reuven's eyes. Or maybe it was the smell of medicine. Reuven spotted a box of institutional tissues by the sink, glanced at the door—shouldn't there be a nurse somewhere, or an aide?—then got up and took a wad, leaned over Ash, and made himself dab at the drool. The egg smell rose up, stronger. What did Ash endure every day?

Ash, eyes closed, whispered, "Tell me a story about chicken soup."

Reuven's stomach pitched, a small roll. He looked down at Ash. Could this be a test? *This is your man?* Satan asked God, pointing at Job. *You think he's so upright, so righteous? Touch him and see what happens.* Reuven the vegetarian tossed the wad into the trash, sat down and closed his own eyes, and saw the soup: the pimply skin floating in the water, fat globules colliding and collecting at the top, the bones falling off the flesh and then bobbing, naked, in the pot— feet, claws, ribs. Then he saw the chicken running, its neck broken, and then headless, through someone's yard. He could be that chicken, running headless through life. Where, though, was the chicken's head now?

"Mmm, Shulman's soup," Ash said.

Reuven opened his eyes.

"So, Rabbi?"

Reuven took a breath, gazed around the cheerless room. What had he heard lately? There was no chicken soup in the Elijah stories, no soup in the Black Forest where the Baal Shem Tov had his visions. He looked at the window, at the neat lines of sunlight between the blinds, his mind aimless and wandering, his mouth leading, a mouth without a body. He was the chicken's head now.

"Once there was a man who loved to make soup, especially chicken soup. He made it for all his friends. But one time where he lived, there were no chickens. There were not even ducks or geese or turkeys.

"But there were lizards. Lots of them. Green, scaly lizards with long tongues and flapping tails. So he caught a couple and brought them home, dropped them in boiling water, added carrots, an onion, celery, and cooked it up. After removing the bodies, he served it to his friends. 'Wow! Great soup!' they exclaimed with gusto. Then they went on to tell him it was the best chicken soup they'd ever had."

Silence. His stomach was close to heaving right there on the floor of the sick man's room. He hadn't been able to stop himself. A story about lies; about perpetuating colossal, disgusting lies.

It was a curse. He couldn't open his mouth without the pestilence of his own life pouring forth. He forced himself to look at the bed. Ash's eyes were still closed, a faint whistling coming from his nose. Maybe Reuven would be lucky again; maybe Ash had fallen asleep.

"That was one sick dude," Ash murmured, nothing moving but

his chalky lips. "Sicker than me, I think." He took a few shallow breaths, pushed his words out with effort. "Come up with something a little different next time, will you?"

WHAT NEXT TIME? How could there be a next time? Reuven hid under his covers the next morning, his tefillin untouched on the dresser. He couldn't go out, couldn't go to the hospital, couldn't look into Ash's dying face and listen to himself mocking not only the sick man, who loved Shulman and his wonderful soup, but also the good intentions of the Rebbe and his other teachers. Innocent men who had no reason to care about him other than some stubbornly held belief in the worth of every human being. Even Reuven.

A door closed softly in the corridor outside. Someone leaving for a class, or a job, or wherever the other men went every day with their tormented souls. Privacy was an unspoken rule; no one intruded, asked personal questions, the burden of being yourself heavy enough without having to worry about what anyone else thought. He pulled the covers over his head—*All your deeds, do them with a pure heart*—opened his eyes to blackness. This was the color of his heart. He squeezed his eyes shut: darker still. The girl downstairs had been no more than eighteen, his sale an injectable cocktail he wouldn't have given to a dying horse. First they had sex, then he left her the stuff. At her bird weight, half her systems already shot, it was probably over in half an hour. Although it took until the next day for the police to come, find the body, the stench in the hallway like nothing he'd ever imagined.

He turned to the wall, the stink from that downstairs hall coming to him as though it were outside in the corridor now, and pulled the covers down onto his face, trying for the smell of starched cotton. Maybe he could sleep.

Sleep? How can you sleep? the sailors screamed at Jonah, the sea a raging torrent. *It's your God who's making the storm! Get up and pray!*

Pray? What for? He held his breath against the remembered stench. There was a poison ocean inside him. What else could explain what was escaping his lips in Ash's room? It was his soul rising up and reminding him of who he was; who Reuven Schweller really was without the tzitzit and tefillin, without the Rebbe.

Get up! Pray to your God and make him stop!

But there was no stopping this. He forced the covers tighter onto his face and, like Jonah, tried to shut out the screaming.

NIGHT. HE HADN'T turned on a light. Quickly, he got out of bed, dressed, grabbed his coat. The corridor was empty, everyone at maariv or the evening classes.

He was starving. Out on Bell Boulevard he shoved his hands into his coat pockets, a package of crackers in one, kept for emergencies when he was too far from the yeshiva, not near a place where he could eat. In an instant he was inside the Bluebell Diner, under a *Take Out* sign.

"Help you with something?"

"Bacon cheeseburger."

The man behind the counter raised his eyebrows, glanced at Reuven's yarmulke.

"What are you looking at?" Reuven shot back. "A costume party, all right? I'm on my way to a costume party."

The man shrugged, went to the back. Reuven put his hands back in his pockets as if he were hiding something on his fingers—an illicit wedding ring, a telltale stain. When he got his food he quickly walked around the side of the building to the alley, leaned against the brick wall, and took huge bites, like a thief, a dieter on a binge, no handwashing, no blessing, nothing. He ate as he felt, like an animal, expecting to be ill, the food grotesquely taboo. But it was delicious, so good he would have gone back and ordered a second if it hadn't been for the counterman's stare.

He left the alley, walking fast, the sky clear, the stars bright, unheard of in overly lit Queens. In a liquor store he bought a fifth of gin, no looks, whiskey permitted, the Rebbe's humorous story of being refused alcohol once on a plane, the stewardess certain that, as clergy, he wasn't allowed. *So many things from which to abstain, and the stewardess thinks of yet another!* He hugged the paper bag to his chest and hurried down the street.

There was plenty of room under the overpass, the headlights from the Expressway dizzily illuminating the dead ground. A few drunks huddled together by a stone divider no more than forty feet from him, warming themselves over a primitive fire. Two of them turned, gave him a quick look, turned back. Reuven sat, opened the bottle, took a long drink. They couldn't have seen him very clearly but even if they had, there, by the highway, appearance would mean nothing, his beard nothing, his suit nothing, even his tzitzit would mean nothing. Who would expect him to look heavenward now, nursing a bottle of cheap liquor among the used rubbers and ravaged cans and broken glass? Dope, too, if he wanted to look; if he wanted to put his nose down into the dirt like a dog and sniff, then stuff the unfinished ends of joints into his pockets, fill them if he wanted to.

The damp seeped through his raincoat. He twisted the bag

tighter around the bottle and took another drink. Why had the Rebbe sent him to the hospital? It was too soon. Certainly it wasn't some morality lesson: *There but for fortune go I.* That was not the Rebbe's way. *I don't change people. People change themselves. Or they don't.*

He took another pull, then another, the liquor burning his chest. The shadows by the pillar were moving, drifting in his direction. The drunks. After they took the girl's body away the police questioned him. Did he know her name? Had she ever mentioned parents, a home address? There was so much bodily damage—heart attack, needle tracks, a plastic bracelet, the girl was a diabetic—they weren't even going to try and name a cause of death. *What's the difference, eighteen, a wasted life.* And then, the two of them on the way out, their blue policeman backs to him: *He doesn't look so good, either. I give him six months.*

A rustling of paper bags, the rancid smell of clothes that never got washed. They loomed over him, four big men, the stink of booze and urine on their shoes, four men like trees. His breath turned shallow. Maybe they would kill him. He had a good watch and a wallet. People had been killed for less. It was a fair trade, his life for hers.

One of the men bent down, getting a closer look, almost sniffing him. Could he smell Reuven's foul meal, the oily coins in his pockets? The rot that had settled deep in his core and that now refused to be covered up by his feeble efforts at prayer and good deeds? The man leaned closer, the stench from his clothes, from his matted hair and partially open mouth seeming to hover around him like an aura, a haze that separated him from the black night and the world of men. Reuven didn't move, the sounds from the highway suddenly ceasing, the headlights gone, everything still except for the flickering of the fire, nothing in the universe but Reuven and the man and the watching stars. The man started to put out a hand. Reuven's chest pounded wildly. He could die from the feathery touch. Then the man seemed to change his mind, took the hand away, and the four of them stumbled on, moving aimlessly, not back to the stone pillar, not anywhere, just moving.

A truck rumbled on the highway. Reuven let out a breath. Above him clouds were moving in, a soft gray that was obscuring the retreating stars. Maybe the next day it would rain. He felt his heart slowing. Why was he still alive? How was he supposed to live?

He pulled himself up. The drunks were gone, the fire out, as if it might never have been there. He left the bottle upright on the ground—an offering—then reached into his pocket and found, not only crackers but, miraculously, gum. He had fouled his breath with forbidden foods and whiskey but now there was gum. Quickly, he unwrapped two pieces and stuffed them in his mouth, then immediately pulled them out—*He who subdues his impulses is called a man*—uttered the blessing before putting them back in.

The night had turned warm, a thin reed of spring floating in from somewhere, the smell of flowers. He took off his damp raincoat, dusted the dirt from his pants. Ash. He needed Ash. Needed to sit before that mirror face and listen to the truth of his life. And might not Ash also prefer having Reuven there to lying in bed alone, dying in a ten-by-ten room thousands of miles from wherever he had once called home? *One who visits the sick extends the boundaries of heaven.*

The sounds from the highway rang, vibrant, across the open ground. Reuven began to climb the embankment to Bell Boulevard and the Q-13 for the hospital, his coat joyful over his arm. *Within the sickness lie the seeds for the cure.* Quickening his pace, hurrying to get there while Ash could still be counted among the living.

THE LAMENT OF THE
RABBI'S DAUGHTERS

THE RABBI HAD four daughters. One became an actress, moved to Los Angeles, gave up the tradition—it was in the way!—slept with producers. Why not? Her father said never do things halfway. The whole hog, he would've said if he could have brought himself to utter the word. She took singing lessons, dancing lessons, and went to restaurants and bars and parties where studio moguls hung out whenever she was invited. Even if she wasn't invited. You had to be aggressive in this business.

She was not, however, without talent. She had talent. It was evident when she was a little girl. Rena, now Rianna, prancing on the stage of the yeshiva's empty auditorium, nudging the PTA ladies in the back to watch. How could they refuse, the rabbi's daughter? They smiled, nodded, patted her on the head with forbearance, gave her a cookie. The child was in need of such attention! But what can you expect, a father preoccupied with—what? The obscure, the arcane, his feet hardly in this world, and a mother who—never mind, it's not nice to talk, so she's not the type to play rebbetzin. Okay, okay, but did they have to be the surrogates?

Rianna, coming by her nerve and talent naturally, used it to full effect, grimacing in the mirror of her dingy apartment on Beethoven

Street preparing for auditions, snagging a few commercials to pay the rent—Rinses away plaque and leaves your teeth whiter than white!—and scanning the pages of *Variety*. It wasn't a bad life. At least it was hers, she told her sisters on the phone. Is yours? Be honest: can you truly say it's yours?

NONE Of IT is ours, Ilana, now Iyervasana, answers, trying for serene but coming out irritated. Rena was always so self-absorbed! Still, Iyervasana loves her, her exuberant embraceable sister, Rena the Irrepressible, Rena the Bold. Iyervasana stills her irritation, folds it back into herself. Breathe deep, close eyes, take another breath. She inhales the fragrance of the day—which did she light? Face of the Moon? Iridescent Star? It sits on the mantel of her carefully hushed studio on Sixteenth Street, a thin river of smoke rising to the ceiling. She knows she looks like a caricature but what was she supposed to do—deny herself her true faith just because people have turned it into a joke? *Where's the best place in New York to look for a minyan? In an ashram on Eighth Avenue.*

How are the auditions going? Iyervasana asks, calm now, the startled flutter of feeling quiet and limping, like an injured bird. It's the only way. Any other way is so exhausting. It used to wipe her out.

Shitty, Rena says, and exhales. She's probably smoking, Iyervasana thinks, and hears tapping, Rena drumming a tabletop, or the phone. The idiot producer I slept with last week? Rena says. The one who promised to call me for a sitcom? *You'd be perfect! That New York accent, I love it!* Did he call? Did he even e-mail? Rena lowers her voice. Asshole.

Iyervasana concentrates on her breathing. She hates her sister's gutter talk. Even when Iyervasana was still Ilana, still in the material world, still Jewish, she didn't talk like that. That's one consistent thing about her: *You were always on the pious side, I have to grant you that,* Rena said back then when she heard about Ilana's plans. *Two years in an ashram? Without a phone, without visits, right there in the city? Two years just listening to your breath?*

I'm really sorry to hear that, Reenie. I know you've been working hard.

Damn straight. Ach, if I have to do one more mouthwash commercial I'll spit! Suddenly there's laughter, Rena hysterical. Oh God, Ilana, did you hear that? A pun! A joke! Spit! You get it? Rena laughing, then almost crying. Oh God, it's really getting to me!

I get it, Iyervasana says, and permits herself a smile. It's only a small smile, because Rena has always been so funny. If you forgot about her self-absorption and just listened to her, you could really have a good laugh.

SHAINDEY, MEANWHILE. What about poor Shaindey? Iyervasana hangs up with Rena—it's late, eleven o'clock, the evening just beginning on the West Coast but Iyervasana doesn't want to know Rena's plans—and dials Shaindey, who finally has her own phone, twenty-six years old. It was so hard when their parents always picked up.

Oh, Ilana, you're sweet to call, really I'm fine. Shaindey is breathless, as if she had to run to get to the phone. What could she have been doing in her frilly pink room, the same since seventh grade? Iyervasana hasn't been in the apartment in two years, since before the ashram, relations with her parents awkward though not severed, and she doesn't know if Shaindey has anything new, a stationary bike or a VCR, maybe not even those pink café curtains and bedspread anymore. She hasn't asked. All she knows about is the phone.

Well, it must be quiet, Shaindey, with Abba and Ima away.

Oh, it's not bad. Mrs. Kornfeld stopped in yesterday, and Mrs. Greene, from upstairs.

Iyervasana closes her eyes, goes for that serenity again. She has to stay centered. She gets so frazzled when she talks to her family. In the ashram it was easy. Even when she got phone privileges she wrote them that she didn't. They believed her. She thinks they were secretly relieved. What would they have said to her on the phone? *So what's the story with all those statues with eight arms? Is it true, do Hindus really think their gods are like octopi?*

Mrs. Kornfeld and Mrs. Greene still live upstairs? Iyervasana says.

Shaindey giggles—giggles!—and says, Of course, where would they go?

An impatient shake of the head, a gesture she has banned, and Iyervasana says, too testily for her own liking, Well, they might have moved, they might have gone to an old age home, or Florida.

Oh of course, Shaindey says quickly. She's upset Ilana, and Shaindey knows it isn't good to upset Ilana. Ilana doesn't do well with upset. Her whole life Shaindey has tried not to get Ilana upset. At least Ilana calls her, still makes an effort. Unlike Rena who, Shaindey knows, thinks she's ridiculous. A hopeless case, living at home. Yes, yes, they're still upstairs, still next door to each other, Shaindey says. Still sit next to each other at shul. Shaindey suddenly drops her voice as if she's said a bad word. *Shul.* Ilana doesn't go to shul anymore. Shaindey hasn't forgotten, she just can't quite get it in her head. How can Ilana have given all that up? Ilana used to love shul, used to daven with more devotion than any of them. Ilana had the spark, the flame, the fire. Where did it go? Abba says nothing about Ilana's new religion but Shaindey secretly thinks Ilana's passion went there, with the Hindus, into their prayer. What is their prayer, anyway? One day she has to ask Ilana, but not yet.

Have you heard from Abba and Ima? Iyervasana says, waving bye-bye to the biting thought pecking at her mind, willing it away on the current of garbage that is constantly flowing out of her head anytime she pays attention. She learned about this in the ashram. So much garbage to float out! In everyone's head, if they only paid attention. This particular garbage-thought is laden with Shaindey's whisper of *shul* and all that it evokes: the claustrophobic preordained life, designed and constructed in advance like a prefab house, the life she was supposed to live. Ilana studying at a girls' yeshiva, Ilana marrying at twenty, Ilana looking up to her scholar husband, Ilana becoming the dutiful rebbetzin, just like her mother was supposed to have been. Screech! Stop! Brakes! Breathe in, breathe out. Iyervasana pushes the preordained life out with each exhale. Are they having a good time? she asks Shaindey, between breaths.

I think so, Shaindey says, tentative. Does Ilana want to hear about the relatives, Uncle Nathan and Aunt Aviva in Har Nof with their fourteen children? Aunt Aviva is forty-five and still having children. *Pregnant at the same time as four of her daughters,* Ima told Shaindey on the phone. *It's not nice.* It's Purim, Shaindey says to Ilana. In Israel they're having it for three days. Three days! First in Petach Tikva, then in Jerusalem, a walled city, so that's a day later from the rest of the country, and then on top of that, it was Shabbat, so that extended things.

Ilana murmurs something. Does Ilana care about this anymore?

Shaindey finds it fascinating, endlessly fascinating, that in Israel you can have Purim for three days! It is so interesting to Shaindey! Abba and she studied it before the trip; they sat together the night before and read Tractate Megila at the dining room table, Abba so happy she was interested. Face it, the tradition was dying out in this family. Only Shaindey kept it alive. She should have gone to Israel instead of Abba and Ima—a thought which Shaindey has just this moment registered and which of course she will never utter to anyone.

Purim has long since been dropped from the conversation and Ilana is now reporting on Rena, but Shaindey isn't paying attention. There's been a knock at the door.

Someone's at the door, Ilana, I'll have to call you back.

I can hold, Iyervasana says, and thinks: A knock at the door at eleven-thirty at night? What is that?

No, no, let me call you back. Really.

I'll hold, Iyervasana says, more insistent. Iyervasana should wait, make sure Shaindey's okay, listen for noises, sounds of strangling or—breathe in, breathe out—she's working herself up.

No, really, Ilana, I've got to go, Shaindey's voice almost harsh, the first time Iyervasana's heard such a voice from her sister. I'll call you back. If not tonight, then tomorrow. Then a click, and Iyervasana's line goes dead. Cut off by never-hurt-a-fly Shaindey.

IT IS MIRI. Miri, who's been gone, missing, for fifteen years. The oldest daughter, disappeared, poof, vanished in a puff of smoke, a pillar of fire. For years the family looked everywhere—Israel, Mexico City, Montreal, anywhere they had relatives, anywhere Miri had been. Later Ilana and Rena flew to Oregon with Uncle Nathan to check the cults. They even tried to get in one—it wasn't for nothing Rena had taken acting lessons! she announced to her desperate parents. No sign of Miri. The cults even cooperated. We feel sorry for you, they said. We're sad you've lost your sister. If you lived a more meaningful life, without emphasis on material gain and personal success, she might not have run away. Ilana and Rena rolled their eyes. Maybe they should have brought Shaindey. Shaindey, sixteen then and already in love with God. Shaindey would have made the cult man run in the opposite direction.

How was your walk? Shaindey says to Miri. It's not quite spring, and the weather is temperamental. Some days are warm, others still feel like winter. Always, rain is in the air. Miri wears Shaindey's winter coat, which is a little short on her—Miri is tall, like their mother—and keeps it on after she's inside the apartment. She's brought a jacket with her but it is too thin for this cold March night.

Miri says, Fine, thank you, the walk was pleasant, and Shaindey nods, moves to the kitchen. She doesn't know what to ask Miri so asks only practical things: Are you hungry? Do you want to rest? Do you need some clothes? Miri is a legend, a myth, to Shaindey, who was eleven when Miri disappeared. Miri was twenty-one. Now she is a thirty-six-year-old stranger who vaguely resembles their mother but could be someone Shaindey has never seen before. When she speaks, which isn't often, at least not in the twenty-four hours since she appeared, she has traces of various accents—British, Australian, South African—which Shaindey recognizes because of her post–high school year at Machon Gold, the religious girls' seminary in Jerusalem that specialized in girls from English-speaking countries and where Shaindey learned to knit kippot and make cholent without ever opening a page of Talmud.

I'll make us something, Shaindey says, putting up the kettle, even though it is late, almost midnight, and ordinarily a person shouldn't eat or drink at this hour. But Shaindey hasn't been able to sleep since Miri arrived, called in sick to work this morning and plans to call in sick tomorrow, too. Her boss, Mr. McMahon in Litigation, told her to rest up, lots of flu going around, Anne-Marie or one of the other girls will cover for her.

Oh, that would be nice, Miri says, hugging herself, rubbing her arms through Shaindey's coat. She sits at the Formica table and looks at the specks in the surface. Still the same table, she says.

Shaindey takes from a cabinet a package of cookies, a box of tea. You remember this table? she says, not looking at her sister.

Oh yes.

Miri has asked Shaindey not to tell Abba and Ima she's there, it would be too much of a shock. Also Shaindey shouldn't tell Ilana and Rena. Not yet. One day soon, but not yet.

I remember everything about this apartment, Miri says.

Shaindey carries over the cookies, teapot, milk, sugar. Miri makes tea the British way, putting milk into her cup first, then the brewed tea, then the sugar. Shaindey thinks Miri must have lived in England part of the time. The tea, the accent, the reserve.

Miri lifts her cup to her lips. Mmm, good, she says. The steam rises, casting a little rosy tint on her cheeks. She is beautiful, Shaindey thinks. Thank you, Miri says, looking at Shaindey over the rim. You're being very kind. And very patient.

Shaindey feels herself blushing. Miri has said nothing about where she's been, what happened to her. She has asked Shaindey to be patient, she realizes it's a matter of importance and that the sisters are entitled to know.

It's okay, Shaindey says, lifting her cup, a small smile. The universe has altered and this, for Shaindey, is good news. Something big is happening, something big and important and true, because people don't reappear as Miri has unless it means something—a sign, a portent. A word, even, from the heavens. Shaindey understands now why she needed to be home alone, without Abba and Ima. Because though she only now realizes it, Shaindey's been waiting for such a sign for some time.

IN THE MORNING, six o'clock, Shaindey's phone rings. Her answering machine picks up.

Shaindey? This is Ilana. I'm worried about you. Who was knocking at your door at midnight? Call me when you get up.

In L.A. seven hours later, Rena's answering machine also takes a message. It is ten o'clock in the morning Pacific Time but Rena is in a dead sleep, a late night with Joe Maginnis, a fledgling producer too fledgling to be an asshole—yet. Rena actually likes Joe, and thinks he might like her, and thinks also she might have slept with him for not entirely opportunistic reasons. Joe, however, left in the middle of the night because staying over, dealing with the morning, anyone's real life, is just not something anyone does on a first date.

Two rings, then the beep.

Rena, this is Ilana. You're probably sleeping, so okay. But listen, call me when you get up. Something's up with Shaindey. She's okay, don't panic. But Abba and Ima are away, and she sounded all rushed and adrenalined last night on the phone, and that's not Shaindey. I've never heard an adrenaline rush from Shaindey. Call me. You have my work number.

Ilana, alone in the store, hangs up and tries to calm herself, not get all worked up over the critic in her head who isn't happy she's slipped and called herself Ilana and is calling her parents Abba and Ima. She's been Iyervasana and they've been Mother and Father since the ashram because she really needed to cut that cord, that intimate Hebraic cord. But her carefully constructed new self isn't holding together lately, the whole thing starting to come apart, and here they are again, the old names, seeping into her talk.

Okay, okay, no sense beating herself up over it. She brushes by the racks of dresses, skirts, blouses, imported from India, Pakistan, Sri Lanka, the faint tingling of bells coming from some of the hangers, and goes to the little kitchenette in the back to brew some Mellow Mint. But she's so upset—the names, Shaindey, the customer who came in this morning and accused her and the owner, Patrice, of selling goods made by child labor—that she might have to have something else.

She stops at the sink, reaches up to the cabinet where Patrice keeps a stash of stuff she thinks Ilana doesn't know about and pulls down a jar of Folger's crystals. She opens the jar, takes a whiff. It's bitter, awful, instant, she hasn't had anything like it in two years, but it's all she's got. She finds a mug, a spoon. She'll have it, and later she'll have it again, better, at Starbucks up the street, double latte, extra large.

RENA IS PUKING in the bathroom. For once, she didn't drink too much, and there wasn't any weed. Which leaves only the food. What was the problem last night? She's had mu shi pork a zillion times.

When would her system shut up and learn to adapt? I eat pork now! she shouts to her intestines, but it doesn't help. She throws up one more time into the toilet, then staggers to the sink.

What a wreck. She leans into the mirror and tells herself she'll be lucky if Joe Maginnis nods at her on the street, let alone ever calls her. Though she didn't look half bad last night; in fact, she looked pretty good, little black skirt, beaded orange vintage top from The Second Hand. She even looked cute. Pert. A word she loves and could never use on herself. Rabbi's daughters were not allowed to be pert. Not her father's daughters, anyway. They had to be *thoughtful, considerate, responsible.* They had to do *acts of charity, good deeds, repair of the world.* Fun was not a word to be used in the same sentence with how they were supposed to spend their time. But there is fun! her parents insisted. Fun was making decorations for the sukkah, wearing a costume on Purim, making her fiftieth clay menorah. At fifteen fun was—what? Looking at *Glamour* was not acceptable, playing with hair dye not acceptable, going to parties not acceptable. There was no more fun after about age ten, in Rena's book. She loved her family, but she had to go away to make her own fun.

She washes her face, brushes her teeth, then stands back, looks at the whole tired picture. Buck up! Pinch those cheeks and get some color! She makes herself stride to the kitchen. The answering machine light is blinking. On off, on off. Hope. Maybe he forgot his wallet, his underwear, his extra condoms. Maybe he wants to take her to Luigi's tonight for a candlelight dinner.

She tightens the sash of her ratty robe, tosses back her hair as if someone were filming her that moment, and presses Play. Ilana's voice propels itself into the room.

FROM HER BED Shaindey watches the sunrise. She's hardly slept, and the sky is now light, almost white. Shaindey has always liked the early morning. It reminds her of Jerusalem and the birds. Huge flocks, loud and raucous, that appeared at both ends of the day, dawn and dusk, swooping over the rooftops like messengers. Wake up! Wake up! And later: Go home! Go home! They were like the muezzin, faithfully calling. She loved that muezzin sound, the way it hovered over the city, floating up to God's ear. She should have stayed in Jerusalem after her year at Machon Gold. Why did she come back? Because how could she live so far from Abba and Ima, the youngest daughter, the only one not lost? She would have broken their hearts.

In Ilana's old room across the hall Miri is murmuring in her sleep. Shaindey gets up, tiptoes to Ilana's doorway. The door is partly open and Miri is sleeping on her side, one leg hanging over the bed, long and smooth, no nail polish. Strips of light slice through the blinds. Miri is neat, nothing lying around, a blue flannel bathrobe carefully draped over a chair, a black canvas suitcase by the dresser. Shaindey could search through the suitcase for clues to Miri's past, she's had plenty of opportunity in the last two days, but she knows she won't find anything. Miri's silence about where she's been is thought out, careful, deliberate, and she's not about to leave a suitcase full of hints lying around.

Shaindey turns to leave, then takes another look at the robe. It is so familiar. Then she knows: it sold all winter at Macy's and just went on sale, she saw it there last week, a whole rack of them at the front of the lingerie department. Miri has just bought it. Probably everything in Miri's suitcase has just been purchased, probably right here in New York, including the suitcase itself. As if Miri has dropped down from heaven or come up out of the sea after vanishing, no traces, off the face of the earth.

YOU KNOW, I could really use a vacation, Rena says to Ilana. Rena is on the couch, holding up the phone with her shoulder. She's still in her robe, and her stomach is jumping around like it wants to go somewhere without her. What's her life? She hasn't had a callback in a month, the toothpaste gig is about up, she has no prospects, and everyone she knows is out of town. Meaning they've packed their suitcases and sublet their places saying they'll be back in a few months, then gone home to Des Moines or Milwaukee to become schoolteachers or waitresses or drama coaches at summer camps.

Please don't change the subject, Ilana says. Ilana's been filling Rena in on Shaindey, who called her back this morning and was on the phone about five seconds before saying she had to rush off to work. But Shaindey didn't go to work, Ilana checked, and now Ilana needs Rena to pay attention and use her considerable brainpower for something other than figuring out which guy on the nameplate is the producer.

I'm not changing the subject, Rena says, leaning back and swinging her legs up onto the sofa. There's something hard under her head. She pulls it out from under the cushion. The cheese platter from last night. Little orange cubes have dried onto the fabric and left a moldy smell. She'd made a little plate for Joe and herself, cheese and crackers and grapes, and carried it out, nervous. *This is very nice,* Joe said. *It looks like afternoon tea* is what she thought. That's why he'd never call her again: her idea of seduction was bridge mix and a fruit platter.

So what about Shaindey? Ilana says. What should I do? Keep pestering her, calling?

That's what I've been trying to tell you, Rena says. I'm going to take a vacation. Come east. Help you. She bounces off the couch. Tomorrow, the red-eye, she says. There's nothing on her calendar for the next two weeks or, say, the next two years. In fact, it's crystal clear that she needs a change, that it's time to leave L.A. She hangs up with Ilana, tosses her robe over a chair on the way to the shower, ticks off the names of at least four people she knows who, right now, would sublet her place on a dime.

EXCELLENT, MIRI SAYS, watching Shaindey hang up the kitchen phone. Shaindey has just talked to Ilana. Rena is coming to visit, won't it be great, they'll all be together, first time in years, let's have dinner Friday night, Rena and Ilana will come to the apartment. Shaindey knows Ilana is being fake—fake enthusiastic about a big reunion, fake casual about Shaindey's phone behavior lately because Shaindey has never talked to Ilana so hurriedly and, well, rudely. Shaindey kept her eye on Miri the whole time she was talking, Miri nodding, understanding both sides of the conversation though she didn't pick up the extension.

What should we make for dinner? Shaindey says, sitting down to write a shopping list. She wonders if Miri knows how to cook, hasn't been able to help but notice that Miri doesn't seem particularly at ease in the kitchen. Some of the appliances seem foreign to her— the disposal, the ice maker, the timer on the stove—a hesitation, as if Miri were figuring out how something operated from a manual in her head.

Shaindey mostly knows traditional cooking, like Ima's, she tells Miri. She can make various soups, chicken or brisket or turkey, chocolate cake.

Sounds fine, Miri says. But what about Ilana, she's a vegetarian.

How do you know that? Shaindey says, a quick look up from the list.

Miri tips her head.

Shaindey regards her sister. Something about Miri is beginning to vaguely assemble itself in Shaindey's mind, but Shaindey can't quite make out what it is. Have you visited Ilana? she says.

No.

Rena? Have you seen Rena?

No.

Then how?

I'll tell you soon. I promise.

Shaindey nods slowly and Miri smiles, and Shaindey feels a current like something electric running through her, from her chest to her knees; she's not sure she could stand right now. Would you mind if I took a shower? Miri asks.

No, please, go right ahead, Shaindey says. Miri leaves and Shaindey stares out the tiny window over the table, steadies herself with her breath. Who is Miri? The window is shut tight. But it doesn't matter, there are no birds like in Jerusalem, no great swooping flocks. The sky is empty, colorless. Why did she come back?

The shower comes on in full force—Miri likes the pressure they get in the apartment, she's told Shaindey, the way the spray slaps her back and tickles her toes—and Shaindey pulls herself up from the table and puts on a pot of water to boil. She isn't hungry, has hardly eaten in days, but she'll make something for Miri. Miri's arrival has stunned Shaindey in a way she cannot understand except to say that it's like falling in love. Like the way she felt in Jerusalem. After she got to Jerusalem she couldn't eat, couldn't sleep, was never tired. For twelve months she lived on air.

And now this feeling again, this stunned, full feeling that makes eating unnecessary, sleep unnecessary. Something is happening and she must pay attention. She measures out rice and pours it into the boiling water, food for Miri, because she, Shaindey, isn't hungry and no longer needs food. Like the angels, Shaindey thinks. She stirs the rice, feels herself hovering near the sphere of the angels.

IYERVASANA IS MEDITATING. Rena will take her sanctuary by storm, will shatter all the calm and leave little armies of nail polish bottles and French perfume everywhere. She'll bring in Chinese food and barbecued ribs and cuts of meat Iyervasana hasn't pronounced, let alone eaten, for three years. And that's just the material side. Who knows how Iyervasana will cope with Rena's hyper personality? They talk on the phone but, face it, having someone stay in your apartment is different. Iyervasana feels an itch in her foot, tries to let it float away, to put it on the barge laden with Rena-thoughts to float down the river and out from her mind. But the barge is so loaded, it can hardly move, and there's no room for the itch. She leans forward to scratch it, and the phone rings.

It is Ima. Iyervasana's chest pounds. Ima, calling from Israel. Where? You're in Netanya, you and Abba are at the beach? The pounding is like a gong. Gong, bang, bang, gong. Ima hardly calls her from twenty miles away, what's she doing calling from the other side of the world?

I have regards for you from Shimmy, Ima says. You remember him?

Shimmy. Shimmy Birnbaum who lived in the next building, Ilana's first boyfriend. She was sixteen, Shimmy seventeen. *When I get older I will make my parents call me Shimshon, or Samson.* His father was an even bigger rabbi than hers, stern and formidable. Shimmy went to Israel, turned secular, fought in Lebanon, then went to India, to Ecstasy Beach, to get high and zoned out with all the other messed-up Israelis. That was eight or nine years ago. Suddenly she wants to know all about him.

Where did you see him? Iyervasana says.

Here, in Netanya. He works here.

Netanya? What does he do there?

Diamond business. He came to our hotel, they have a gift shop in the lobby. He recognized us.

You didn't recognize him?

How could we, it's been so long. Plus he looks different. No beard, no yarmulke, an earring in one ear. Still—Ima hesitates—he's a nice boy. Boy. What am I saying? Man. A grown man.

Iyervasana feels a vibration in her lower back, like a guitar string. Shimmy, of all people. Why did she break it off? Too familiar, too close, the preordained life rising, treacherous, before her. But he wouldn't have wanted that, either. The string stirs again. She should find Shimmy, talk to him.

Your father wants to come on the line, Ima says. Hold on a minute, he'll pick up the extension.

Something is off. Abba never gets on the phone; Ima always pretends to send his regards.

Ilana? This is Abba. Just wanted to say hello.

It's Abba's voice but far away, like an echo, or from underwater.

Hi, Abba, she says, her mouth dry. He's hardly talked to her since the ashram. Suddenly she misses him, misses the gravelly softness of his voice. Enjoying your trip? she says.

Oh yes, Ima and Abba answer together.

Iyervasana's tongue is the size of a whale. Great, she says, the tongue now pushing to leave her mouth and swim out the door and head for the East River and the ocean.

Listen, Ilana, Abba says, then Ima is speaking, too, a double voice, in unison. This trip has us thinking. We just wanted to tell you that however you live your life, it's fine with us. Whatever you choose. Jewish or not Jewish. Religion or no religion. Marriage or no marriage. You decide. It's your life, not ours, and we love you no matter what, and we should have told you this years ago.

Iyervasana opens her eyes. She is in position on the floor, the phone untouched on its cradle. It has stopped ringing, and of course she never picked up, of course that wasn't Abba or Ima on the line. Iyervasana never picks up while she meditates. She doesn't even leave the answering machine on, afraid it will distract her even with the volume turned all the way to off. She is trying to increase her discipline, to keep her concentration on her breath even when the phone rings.

But her discipline has failed her, as it has, repeatedly, in the past two days. As if there were some sort of interference. She had perfected a high level of concentration over the years and now, all of a sudden, there's been a disruption, atmospheric static. A disturbance in her psychic waves. Thoughts of her parents, bits of conversations she'll never have with them: *Iyervasana—what a lovely name.* Yesterday an old song coming to her in Ima's singing voice: *If you want to be free, be free. And if you want to be high, be high. You can do anything that you want, you know that you can.* And earlier today, a fleeting vision of her lost sister Miri—Miri, Miri, wherever you are—Iyervasana as a marionette and Miri, pulling the strings, the puppeteer.

She gets up out of position, frustrated. And now this latest fantasy, Abba and Ima and Shimmy Birnbaum. She is irritated, feels the interference coursing through her body, an agitation demanding that she let go of something right now. She shakes her head, then her hands, then does some jumping jacks for no reason. One two, one two. Outside, a light rain is falling. She jumps faster, clapping her hands over her head, back and forth, over and over, until her arms ache.

THE MAN NEXT to Rena is movie-star handsome. Gorgeous in that casual way, as if he's always looked good in a shirt and tie, always had his hair perfectly tousled. Relaxed and thoroughly at ease, and Rena will be sitting next to him for the next seven hours.

It's eleven P.M. and half the plane is already sleeping. Rena's food sits doll-sized on her tray. Mr. Handsome, next to her, is eating his meal with gusto.

You're welcome to my dinner if you want more, she says to him, smiling. She shrugs her cutest shrug. It's the chicken dish. I ate before I left.

He smiles at her. His teeth are as white as hers, and he probably doesn't make his living doing mouthwash commercials. Thanks, he says, and looks down at her tray. I might take you up on that.

Friendly, Rena thinks. I'm Rianna, she says. Rianna Powell, she adds, tossing in a last name. She never thought she'd do that, waspify her last name, too, Hecht, how low can you go, but what the heck— heck! Hecht! she can't help herself! she really is funny!—she'll never see him again, it's only an airplane. Besides, the real names aren't working. She's failing with the gentile guys as Rena Hecht, hilarious, over-the-top, noisy Rena Hecht, and as for the Jewish guys, forget it, guys only willing to go out with dress sizes two and four. So I guess you didn't have dinner? she says. Board straight from work?

Oh, I ate. But free food, it's hard to pass up. He looks at her and does this adorable thing with his shoulders, a half shrug, half shimmy.

She senses a joke coming on—*Free food, pass up, pass out, airplane meals are food-free*—and stifles the impulse. Sure, Joe Maginnis laughed at her jokes but he probably couldn't wait to get out of there, was probably thinking, *What is it with her, everything has to be a big yuk, why can't she just be like other girls, batting their eyelashes and waiting for me to say all the clever stuff?*

Free food, a cultural thing, Handsome says, looking over at her tray. You sure you aren't hungry?

She does a cursory head shake and waves off the tray. Rianna Powell eats like a bird.

So, cultural thing? Rena says, hands folded, while he works on her roll.

Oh, it's kind of an ethnic joke, he says.

Joke? She cannot afford to register the word. She sits up straight, does her best to seem rigid and uncomprehending.

He makes a quick smile, then reaches across with his fork, stabs at her fruit cup. A little electrical charge flashes along her arm as his brushes hers. She catches a whiff of laundry detergent and beats back a wild urge to lean over and sniff that crisp, white shirtsleeve. She loves men's shirtsleeves. He nabs a canned peach slice and pops it in his mouth. He is adorable and she wants to smile but can't.

She's become a statue, her face frozen, the most humorless, most expressionless person on the planet.

Handsome makes another little smile. She stares at him, unable to thaw out her face. In her head she calls to her old self. Rena? Hello? Anyone there?

You know, I guess I'm not all that hungry, Handsome says, finally dropping the smile and sitting back, his body language unmistakable: *Nice talking to you. Let's not exchange phone numbers, okay?*

What about the joke? she says, her voice strangled. Rianna Powell is holding Rena Hecht hostage somewhere in the back of her throat. *Give me back my face!* Rena Hecht yells to Rianna Powell. *No! Rianna Powell yells back. No! Yes! No! Yes!*

Oh, that, he says to the ceiling as he reaches up to turn off the little light. It's not very funny. And anyway, you'd have to be Jewish to understand.

MIRI HAS RETURNED from her evening walk. She knocks softly and, when Shaindey doesn't answer, lets herself in with a key. The lights are on; Shaindey has fallen asleep on the couch. Miri gently drapes the afghan over Shaindey, turns off the lights and sits in the easy chair, watching her sister. Shaindey sleeps quietly, without moving, which amazes Miri. Miri was a noisy sleeper, restless in life as she's been in death, and Shaindey's stillness surprises her.

Outside, a taxi honks wildly. Miri gazes around the room. Nothing has changed—the coffee table, the pole lamp, Abba's books, the piano. She hugs herself in Shaindey's coat. She was not happy with how she left, dying in a plane crash so soon after she went away, a foreign passport and a changed name. She'd always planned to contact the family after a little more time had passed, but then it was over, just like that, her life ended with a single great swath of the shears. She'd been petitioning ever since to be allowed to come back and try to make things right, be the big sister she never was, help her sisters find some happiness. She glances over at Shaindey. And so far things seem to be going pretty well. *You can never be sure,* they told her, a warning. *You do what you can, but you can never be sure.*

Shaindey sighs and Miri pulls herself out of the chair and stands over the couch, brushes a hair off Shaindey's face. In Ilana's old room Miri takes off the coat and climbs into Ilana's old bed with her clothes on. She would like to dream. If she dreamed, she would dream she was still in Victoria with Jodi. Jodi, with her beat-up cowboy boots and beautiful red hair. She loved Jodi, her first and final love, furtive, in the dormitory at Barnard. If Abba and Ima had found out they would have killed her, well, not killed her, but made her marry one of the yeshiva boys, as good as killing, Ima murmuring, *You don't have to like it, you close your eyes and think of other things, you think women have always liked it? You have children, then he'll leave you alone. You have to have dignity in your life. Dignity is more important than happiness.*

She pulls the quilt up to her chin. If she dreamed, she'd dream about what she never got to finish out. Children, and a house by a lake, a glass of milk left on a table, a stack of bills to pay, the dog in the yard barking to be let in, block parties and summer dances and backyard barbecues, warm nights in a mauve bedroom with fresh-smelling curtains that moved gently with the breeze.

She closes her eyes and waits. A few hours will pass and then she will waken, briefly, into this world again, because she has heard the lament of her sisters. Their cries went up, and she pled in all her petitions, *Can't you hear them? Can't you all hear them? Surely they're entitled to something?* Until finally they told her, Go. For we have heard their cries, and sometimes we must answer.

IN SHAINDEY'S DREAM Jerusalem walks toward her, arms open wide. She is in Gan HaShoshanim, the Garden of Roses on HaPalmach Street, though there are no roses. It is a fallow season, Jerusalem tells her, and Shaindey can't find a bench to sit on, all the benches missing or taken away since she was last there. It's all changed since she left, Shaindey sees, scanning the bare garden, the broken squares of gray slate along the paths, but it's not hopeless, there are some bushes with buds over there, and yes, now she sees it, a bench at the edge of the park. Miri is sitting there, smiling, looking pleased, like a matchmaker approving her work. Shaindey walks toward her sister, holding Jerusalem's hand, and when she feels Jerusalem run its light fingers over her face and smooth back her hair, she holds her breath, that rapture, that ecstasy, waiting for the thing to happen, whatever the thing will be. A bird flies overhead, and they walk on, and Shaindey is certain this is right, that the bird is telling her she is not alone, not without protection, and that being with this city is the right thing to do. The only right thing, this is the one right thing in her life.

WAKE UP! RENA says to Handsome, tugging on his shirtsleeve. She has gotten her face back and has banished Rianna Powell forever, thrown her out the window over Kansas and told her never to come back.

What? What? Handsome turns to her, squinting. Is something wrong? You need me to get the stewardess?

I don't need the stewardess! Rena whispers. Someone across the aisle shoots her a look. It's probably three in the morning. She hasn't slept a wink, and a tall woman, another wide-eyed insomniac who looks, strangely, like her vanished sister Miri, has been walking up and down the aisle, passing Rena's seat several times. I'm Rena Hecht, Rena says to Handsome, urgent. I'll get the joke because I'm Jewish, I've had a major life shift while you were snoring over Colorado, and I'm starving because all this thinking burns up a lot of calories. I know it's late but you might as well listen because I'm really very funny and fun to know, okay? Please? Okay?

Handsome rubs his eyes and takes another look at her, then digs in his pocket and pulls out a candy bar. A Milky Way. Oh God, her favorite. She smiles, though she's close to crying, too. Why is it that things happen when you're high above the earth that would never in a million years happen when you're plodding along, weary and hopeful, on the ground?

IYERVASANA WAITS IN a plastic chair at the TWA terminal. She hasn't been to an airport in ages because they make her tense and because she's afraid of flying, but this time she finds the place interesting, the thought of going on a plane bizarrely appealing. In the last two days she's had thoughts of packing and closing up her apartment and going somewhere far away, the apartment, maybe even her whole life, suddenly seeming stifling, precious, fake.

She gets up, studies the arrivals monitor, strolls to the ticket counter.

I'm curious, she says to the woman behind the Plexiglas. The woman is tall and vaguely familiar. Competent, calm, reassuring, like someone you'd find working at a hospital, or a courthouse. Do you fly to India? Iyervasana says.

We do.

A place called Ecstasy Beach—have you ever heard of it?

The woman does a quick eyebrow lift, glances over at Iyervasana's feet. You have luggage? she says.

Oh, I'm not thinking of going now. Maybe in the future.

The woman leans toward the Plexiglas. She's older than Iyervasana, thirty-four, thirty-five. Let me give you some advice, she says. When you buy your ticket? Don't mention Ecstasy Beach. You'll be searched. She tips her head. You know what I mean?

Iyervasana nods. The woman straightens herself up, taps into her computer, reads the screen. You'd need to fly into Bombay, she says, then jots down some figures and hands it to Iyervasana. Iyervasana thanks her, goes back to the monitor. Rena's plane is landing.

Iyervasana slips the paper into her pocket and heads for the gate. An electric cart passes by, an elderly woman facing backward in the seat, anxiously gripping the sides. On an impulse, Iyervasana smiles and waves at the woman, who, flustered at the greeting, tries to wave back and loses her balance and spills, gently, out of the cart.

SHAINDEY ISN'T THE least surprised that Rena and Ilana don't believe her, but it doesn't matter. The table is set, the food is cooked, the three of them are together. And there's no point in waiting for Miri to come back with the bottle of wine she left three hours ago to buy because Shaindey understands now that Miri isn't ever coming back. Plus, Rena's brought wine, which Shaindey thinks might not be an accident.

Shaindey has shown Rena and Ilana the black canvas suitcase, but of course there is no identification, no way to prove the contents are anything but clothes of Ima's or Shaindey's. The bathrobe had been neatly packed, and though Shaindey pulled it out and held it up to her nose, trying to capture an essence of Miri, it smelled only of the factory stuff they spray on new clothes. Rena and Ilana exchanged glances while Shaindey sniffed, but Shaindey didn't mind. Off the hall, in her frilly room, Shaindey has packed her own suitcase. She will leave tomorrow night and fly to Jerusalem. She has closed her bank account and mailed letters to Mr. McMahon in Litigation, and to Abba and Ima care of Uncle Nathan and Aunt Aviva, and to Ilana and Rena at Ilana's apartment. She understands Miri has something to do with her leaving. Something she cannot yet know. But which, one day, where she's going, she might.

Two pairs of candles flicker on the dining room table. One for each of us, the rabbi's daughters, Shaindey says, motioning for her sisters to sit, and though Miri's chair is empty and her place setting untouched, no one contradicts her. Rena pours wine, and Ilana inhales the aroma of the soup and tells Shaindey it is very good. Butternut squash, Shaindey says, vegetarian for you, and Ilana nods and appreciates it since it is the last soup she will have in that apartment for a long time. In three days she will go to Bombay, where Shimmy Birnbaum lives alone and works as a drug counselor at the Jewish Home Clinic, so happy to hear from her, it's been such a long time, I can't believe you met my grandmother at the airport, the poor woman, such a fall, Ilana, Ilana, where have you been. Come, yes, please come.

And you, Rena, how are you? Shaindey says, and Rena smiles as if maybe she doesn't think Shaindey's life is so hopeless after all and says, Fine, thanks, Shaindey. Actually, I'm thinking of staying in New York awhile.

Oh, that's a good idea, Ilana says. You can stay at my place, she adds, because she was wondering what she would do about the apartment and isn't this perfect.

Yes, very good, Shaindey says. Of course, there's lots of room here. She sweeps a hand around the dining room. But you wouldn't want to stay with Abba and Ima.

Rena is beaming. Her sisters are so generous! Later, after another glass of wine, or maybe tomorrow or next week, she will tell them about Handsome, whose name is Greg and who lives five blocks from Ilana, and who squeezed her hand in the terminal and said, Call me as soon as you can, you must call me. Rena is dying to tell her sisters now but she doesn't want to hurt them, wishes so much they could have love, too. Couldn't they all have love? Was that too much to hope for?

Well, this calls for a toast, Shaindey says, reaching for her wine. Rena and Ilana nod, and the candle flames surge, grateful, with the sudden lifting of the glasses, the stirring of the air, the great exaltation of the sisters' collective breath.

THE SEVENTH YEAR

IT WAS THE Seventh Year, a time when the land was supposed to rest.

Nine times Boaz Deri had lived through such a year—he had been born during one, his age forever in sync—and now this would be, God willing, his tenth. No planting, no reaping, no nothing: *And the seventh year shall be a year of solemn rest for your lands, and you shall neither sow your fields nor prune your vineyards, and the grapes of your untrimmed vines you shall not gather.*

Boaz unlocked the door of his apartment, an envelope in one hand, a bag of oranges in the other, winded from climbing the three flights, his building one of the last in his Jerusalem neighborhood without an elevator. The strains of a Mozart sonata seeped into the hallway from the apartment next door. He let himself in, put the oranges on the coffee table, and looked at the envelope. More clippings from his friend Chaim in New York, something from the *New York Times* or the Jewish papers—Israel's cultural vacuum, the plight of the Ethiopian immigrants, the sliding of the Seventh Year. Especially the Seventh Year. It was not a popular custom; Boaz's friends would be surprised by his attachment to it, the papers running editorials, the secular having their say: it wreaked havoc on exports, a ridiculous throwback that had no business in the global economy that was the modern State. Boaz understood. Who, other than the ultra-Orthodox, would be interested in such a thing nowadays, the whole country worshiping the God of Productivity, incubators that had nothing to do with furry little chicks springing up weekly in Tel Aviv, a telephone the size of a billfold in every pocket? Even the kibbutzim were not immune, the second page of Friday's *Ha'aretz* featuring a collective that was selling stock, getting itself listed on the Canadian Exchange. Did anyone in such a country want to hear that the land, like a person, might get tired?

Boaz let himself down into an easy chair and gazed out the big window, a construction crane for a view, the city a constant boom where nothing was ever finished. The crane sat immobile, the late afternoon light streaming past it and into the room like an overdue visitor. March, and though it was beginning to turn warm, Boaz was cold—age, and the fact that his apartment only had heat in the mornings and again for a few hours every evening, building policy, and he hadn't wanted to spend the thousands of shekels to put in a private system. And now it was too late. If he hadn't put in the heat for Adina, hadn't done it when she asked, how could he do it now? He'd rather be a cold widower than a guilty one.

He pulled the cuffs of his sweater over his wrists and unfolded Chaim's letter. A clipping in English that he couldn't read fell into his lap. Israeli landowners were looking for loopholes around the Seventh Year, Chaim wrote. Had Boaz heard what they were doing, young hot shots and retired Army colonels who'd been buying up property left and right as if socialism had never existed? They were selling their land on paper to gentiles abroad, shamelessly advertising come-ons that were an embarrassment to the knowledgeable eye: *Buy a piece of Holy Ground, yours to own during the Holy Seventh Year!* The fact that Chaim hadn't lived in the country for forty years had not stifled his indignation. Nor did it bother Boaz. Chaim was entitled to his outrage. The two of them had come to the country together from Vienna, children, their parents still behind, doomed, then been packed off by the visionaries in charge first to a youth village, then to a mosquito-infested collective by the pitiful Yarkon—a trickle, God's spit, not a river. Together, they spent twenty years cursing the stubborn soil, first trying melons, then roses, then sunflowers, the ground refusing them at every turn. Now Boaz heard they made those sticks with the terrible names there—tongue depressors. The largest exporter of tongue depressors in the world. For this he and Chaim gave nearly a quarter century of sweat? Who could blame Chaim for slipping out of Haifa port under cover of darkness, huddling on a boat to America because he and his Frieda *had had it with the bugs, the shortages, the snipers, this impossible life*?

Boaz reached the end of the page. Chaim was coming to visit, alone; Frieda wasn't up to it. The urge had seized him and, one-two, he bought a ticket, nothing, Boaz couldn't help but notice, like his last trip two years before when he and Frieda had come on a whirlwind fortieth anniversary tour. Within six months of toasting each other's continued marital happiness, Adina was dead, a cancer in the ovaries. Should they have had more children? she whispered to Boaz near the end, guilty for having had only two when there were so many dead to make up for. Were the life forces that hadn't been given the chance to flower turning against her, the impulse to procreate gone horribly awry?

He set the letter on his lap. The crane began to whine and stretch like an animal coming out of sleep. He loved Chaim, his oldest friend, the only person in his life to have known his parents and two sisters, the single other witness that once such people had lived; but for forty years he and Chaim had been together only in the company of Frieda and Adina. Now Adina's absence seemed to fill the room with an iron-cold emptiness he could almost touch, the couch, the coffee table, the coat stand all suddenly confused and without purpose, as though she had never sat there, put her teacup there, hung her coat there. As though being with Chaim again as they had when they were young—before Frieda and Adina and the children, before their lives diverged onto different continents like opposite branches of a tree—meant the intervening years might never have existed.

IT WILL BE good to be back, Chaim wrote now, but in 1959 he could hardly wait to leave. And not just on account of Frieda. Did it matter where they lived? Chaim said to Boaz then. Europe was a grave-yard, and as for this country, did they belong here any more than they belonged anywhere? They had waited out the war together, teenagers, then scanned the lists coming out of the DP camps, the ship manifests; searched the family names, every possible spelling, posted in the papers identifying people who were wandering the country looking for each other. No one from either of their families ever appeared, eventually a letter or two arriving from some distant relative who'd made it to England or South America. It was a delu-sion to believe in belonging, Chaim said in 1959. What did anyone think they belonged to—a particular piece of ground, call it a home-stead, a village, a country? Hadn't they learned that lesson already?

Boaz washed, fortified himself with a glass of tomato juice, picked up the envelope, and stepped out into the hall. He smoothed back his hair, still thick and full, and knocked on the door next to his. The Professor and his young wife, where Boaz went for translations.

OUACHITA TECHNICAL COLLEGE

The door opened and he heard the distant sound of a piano con-
certo, felt a little spreading glow in his chest: Rachel Locke, who
appeared in the doorway like an angel and who caused in him a reju-
venating joy he could not regard as sinful. Could not an old man
admire beauty without the lust of possession?

"Mr. Deri," Rachel Locke said, red lips over pearly teeth, her
good fortune to be born into a prosperous family that could afford
conscientious dentistry, a faint wisp of mint floating into the hallway.
"What a nice surprise." She glanced at the envelope. "You have something that needs translating?"

He followed her, nervous, like a schoolboy, to the living room,
where she gestured to the sofa, then reached over to the radio on a
side table and switched it off. The room was hushed, an air of dusky
calm, the door to the Professor's study in the back closed. Either Yosef
Locke was deep in thought—philosophy or philology, Boaz couldn't
remember, or maybe it was his hearing—or perhaps he wasn't there.

"Some tea?" Rachel Locke said, sitting down in an armchair opposite him. Her hair was a pale gold, unnatural, Boaz suspected, the
coloring of the Austrian girls of his youth. It was the rage in parts of
Israeli society, the newspapers said, dark-haired women turning themselves blond and blue-eyed, an Aryan assault to the aging remnants
still wandering the streets. Boaz had been furious when he first read
about it. The insensitivity of these women! The national amnesia! Until
he saw Rachel Locke. Was imitation such a bad thing? Was this not
the natural outcome of a nation striving for normalcy, trying to be a
country just like any other, Jews wanting to live like everyone else?

"Tea, Mr. Deri?" She was smiling at him, waiting for an answer.

"Oh no, no thank you," he stuttered, ten again, in knickers and
socks.

She gestured to the envelope. He opened it, passed her the clipping. He was entirely in her hands, which he now saw had a coat of pink polish on each nail. No manure-spreading and peach-picking for her, a degree from Hebrew University, a master's from somewhere abroad, a handsome husband with a secure appointment. And a modern apartment twice the size of his with all the conveniences, including, he couldn't help but appreciate, sufficient heat. His fingers relaxed for the first time all day, the invisible warmth loosening their grip. How would Adina feel about his putting in heat if it helped his hands? Would that be less terrible, his greatest regret over his marriage that he hadn't acquiesced to her pleas to put in the heat? Had he been a bad husband? Or just stubborn, a sturdy pioneer who didn't need conveniences, luxuries? What kind of softness would they be inviting if they had private heat? he'd thought then. They would lose their ability to adapt, endure. To pull together in times of trouble, put the good of all before their own. It was a matter of character.

Rachel Locke shifted her feet, her free hand resting on her soft gray lap, an expensive dress suitable for a woman who held a high position in a bank and listened to Mozart on the radio. What about Rachel Locke's character? Could he have been wrong all these years? Was backbreaking labor and austerity the only way? Maybe even the wrong way, preventing him from providing his wife with the one bit of comfort she'd ever asked for?

"It's from the *Wall Street Journal,* Mr. Deri," Rachel Locke said, her native Hebrew almost musical, he forever stuck with a plodding German-tinged sound. "An article about the Seventh Year." She looked up. "You're interested in this?"

He tipped his head. "You might say that."

She seemed to consider for a moment. He could see she was

straining to be polite, suspicious of anything old-fashioned or, heaven forbid, from the religion. She was like so many of the young people now, his sons Doron and Avishai, too, a generation of technical wizards putting their faith in the power of human engineering. "It says Israeli landowners are looking for ways out," she said. "Setting up trusts and land corporations, all sorts of novel legal entities." She handed him the clipping. "I don't blame them, they're really quite primitive, these Seventh Year prohibitions. Don't you think?"

Boaz tipped his head again, noncommittal.

"You don't agree, Mr. Deri? You think it makes sense, the Seventh Year?"

Boaz made a weak smile. What could he say? That sometimes it might be good to stop all the striving? "Maybe it's good to give the world a little rest," he ventured. "A chance to rejuvenate on its own."

"But isn't that what the growers already do?" she said, irritation edging in on her reserve. "Rotate the crops? But on their own schedule, Mr. Deri, not some seven-year cycle dropped down from heaven. What could possibly justify such an outdated practice, especially now, with the situation with the Arabs, the economy suffering as it is, so many other priorities?"

He tried again to smile, pulled himself up from the sofa. Behind him, Rachel Locke's heels clicked on the tile. He was not a religious man. Dogma didn't interest him; the ritually correct, with their absolutes and ponderous judgments, didn't interest him.

But the explanation, the justification, was right there, in the same sentence as the prohibition itself. An explanation that helped make sense out of the seventy years in which he had lived, when human beings had demonstrated over and over their inability to run even the smallest corner of ground. Which assured him that the human spirit was not entirely in charge. *For the land is mine, and you are only sojourners here, with me.*

But this he would not tell Rachel Locke. Just as he would not tell his sons, certainty the fleeting privilege of the young. "Thank you, Mrs. Locke," he said at the door, the visit redeemed at that moment by the beam from her postcard smile.

IN THE LOBBY of the Jerusalem Hilton a week later Boaz waited for Chaim. Two hours earlier Chaim had called from the airport, the connection crackling with static, Boaz probably the only person in the country, maybe on the planet, to still use a rotary phone. There had been a mix-up with the luggage but he was on his way, Chaim said, his Hebrew as good as the day he left. The language had taken a viselike hold on both of them from practically the hour they'd arrived, intense propaganda—*Hebrew land, Hebrew labor, Hebrew language!*—mixing with their fierce personal determination to eradicate their native tongue. Even their names were not immune, the visionaries urging them by the late 1940s to take new ones that were better suited to the muscular New Hebrew who was emerging from the ruins: Berel became Boaz, Dershovsky became Deri, all identifying signs of the stooped-over shtetl Jew shed like an unwanted skin.

"And I brought a surprise," Chaim, formerly Mendel, said, the phone line a staccato of bleeps and buzzes. "Noah."

This would indeed be a surprise. Boaz wouldn't recognize Noah, Chaim's son. Unless he looked like Chaim, whose appearance at thirty, about Noah's age, Boaz could still conjure despite having seen Chaim more than fifteen times in the intervening years. Broad-shouldered, with a thick neck and strong features—like a movie star,

Frieda used to say—Chaim should have remained as the sturdy pioneer, not Boaz, who tended to a pale thinness, despite the almost constant sun, that had made Adina worry. Was he getting enough meat? Vitamins? Adina had never fussed unnecessarily, but to the essentials she paid attention: nutrition, good shoes, fresh air. Now his sons took over the worrying, Boaz eating less and less as time went on, his tastes simpler by the day. A boiled egg, a sliced tomato, some bread. It was really quite a paradox: just as things seemed to improve—no sickness on his doorstep, his pension secure, even sufficient—he found he had fewer wants than ever.

From a loveseat near the entrance he watched the revolving glass doors, an American group collecting excitedly by the front desk, *Houston Baptist Mission* stenciled on the tour agency's shoulder bags. There were more Christians than Jews visiting the country these days, the papers said; he heard one woman tell the clerk it was her fifth visit in two years. The clerk leaned across and said something in return, and the woman laughed. Chaim and Frieda always stayed here once they could afford it, or at another hotel a few notches down when they couldn't, no matter how much Adina had pleaded. *What kind of friends let friends stay in a hotel?* insisting there was room, even in the leanest times, the three-room flat on Tchernikovsky and the one after that on Aza, the boys would sleep in the living room. But always Chaim demurred, Frieda's asthma or his erratic insomnia, he'd say, inventing some excuse, unable to say what all of them knew: *Please, your life is already so hard, already so stretched.*

A giggle rose up beside him, and he turned. Catty-corner in matching armchairs, two Cokes on the little cocktail table between them, a Hasidic couple was on a date, the girl tossing her head back, flirtatious, the boy, maybe twenty, somber-looking in a dark suit and hat but unable, it seemed to Boaz, to take his eyes off the girl. And from her tone, a kind of brimming vitality and anticipation, it sounded to Boaz like a successful match. He turned away and found himself hoping he was right and that in five or six weeks there'd be an engagement, then a big celebration, a baby every year.

One of them made a slurping noise with a straw. Children still! Yet why not marry in the full bloom of youth, when energy and passion ran highest? It was a blessing to find your *bashert* when you were young. He had. Eighteen, he and Adina both, married four months after meeting. What was there to wait for? Some pretext of propriety? They had even considered forgoing marriage entirely dozens of their friends were doing it, why not, they were starting a new society, a new world—but something, he didn't remember what, made them go ahead. He closed his eyes and saw her then: a borrowed yellow dress, her dark hair unbraided, and red lips, she must have found a lipstick. Then afterward, juice and cookies, a pilfered bottle of Scotch, some singing and dancing in the parched field behind the chicken houses. The next day they took the kibbutz car and drove to Ein Gedi for two days. Within three weeks Egypt and Syria attacked, and the Arabs had declared war.

A scraping of chairs on the marble. He opened his eyes. The couple was getting up, walking to the door, the boy pausing, flushed, as the girl stepped in. Then, astonishingly, breaking all the rules, the boy put his hand on the small of the girl's back and, instead of waiting for the next little compartment, stepped in with her, the two of them squeezing together, the girl giggling as if it were a merry-go-around, until they were on the other side, out on the street. In that instant, Chaim and Noah came through and into the lobby.

They were father and son, there was no mistaking it. But while Noah had all the robustness of Chaim's early years, Chaim had aged drastically since his last visit, when he'd seemed to Boaz to look fifty, not sixty-five, and Boaz had wondered then if that's what happened in America: you drank from the fountain of youth, nothing to worry about except who won the World Series. Now life had caught up with Chaim, even in the new Garden of Eden.

"Don't even say it, I know I look terrible," Chaim said, pulling away from their hug, a matter-of-factness in his tone as if they'd had coffee last week or still lived ten minutes apart, Chaim simply returning from a long trip. They were like brothers who picked up where they had last left off, despite four decades with six thousand miles between them. "I've been sick but I'm better now." He stretched an arm out toward Noah, who had stood back, giving Boaz and his father room. "That's why I brought Noah, a chance to spend a little time together, show him my old haunts."

Noah smiled, shook Boaz's hand. The boy was rugged and handsome, like his father had been. "I saw you last—when?" Boaz said. A summer during college? On his way to Jordan, maybe, Petra back then the latest exotic destination? It had been Adina who'd kept track of their friends' children, remembering their birthdays and graduations, providing a home away from home when they visited the city. She would have known exactly when he'd last come, and with whom, and where he was headed.

"You were sitting shiva, Boaz," Noah said softly. "I came with my father, I happened to be in the country, on my way to Egypt."

A hand came down onto Boaz's shoulder. Chaim. Chaim had come for the funeral, but Noah? Noah must have talked to Avishai and Doron then; perhaps they'd even told him later that Noah had been there. His memory of the weeks after Adina died was of a hollowness that inhabited him, moving into his chest and pushing everything else out, even breath.

"Is this true?" Boaz said to Chaim. "Why don't I remember?"

Chaim squeezed Boaz's shoulder. "It's good Noah's here with us. Good to have a young man travel with us, help us see things again, through his eyes."

THE LAST ONE out of the bus, Boaz climbed down onto the parking lot at Kibbutz Doron, once the site of the youth village where he and Chaim had spent their first months. All the old buildings had either been torn down or remodeled beyond recognition, except one. Chaim and Noah trekked off to find it.

The weather had turned springlike, and Boaz took his hands out of his pockets, letting the sun warm them like a pair of undernourished plants. Behind him another of the ubiquitous cranes whined, single-family houses going up on some of the hundreds of dunams the kibbutz had sold to developers, its only salvation despite the green lawns and sparkling blue swimming pool. Kibbutzim all over the country were going bust. Socialism was dead, communal life dying. Who wanted to eat in a common dining room every night or wait for the central committee to approve your daughter's dancing lessons when you could live in isolated splendor in Tel Aviv or Haifa or anywhere, every decision, every meal, your own?

He walked a gravel path, a wooden bench nestled among pots of red geraniums at the top of a little incline, and sat, the geranium smell sharp, even bitter. It was quiet, the hum of the crane remote, as if what it was doing didn't have to matter to him the way the newspapers insisted it should: the loss of open space, the mindless imitation of American sprawl. A group of tourists had collected in front of the administration building. Dutch? Swedish? German? Boaz closed his eyes, listened—German—then opened them and gazed out at the hills. They could rage in the papers about the alteration of the landscape but in the long run it didn't matter. In a thousand years it would all be covered in sand anyway, gentle rises formed over the congested highways and ugly Paz gas signs, grown over with grass and trees and waiting patiently for the archaeologist's knife. They were all living on the rotted wreckage of someone else's past, every new civilization building itself on top of the one before. Which was a comfort, he supposed. There was always another chance.

The low murmur of German floated up the path. The group clustered ten or twelve meters from him, looking out over the kibbutz grounds with their guide, agriculture long since abandoned in favor of plastics manufacturing. One of the tourists glanced at Boaz, then quickly turned away, embarrassed, it seemed, for being caught not paying attention. What did they make of this country?

Footsteps on gravel. Chaim and Noah appeared on the path.

"So? Did you find anything?" Boaz said.

Chaim sat, out of breath. Noah gazed at the sloping hills, a camera around his neck. He had taken half a roll before they even got there: Boaz and his father outside Boaz's apartment, in front of the café where they had lunch, boarding the bus. "What was left," Chaim said. "A little building, maybe it was the infirmary, I don't know. Now there's a lot of pictures on the walls. I didn't see either of us in any of them but who knows, I might have missed something."

The Germans were moving off. Carefully, they walked down the path, watching their feet, afraid to disturb anything. "Do you remember this?" Noah said, sweeping up the vista with one hand. "It's really spectacular, the views of the hills and the valley, all those tiny wild tulips out there."

"I don't remember it," Chaim said. He looked at Boaz. "Do you?"

Boaz shook his head. Nothing was familiar, not the scenery or the buildings, not even the smells. Was it possible he'd once lived there? Was memory that selective, that easily crowded out? Noah had stretched his arms out wide and was taking deep, deliberate breaths. He lived in Manhattan, he told Boaz on the bus, and never got enough air.

"He reminds me of those morning exercises," Chaim said, looking at Noah. "You remember, Boaz? Those calisthenics they made us do?"

Noah turned around. "What? What was that?"

"Those thin-lipped ladies," Boaz said, staring off into the distance, seeing again the grim women in their gray shirts and thick shoes. Functionaries from the relief agencies whose job it was to acclimatize tender European children with their brusque staccato Hebrew. "Five-thirty in the morning. They'd bring us outside, whatever the weather."

"Wasn't there also a hike, some march they made us do?" Chaim said. "We had those lace-up shoes, remember? It took forever to get them done up, and they'd be yelling at us to hurry."

"A march?" Noah looked out at the grounds. "Do you know where?"

"No, but I can tell you why," Boaz said. "For color. To put color in our cheeks. A parade of half-starved city children, and they were going to give us rosy cheeks with walks, we should eat the air." He turned to Chaim. "Except you. You always looked healthy." He looked at Noah. "Your father was always strong. An ox, we used to say."

Chaim shook his head. No one would call him an ox now, his skin as pale as Boaz's, his cheeks sunken. Even until his last visit he'd had the body of a wrestler: firm, compact, muscled. Now he seemed to Boaz shrunken, the muscles not gone to fat but instead seeming to have disappeared altogether.

Noah lifted his camera and looked through the lens, panning the fields for something to capture. "Anyhow, we got used to it," Boaz said. "After a few months they pronounced us healthy and shipped us off to kibbutz, and we got used to that, too."

"Those early years," Chaim said. "No frills, no extras, no nothing. It was heroic, really. Not like now, with our fancy cars and big houses." He pointed to himself. "I don't mean your life, Boaz, I mean mine. Soft and easy and spoiled."

Heroic? Age had clouded Chaim's memory like a cataract. They hadn't felt heroic then; they'd only felt terrified. Afraid of the raids. Of the miserable winters. Of dying from malaria and influenza, and suffering from things that would plague them the rest of their lives. Weakened nervous systems, unchecked diabetes, digestive disorders. And more. Adina hadn't been the only woman to lose a pregnancy during those years. Frieda, too, or had Chaim forgotten?

The Germans were walking in single file near the factory buildings, the corrugated metal roofs glinting in the sun. For an instant Boaz imagined they'd come to do penance, to work in the factory before moving on to some more terrible destination. Noah snapped a picture. "It wasn't heroic, Chaim," Boaz said flatly, staring ahead, listening to his own voice as if he were hearing someone else. He sounded almost cruel, and didn't mean to, was talking to himself as much as to Chaim. Or the Germans. "It's just how it was, and we had no choice."

Chaim waved a hand. "But doesn't that count for something? Doesn't courage count? Bravery? The willingness to sacrifice?" Noah moved next to his father, rested his palm on Chaim's shoulder. A good son, who could see the valor buried in his father's long-gone past. "It can't have been for nothing," Chaim said, a rising distress in his voice. Seventy years old and looking for meaning in his life. Boaz understood. He was doing it, too. "Not that I would know. It was you, Boaz. You, who stayed and sacrificed. I left."

"Don't be so hard on yourself," Boaz said, more softly now. "You had to live your life." Boaz took Chaim's hand between his own and patted it the way Adina used to do with the boys when they needed solace. "Believe me, Chaim, you didn't miss anything by leaving."

BOAZ GAZED OUT the bus window, Chaim dozing beside him, and watched the passing fields. Unharvested corn that fell to the ground for the birds, olive trees naked without the sacks that hung from their trunks to catch the delicate fruit, groves of yellow citrus, lemons dotting the ground like fallen petals. Wild abundance that both teased and reassured: *Do not touch, but look what the earth can do.*

The bus climbed, giving Boaz, and Noah in the seat in front of him, a view of vineyards below. In the gathering dark they could make out hundreds of rows, a stillness there—no workers, no tractors—that made the fields seem frozen in time. Carefully Boaz slid open his window, the air fragrant with the excesses of early spring, and squinted at the winery buildings as if it were 1929 and Rothschild himself were down there with his specially imported grapes and foreign workers, his personal largesse and pity. What would Rothschild think now, the vines heavy with fruit, the air so ripe it was almost too fragrant, too much?

Beside him, Chaim shifted, murmured in his sleep. Was he dreaming of Frieda? Of his vanished past? Could they go next week to Rafa or Abu Ghosh to buy produce from the Arabs like they used to during the Seventh Year? Chaim had asked Boaz at dinner.

It wasn't safe, Boaz had to tell him. You didn't go to Abu Ghosh anymore, to Rafa. Not without a bulletproof car and a soldier with a gun.

But that was the best part, those outings to the villages to buy vegetables and trinkets, speak your few words of Arabic.

Gone. All gone.

Noah turned in his seat, looked out Boaz's window at the neat rows of trees. Apple, maybe, or perhaps those small pears. "It's amazing, all this plenty," he said. "Like nature on display."

"Some people find it frustrating, even unpatriotic," Boaz said.

"Oh, I'd like to photograph it," Noah said. "Ride around the country and take pictures, the whole place bursting. But not just when it's full. When the fruit is rotting on the ground, too. And the fields when they're fallow. The whole cycle, without anyone meddling." He leaned closer to the glass. "I could see a whole series, shots of all the different stages." His finger tapped at his lips, the idea taking root like a seed. Sometime during dinner it had come to Boaz that he remembered seeing Noah at the shiva. And thinking then: this is consolation, Chaim as witness but his son as witness, too.

"Thank you for coming to see me when Adina died," Boaz said.

Noah looked over at him. Outside, an orange grove thickly lined the road, the fruit like little suns in the passing headlights. "My mother couldn't come. She wanted to, but some people are too close, she told me. She felt terrible and selfish, but she said she couldn't bear Adina's dying, and that she'd be no comfort to you at all."

Boaz nodded, and Noah shifted back around in his seat. When Chaim and Frieda left for America, Adina wept every night for a week, the only time he'd seen her cry. *Like a sister,* she'd said to Boaz, an old wound reopened, losing her family all over again. Now the breeze from the open window was blowing Chaim's hair into little feathery wisps, and Boaz gently slid the glass closed so as not to wake him.

RACHEL LOCKE WAS at the mailboxes downstairs, a bag of groceries at her feet. From the stairwell Boaz saw her fishing in her purse for the little key. He had only gone downstairs for something to do; now that Chaim was in the country, his mail had dwindled by half. Who was there to write? His sons called, Doron traveling back and forth all the time between Tel Aviv and New York, Avishai in Sydney this year with his in-laws, his wife worried the grandchildren wouldn't know her parents. *What's the difference where I am,* Avishai had told him. *With a computer, a modem, a phone, I could live anywhere. Same job, same company, what's the difference which country?*

Softly, Boaz went to the mailboxes, extracted a few anemic-looking envelopes from his cubby. Chaim and Noah had gone up north to visit Frieda's relatives, then for a little sightseeing along the coast. Boaz had declined, not wanting to intrude.

"Mr. Deri, how nice to see you." Rachel Locke was holding an armful of mail—manila envelopes, for the Professor perhaps, and a stack of regular white ones, letters from globe-trotting Israelis like Avishai who could be writing from Hong Kong, Los Angeles, Stockholm, living anywhere, indifferent to the terrain. She bent down, a weariness in her movements, hints of darkness visible beneath the golden shine of her hair, and took something from the grocery bag. Fresh figs in a little cardboard box. Deep blue, with delicate pointy tops. "Please, try one."

He hesitated.

"From California," Rachel Locke said, biting into hers. She showed him the soft green pulpy inside, the tiny red seeds. "Not bad." She moved the box toward him.

He took one, held it carefully by the little stem. The first time he'd been in the country during a Seventh Year—1945, he was four-teen—he didn't have a fig for ten months, or nearly any fresh fruit at all. A bad growing season for the Arabs, and of course there were no imports. The following year it was worse: 1952, four years after Independence, half the Arabs gone, the other half waging sporadic war against the Jews from their villages at home. That year the only fruits they had on the settlement were tomatoes and occasional peaches sold to them by the Druze, and strawberries that grew wild on the perimeter in the spring.

"Go on, Mr. Deri. Have a bite."

He bit into it. It was more than not bad; it was wonderful, the best fig he'd ever eaten. "It's delicious," he managed.

"I'm glad you're enjoying it," Rachel Locke said. "Have you been able to get good produce? It's getting harder and harder in this neigh-borhood, all the vendors worried about losing their religious cus-tomers, carrying only what's imported, and for such high prices."

"Oh, I've been fine," he said. Did he dare tell her about the early years? What was more tedious for anyone than to hear about the past? To have their own deprivations diminished by hearing them compared to worse, and likewise their joys? *You think that's so wonderful, let me tell you about wonderful.* "No complaints," he said, smiling.

"Well, yours is a rare spirit, Mr. Deri," Rachel Locke said, shaking her head. She seemed worn, a sadness about her he couldn't match up with her usual crisp self-assurance. "I wish I had some of your serenity." She picked up her bag and made a weak smile, then went to the stairs, her heels clicking on the tile. Beside him, her perfume hung like a cloud, a defeated spirit waiting for a strong wind to take it somewhere it couldn't manage to get to on its own.

THE APARTMENT WAS too quiet. Boaz felt hounded by his solitude. He tried to eat—a tomato, cheese, bread—lost interest and went to the easy chair to read. Within ten minutes he was up and in the hall.

He collected his breath, looked at the Lockes' door. Should he knock? He had nothing to translate, his only reason for the half a dozen visits he'd made there in as many months. Apart from that, he hardly knew Rachel Locke. But something had propelled him into the hall, and it wasn't just the tasteless meal. There had been a melancholy about Rachel Locke that afternoon, and it had nagged at him. What, then, did he have to lose? His dignity if she refused his company? At his age such considerations had long ceased to be an issue.

"Mr. Deri," Rachel Locke said, surprised. She glanced across the hall at his door, then at his empty hands. "Everything all right?"

He waived aimlessly. "I just thought I'd come by. Though perhaps you're busy, perhaps you and your husband are having dinner soon, or going out."

She shook her head and stepped aside to let him in. In the bright light of the hall fixture she looked tired. "My husband is out of town. Please, come have some tea."

He followed her to the kitchen, glancing at the study on the way as if waiting for confirmation, for the silent door to open and close in agreement. "He's away? I'm sorry, I didn't realize."

"Yes, all week," she said, filling the kettle, a worry in her tone as if she'd said *all month, all year.* The counters were immaculate, white tile with bits of sea blue, the only sign of use a half-filled bowl of soup in the sink, as if someone had taken a few spoonfuls and stopped, no appetite. "He's in New York giving a paper." She hesitated, a little catch in her voice. "It's very lonely without him."

He stood by the table, awkward, while she busied herself with cups and saucers, a tray, a plate of fancy cookies. He'd made a mistake, he shouldn't have come; he hadn't meant to get personal, to make her talk about loneliness. She wasn't the kind of woman to broadcast her feelings to anyone willing to listen. She was like Adina that way, a private person who kept her emotions to herself. He wanted to hold up his hand, tell her she didn't have to say any more about it; that they could talk about the weather, the constant news. Even the Seventh Year.

She picked up the tray, carried it to the living room. They took their customary seats. Then he saw it in the corner, on a table in front of the huge window: a white candle flickering inside its little glass.

HE HAD BEEN a pilot in an elite unit, had started to make a career in the Army. She was married to him less than a year. It was the Professor who'd introduced them—she, his student, he, his good friend. Ten months after the wedding he was dead, eight years ago this week. Hezbollah fire, Lebanon. Everyone knew it was a war they couldn't win. It was a bad time of year for her, but she couldn't keep her husband chained to the apartment. He, too, grieved, didn't he?

"About the same age as my son Avishai," Boaz said, looking at the photograph. A good-looking young man in green Army issue, his head tipped a little to the side, cocksure, like all of them, sunglasses propped on his hair.

"How many children do you have, Mr. Deri?" Rachel Locke said. She had a tissue in her cuff, had been dabbing at her eyes.

"Two sons. One in Australia, the other here in Zichron but back and forth all the time to the States." Rachel Locke nodded. He could tell she wanted him to go on, that the conversation needed to be two-way. Otherwise her pain would be worse, the shame of grieving before a stranger only compounding the loss. "My son who's in Sydney says it will be for only a year, his wife's parents are there." He tipped his head. "But you know how it is. Israelis, they say a year, it could be a lifetime."

"And the other? He's married, too?"

"Divorced. His children live with their mother nearby. But it's not the same."

She picked up her teacup and looked inside. "We've been trying to get pregnant. But it's not happening."

"These things are difficult," he said. *Cancer in the ovaries?* Adina had whispered, horrified. *How is it that that which brings forth life can also bring forth death?*

"We probably shouldn't be working so hard," Rachel Locke said. "Should stop being so scientific about it." She looked up and made a small smile. "Maybe I should take a tip from you, Mr. Deri. Let go, and let nature take its course."

He tipped his head again. The candle fluttered, then stilled itself. "Your wife—she lived to see her grandchildren?"

"Oh yes, all of them. Six."

"Six, a blessing. A full life, I hope?"

"My wife?" he said, surprised. "Oh yes, a full life."

Rachel Locke put down her teacup, folded her hands. She was waiting for him to speak. To tell her about Adina. Grief meeting grief. And in some small way, assuaged.

"She got out of Prague with some relatives, still a child," he said. "Then she got herself fake papers to come to Palestine. A strong-willed teenager, full of principle. She left the relatives behind in Glasgow, they had gotten settled, Scotland, things were all right. Why are you going there? they said. We're safe here." He smiled. "Safe, she didn't want."

"A brave woman," Rachel Locke said.

"Always brave. She served in the Army longer than I did. Fifty years old, she took a degree in psychology. And friends: everyone. Russians, Sephardim, Arabs. From her life, you could make a movie." He gazed at the candle, then at the window above it. "Though you would never have heard that from her."

Dusk was giving way to darkness; he could see the lights of the Old City in the distance. Somewhere a muezzin called. "She loved this city," he said.

"And you brought her here?"

"I did," he said. A flock of birds passed the window, squawking like noisy messengers telling everyone it was evening, time to go home. "At first she thought Tel Aviv, that we should go there. But I persuaded her."

"And she loved it."

The noise was fainter now, the birds passing other windows, other rooftops. "She did."

"So you brought her to a place she loved."

AFTER A MEAL at Chaim's chosen falafel place on Ramban Street, suitcases by their feet, Chaim hailed a cab for the ride to the airport for the twelve-hour flight to New York. Noah was extending his stay, first hiking in the Golan, then traveling down to the Negev to Mitzpe to see the crater. Boaz had told him that when he came through Jerusalem to stay with him, he had room.

"Now you think about coming to visit us, all right?" Chaim said. "A few weeks in the States, it'll do you good, Frieda will treat you well."

"I'll think about it," Boaz said, though it wasn't likely to happen soon. First there might be Sydney, then maybe a week in Greece, for the sun. Plus, the papers were running advertisements for trips to Europe—Kraków, Berlin, even Vienna—guided tours to the old Jewish sections, to restored synagogues and houses, where people could find their roots before they vanished for good.

He waved off the cab, then continued down Ramban, a strong sun warming his neck and hands. He turned up Ibn Ezra, then onto his own little street, a narrow lane overgrown with bougainvillea no one wanted to cut back. It seemed a crime to trim away the purple blooms, each beautiful despite their almost choking abundance. One of the flowers brushed the top of Boaz's hair as he came through the entrance to his building, the vine it hung from arching over the doorway like a fallen crown.

A week later Noah came and stayed a few days before heading to the desert. All spring the papers reported that the fruit trees were particularly full and generous that Seventh Year, enough to carry them into the eighth, though many claimed the papers said that every Seventh Year. Avocados from Spain became popular and much sought after for their unusual nutty flavor. Boaz saw the building beyond his window finally become completed just as ground was broken on another in an adjacent lot.

Three months after his visit Chaim wrote that Frieda wasn't well, it wouldn't be long, a year at most. At the end of summer, Avishai came back with his family from Australia.

And the following year, after the winter rains, Rachel Locke gave birth to a baby daughter.

MEZIVOSKY

THE RUSSIAN NEXT door was driving Koenigsman crazy. It wasn't just the constant smell of potted beef, cuts of meat Koenigsman had never heard of, let alone eaten, which seemed to simmer day and night in what Koenigsman could only picture as a beet-seeping blood-red stew. Or the volcanic music that exploded out the open windows at all hours but most horrifically in the mornings, a five-thirty trumpet call blasting Koenigsman out of bed. These things he could almost tolerate; could chalk up to eccentricity, cultural differences, even passion that was still capable of gripping the Russian heart and soul but had long since been leeched out of Koenigsman and his fellow Americans with roots in the Pale. He could even, if pressed, covet his neighbor's lusty embrace of Rachmaninoff at dawn and fatty borscht at night, any such impulses of his own sanitized away through a hundred family years of soaking in the great washing machine of America.

No, it wasn't the cooking, the noise, the inexplicable habit the Russian had of bringing his garden hose indoors once a day, then returning it outside an hour or two later, dripping, that bothered him. It was the man's insufferable superiority. From nearly the hour since he'd moved in during a sweltering July heat wave that had Koenigsman again questioning why he lived in New England where Yankee stoicism required that no one acknowledge either the heat or the humidity, the Russian had informed Koenigsman that everything about the Mother Country—its language, musicians, pastry, poetry, and the quality of its hats—was better. And that he, Simcha Mezivosky, was the personal embodiment of that supremacy: you name it, he knew everything about it.

Now, on a Sunday morning exactly one month to the day since the cautious Kaloyanides moved out and Simcha Mezivosky and his cowed and sheepish family moved in, Mezivosky was at a picnic table on his patio, tinkering with a VCR.

"Doing a little home repair?" Koenigsman called across the lawn, moving a couple of garbage cans around on his own patio, trying to seem productive, as if rotating the trash cans every now and then served a purpose. Koenigsman hated home ownership and would have been happy to move to an apartment now that his sons were away in school but Arlene would have none of it. To her, apartment renting was akin to adolescence: it was something you grew out of. Or worse, grew into: right now she was in a forgotten corner of Florida helping her eighty-three-year-old father liberate himself from even more of his dwindling possessions so that he could move from a retirement one-bedroom to a studio in assisted living. In two weeks she'd return home desperate to put on an extension or renovate the now archaically named playroom, anything to ward off the fact that the two of them were headed down that same path of divestiture one day.

Mezivosky shrugged at Koenigsman's question and tipped his head to peer more deeply into the VCR. Koenigsman strolled over, bent and put his hands on his knees as if he knew what he was looking at, and said, "Ah, I see."

"Yeah? You see what, Koenigsman?" Mezivosky said into the metal, squinting into the little flap where the cassettes went. Mezivosky's own wife and children were nowhere in evidence, having gone "to the sea," he told Koenigsman, with relatives in New Jersey. Koenigsman had pictured a clutch of awkwardly dressed women, doughy and depressed-looking, like Mezivosky's wife, frying fish and onions over illegal camp-fires on the sand. "A piece of tin junk made by clever Japanese to rip off stupid American consumers who don't know the difference between real machines and Tinkertoys?"

Koenigsman straightened up. A flock of birds took off from the back neighbor's hedge, trimmed flat and perfect as a tabletop. "And you do, Simcha? You know all about it?"

Mezivosky poked a thick finger into the mouth of the VCR and wiggled it around. Koenigsman had a dim memory of Mezivosky telling him that, along with training as an engineer, lawyer, and con-cert violinist, he'd also studied dentistry. "Of course I do," Mezivosky said without looking up. Koenigsman noticed a bald spot on top of Mezivosky's head, a circle the size of a quarter. How old was he? Thirty-five? Forty? "In Russia we didn't have such junk."

"In Russia you didn't have VCRs," Koenigsman said. "You didn't have videos, a Blockbuster on every corner, three bucks a night."

Mezivosky extracted the finger and waved it over his head. "Maybe, but what machines we did have were quality. They lasted."

Koenigsman slipped his hands into his pockets and looked around. The Mezivosky patio, like the house itself, identical to Koenigsman's and to everyone else's in the development, looked like the lot of a junkyard—old console TVs, little RCA black and whites, monstrous canister vacuum cleaners like what Koenigsman's mother used to drag through the house, a couple of rusted lawn mowers. Even stereo parts: a turntable and a dinosaur-age tape player, the likes of which Koenigsman hadn't seen since college when his

Jefferson Airplane tape got stuck and he had to call the dormitory janitor to pry the thing open with a screwdriver.

"What are you going to do with all this stuff?" Koenigsman said, waving at the assortment of metal leaning against the siding.

"What do you think?" Mezivosky's voice was muffled as though he'd crammed his whole head into the cassette slot. "I'm going to fix it."

"Fix it? What for? It's old stuff. You can get new stuff cheaper and better than what it would cost to get the parts for these."

The finger waved again. "No, no, Koenigsman, that's where you're wrong." Mezivosky looked up, giving Koenigsman a full view of his bad teeth and smug smile. "It's only cheaper and better if you know nothing. If you're a useless American who can't replace the toilet paper roller when it breaks." He lifted his chin and nudged his shoulders back, puffing himself up like a fish. "For me, it's nothing. For me, it's second nature. This is what we learned in Russia. How to do everything. How to build and fix and know the inside of every machine. In Russia you learn the whole thing, not just little parts." He puffed himself up bigger. Koenigsman thought of the adders he once saw on public television, venomous snakes that fill with air before they pounce. "You think Sputnik was an accident?"

FACTS, HISTORY, HARD data: none of it persuaded Mezivosky. More than once on the Russian's patio, a long evening ahead after a quick supper alone—Koenigsman secretly allowing himself to indulge in his boyhood favorites, salami and eggs, fatty pastrami from the New York–style deli in the next town, because Arlene wasn't there to see and besides, what were a few days in an otherwise fastidiously cholesterol-vigilant life?—Koenigsman patiently explained to Mezivosky that Russia had lost the space race, not won it, and that half their Olympic athletes had been disqualified for swallowing steroids the size of golf balls. And as for their vaunted poets, who since Pushkin had come along to rival Whitman, Frost, Allen Ginsberg?

Mezivosky dismissed all of Koenigsman's arguments with a wave of the hand and his signature shrug. How do you know? he'd counter, wiping his fingers on an oily rag before sipping scalding tea from a glass, the ever-present beef smell hovering just outside the kitchen window like a nosy relative. Koenigsman could only guess what Mezivosky had done to Kaloyanides' pristine kitchen, the model with the built-in breakfast nook that Arlene mournfully craved; she and Koenigsman had had to settle for the bay window with the two side cabinets instead. Twice, Kaloyanides and his wife had had them over for dinner, immaculately prepared eggplant and chickpea and spinach dishes, for which Koenigsman had reciprocated with a string of boneless chicken barbecues before realizing his neighbors were vegetarian.

About the poets, for example, Mezivosky would say. You can read Russian?

I read, Koenigsman would say, who'd be fudging now, not much of a literary man, a well-read tax man but a tax man nonetheless. It was Arlene who supplied him with the famous names. Word gets out, Simcha, Koenigsman added. Even if it's only in translation.

Phooey, Mezivosky would say, putting down his glass and shoving a hand into the guts of an ancient humidifier. The best don't bother with translations. Too much of a risk. And who needs American readers anyway?

AUGUST WOUND DOWN, the first cool evenings, and the piles of broken junk on Mezivosky's patio grew higher, stretching halfway to the frosted bathroom window. Koenigsman saw it all from where he stood on his own patio ineptly rolling up the hose and covering the grill. Was Mezivosky aware that in three or four months the snow would bury his treasure? That it would hopelessly rust in the rain? And that its accumulation was probably a violation of the town's finicky zoning laws? Koenigsman hadn't been allowed to put in even a birdbath without permission.

Hoisting his rake and strolling across to Mezivosky's yard after a few futile pokes at a couple of leaves in his own, Koenigsman asked Mezivosky, who at that moment had his head inside the maw of a huge vacuum cleaner canister, whether he intended to continue tinkering with all that stuff through the winter.

"Perhaps," Mezivosky said, the *h* clogging in his throat, coming out *per-kchaps* in that inescapably identifiable way that reminded Koenigsman of his long-dead grandmother, whose accent had so deeply humiliated Koenigsman's mother as a child that she forbade the older woman from talking in front of her young friends. Koenigsman's grandmother would wave a bony finger and tell him the story every time he visited, his mother pursing her lips and pretending to be busy with the teacups, her daughter should be *eshemed*. Suddenly it occurred to Koenigsman that maybe Mezivosky had nothing else to do. That maybe the engineering, law, dentistry, and music weren't quite what he'd made them out to be. And that maybe Mezivosky had no real job.

"You have time to do all this, with your work?" Koenigsman asked, looking down at the bald spot. A breeze ruffled across the patio, a hint of crispness; Koenigsman thought fleetingly of storm windows and gutter-cleaning, felt a dim curling knot of dread.

"Of course, plenty time." Mezivosky coughed out a little cloud of dust. "Always time for a *kchobby*."

Koenigsman glanced around the yard. A lawn mower he'd seen Mezivosky take apart in July, now cleaned and shiny and looking capable of running frighteningly well, stood at the property line like a sentry between their houses. Koenigsman heard a nagging rattle of envy inside his head; he had trouble installing picture hooks.

"What kind of work does your wife do?" Koenigsman said. She wasn't back yet; neither was Arlene. It came to Koenigsman that he'd been counting on their wives' return to restore a sense of normalcy. Suddenly he was seized by a panicky vision of himself and Mezivosky living forever side-by-side alone, Koenigsman doomed to watching the Russian perform an endless stream of small machine repairs for the rest of his days.

"Nurse," Mezivosky said. He pulled his face out of the canister. "She's a doctor but here they won't let her. Much better education in Russia for doctors, she knows much more than Americans."

Koenigsman nodded. "Of course. It's always better in Russia."

"I'm not kidding, Koenigsman," Mezivosky said, leaning down and inspecting the hole where the hose was attached. "You know in Russia we don't need anesthetic? We just use ice."

"Is that so? Just send your surgery patients up to Siberia and freeze them before operating?"

Mezivosky waved the hose. Koenigsman couldn't tell if that was to answer him or for purposes of examination. "No, they pack the patient in ice in hospital. Very effective. Stops the heart naturally.

Temporary death but no one's afraid, they always come out of it." He let the hose drop. "Not like here where the chemical can kill you. No such thing as overdose of ice."

The subject made Koenigsman queasy; he was not good with medical details. "What is it, exactly, that you do?" he ventured.

Mezivosky sat up, wiped his forehead on his sleeve. "I fix the vacuum, what do you think I do?"

"I mean for a living."

"A living," Mezivosky said. "A living," he repeated, then shook his head. "Such an American word. So small-minded. As if life was money. As if work was life."

KOENIGSMAN WOKE, SWEATY, dreaming he was trapped up to his neck in a frozen lake; Mezivosky was trekking across the expanse with a hatchet or machete or—no—a chain saw, wielding it like a pro, breaking the ice into movable slabs and shouting over the din to Koenigsman how, lucky for him, he had just that day repaired and oiled the saw to perfection. Instantly Koenigsman recognized the saw as his own, picked up at Sears in a foolish consumer moment and now buried deep in the bowels of his garage. A dead tree in Koenigsman's yard had been running a hotel for carpenter ants in its trunk; too cheap to shell out two hundred bucks to the tree guys, Koenigsman instead shelled out three hundred for the saw, which, from the moment he brought it home, he knew he'd never use. He was afraid of it, teeth like a shark's, an alligator's, a grizzly's, and Koenigsman never so much as plugged it in. Now the never-used tool had buzzed him out of his wretched dream, the last fading image that of a giddy, wild-eyed, rescuing Mezivosky.

Miserable, Koenigsman crawled out of bed. In the bathroom he wrapped himself in Arlene's terry robe, then went downstairs to the kitchen, poured himself a glass of milk, and made a peanut butter sandwich. The grinning Mezivosky bobbed into his head. He despised the man—he was arrogant, selfish, and utterly without charm—but Koenigsman felt a twinge. Guilt. Responsibility. The man was an immigrant, a refugee. Someone who'd endured terrible things. Where was Koenigsman's heart? In the rotating garbage cans on the patio? His own grandparents had come to this country, tormented, with nothing. Now there was a family next door, and they, too, had to eat. What could the forlorn wife be earning, probably less than a nurse, more likely an aide? Plus there were the two children, a pimply boy and girl, joyless teenagers who had skulked around for weeks, misplaced, until their mother whisked them off to New Jersey.

He sipped his milk, took a nibble of bread. A car trundled down the street, the surgical resident at the end of the block coming home, the Korean guy with his god-awful hours. How was Mezivosky getting by? He knew how they got the house. A macher in the temple, Seligman the lawyer, had set up an endowment, interest-free loans and grants for Russian immigrants with a few hopeless strings attached: the children had to go to Hebrew School, the parents to a weekly class with the rabbi to learn about their long-lost heritage. Three out of ten couples complied. The rest used a lifetime of manipulating every system to weasel out: sudden hip problems preventing sitting, job interviews, all inexplicably on Tuesday evenings between seven and nine. They got their houses anyway.

He pushed away his plate. Was it time for him to put aside his petty dislike, his private repulsion, and do something for the man? Maybe even see his supreme annoyance as a gift, a challenge, a chance for Koenigsman to do what was really hard—a good deed in the face of personal distaste? What would Arlene say? *What if it were us? There but for fortune. If the tables were turned.*

He drained the milk. What in the world Mezivosky would do for him was a mystery. Even if Mezivosky was all the things he claimed, Koenigsman's firm didn't need an engineer or a dentist or a violinist. They didn't even need a handyman. Nor could Koenigsman ask Mezivosky to type and file.

It will come to me, Koenigsman thought, turning out the light and shuffling out of the kitchen. At the bottom of the stairs he hesitated. Climbing back up, slipping into an empty bed, sliding under cold sheets to wait for more terrible dreams: he'd skip it. Pulling Arlene's robe tighter around him, he went into the living room and sank into the couch.

IT CAME TO him in the form of a symphony crashing through the window, jolting him off the sofa and into the downstairs bathroom where he could stand with his hands over his ears, waiting for his heartbeat to slow. His breath tasted rancid. He counted to ten, twenty, thirty, then washed his face, went to the kitchen. Outside, an arc of gray was pushing through the darkness. Five-thirty. His glass was still on the table, a ring of sour milk on the rim. He sat, his head in his hands, and stared at the pink sash around his waist, considering the situation: He had to go to work in two hours. He hated Mezivosky. He couldn't sleep because responsibility weighed on him like a pair of stone tablets.

Someone was knocking. He lifted his head. In the dawn, a shape like an upright bear stood at the door.

"I need a favor," Mezivosky announced.

There was no sound, no music. "What's the matter?" Koenigsman said, groggy and foul. "Your stereo broken?"

"No," Mezivoksy said simply. "It's fine. It's the dog."

"What dog?"

"From last night." Mezivosky gestured to the kitchen. "Can I come in?"

Koenigsman stood back, let him inside. Mezivosky looked at the bathrobe, said nothing.

"You want coffee?" Koenigsman said, shuffling to the stove.

"Please."

Mezivosky looked around. "Almost the same." He sounded surprised. Koenigsman glanced over. He didn't know? Hadn't noticed? Mezivosky gestured with his chin to the bay window. "But we have the nook. Very convenient."

Koenigsman rolled his eyes and turned to the stove. "About the dog?"

Mezivosky pulled out a chair, scraping the linoleum. "It came to my house in the night. Sat on the steps and cried. It didn't wake you?"

"No."

"You're lucky. A heavy sleeper. Not like me, I suffer terribly with sleeplessness."

Koenigsman made himself spoon in the granules.

"Anyway, I don't know what to do," Mezivosky said. "I think maybe the other owner, the one before me, the Greek, he had a dog."

"No dog," Koenigsman said.

Mezivosky tapped the tabletop. "You have sugar?" he said when Koenigsman brought him a mug.

Koenigsman got the sugar.

"Also milk?"

Koenigsman brought him the milk.

"It sat, it cried, it howled," Mezivosky said, his spoon clinking against the ceramic. "I didn't like it. I don't like dogs. Plus it stinks. Americans don't wash their dogs."

Koenigsman sipped his coffee. Outside, the light was spreading.

"It's ugly," Mezivosky said. "A face smashed like a boxer. Who could love a face like that? My children will hate it, too."

"Are they coming home soon?"

"The children? Of course they're coming home soon. Today, Labor Day." Mezivosky took a noisy slurp. "A day to think of the workers. So everyone goes shopping."

Koenigsman stared over the rim of his mug. He wasn't going to work, and Arlene was coming home. "Where is it now?" he said.

"Where is what?"

"The dog."

Mezivosky waved toward the front of his house. "What could I do? I had to give it food. It ate, now it won't go away. What should I do, Koenigsman? You're an American, you know what people do about these things."

Koenigsman put down his mug. Finally, he was the expert. He tipped his head. "You probably couldn't get rid of it if you tried."

"Probably not. It's ugly, though, and I don't like it."

"But it's hungry, and it found you."

"It found me."

"You have no choice, Simcha. It's yours."

Mezivosky nodded, finished off the coffee. "That's what I thought." He pulled himself up, gave the table a little decisive slap. At the door he stopped, looked at Koenigsman. Was he going to thank him for the coffee? For the advice? Maybe crack a joke for once, something about Koenigsman looking dainty in Arlene's robe, a border of little flowers on the lapels and cuffs?

Mezivosky pulled a handkerchief from his pocket and blew his nose. Then he went out, banging the screen door on the way.

WHAT WAS A man to do? Ignore the seesaw of right and wrong, the grinding teeth of conscience? Koenigsman showered, dressed, fortified himself with a last breakfast of bacon and eggs, disposing of the packaging like he was getting rid of a body, then strode across the yard. The gleaming lawn mower was at its post at the boundary. On the patio, Mezivosky was stacking a pyramid of microwaves. Beside it, a lumpy blue plastic tarp covered a mound of bulging machinery.

"Look at this waste, Koenigsman," Mezivosky said, waving at the stack of black Lucite and shiny chrome. "All fixable, some not even broke." He waved again. "Some too big, some too small, Americans with minds like sheep. They buy whatever the phony actors on TV tell them to."

Koenigsman stuck his hands in his pockets. "Getting kind of cold to do this sort of thing, isn't it, Simcha?"

"What cold." Mezivosky took a broom and began sweeping the area in front of the microwave tower. "This is nothing. This is mild, warm, healthful."

Koenigsman ran a hand over his hair. "Well, it's harder to stay busy with this in the winter, wouldn't you say?"

Mezivosky shrugged and swept. He brought the broom up to Koenigsman's toes. Koenigsman dutifully stepped back. "I stay busy."

"What I'm getting at," Koenigsman said, watching the broom, "is maybe you'd like a job. Something away from the house."

Mezivosky kept his eyes on the sweeping. "Plenty to do here." He gestured to the tarp with his chin. "You think everything under there will fix itself? Magic?"

"I meant, Simcha, a regular job, you know, for regular pay. Like at a business or a company."

Mezivosky reached for the dustpan. "I wait and see," he said, casual, even, Koenigsman thought, bored. "Someone needs my talents, they come find me."

Koenigsman followed him to the trash barrel. "I'll get right to the point. I'd like to offer you a job. At my company. Where I work."

Mezivosky looked at him for the first time. "I don't know. Will depend if I'm interested." He strode past Koenigsman to the garage.

Koenigsman shook his head. He should go home and forget about it. The man was beyond hope. Beyond compassion, good-heartedness, even cordiality. Why was Koenigsman standing there knocking himself out as if he were the one in need of Mezivosky's help, not the other way around?

Mezivosky emerged from the garage with a long tool, a hoe maybe, or a spade—Koenigsman didn't know the difference—and sat at the picnic table and began to scrub off the rust with his oily rag. The bald spot shone in the morning light.

"Well, I'll be on my way," said Koenigsman after a minute, hands back in his pockets. "See you around, Simcha."

Koenigsman made it to the lawn mower before he heard the voice. "I give it some thought," Mezivosky called out behind him. "What you said." Koenigsman turned. Mezivosky was still scrubbing.

"Speak to me later, I give decision then," Mezivosky said, concentrating hard on the rust.

THAT EVENING, AFTER Arlene showed him a drawing of the wraparound deck they'd always wanted which she'd sketched out on a cocktail napkin on the plane, Koenigsman went next door to the patio and persuaded Mezivosky to let him give him a job. They'd find something, Koenigsman said. Mezivosky supposed he could learn taxes and accounting, it would be easy, anyone could do it. He'd take up Koenigsman's offer, pending of course Mezivosky's satisfaction. But he was good with numbers. Hadn't he ever told Koenigsman he'd once considered taking a degree in mathematics but the course wasn't rigorous enough?

"We'll figure out something," Koenigsman said. A half-moon hung, tentative, in the descending dusk. The depressed-looking wife, still pale despite her weeks at the shore, brought out a tray with a bottle of something stinging and sharp, along with four thick glasses. Arlene downed hers gamely, smiling futilely at the morose teenagers who hung silently along the siding next to a stack of broken TVs. Mezivosky and Koenigsman clinked glasses and toasted to their new arrangement, and Koenigsman swallowed, his throat burning.

Between their houses, the lawn mower was gone. In its place sat the dog, his tongue hanging out, panting, ugly and mangy and content.

SEEKERS IN THE
HOLY LAND

HE HAS CHOSEN Safed because the Kabbalists came
here. The streets are hilly, some of the roads rocky—this is what he
wants, what he came for, the ancient feeling, the hard-to-get-there
feeling—and from time to time he has to pull up on his backpack,
shrug each shoulder through his bulky jacket to keep it from slipping
and pulling him down into the old stones that pave these streets and
could take him under. Though he'd gladly go, that's how much he
wants to know this place. He is tired of Jerusalem, tired of his fellow
Americans posing at the modern yeshiva, not even a yeshiva, an institute it calls itself, to attract the university-conscious who need the
pretext of a graduate school. As if they were there for a credential, a
degree; as if that were what being there was about. He hadn't understood this when he sent in his forms, what did he know, reading the
brochure in his apartment in Boston. An immersion in study. He
thought the other students would be like him, but they're not. They
come to the classes and act like it matters, but really all they want is
to have a good time. To get away from their parents or colleges, hang
out on Ben Yehuda and meet American girls on exchange programs,
and get high and go to Egypt and Petra and then return home after
the year and tell their friends they had a mystical experience.

He has found his way from the bus station to the old section of the city, the streets narrow and winding like in the pictures, like in the guidebooks, like in parts of Jerusalem. The weather is like Jerusalem, too. Cold, the altitude, December, and it can be raw, not like home of course but still raw, wet, you never get warm; his roommates are complaining about the heat in their building, on for only certain hours of the day and never enough. So far he is succeeding pretty well in ignoring the tourist buses clogging the narrow streets. And most of those will be pulling out of Safed now because it's Friday afternoon and there's nowhere for the tourists to stay. They'll go to Tiberias or Haifa to the big hotels. Old synagogues and artists in Safed, that's it, a daytime show, you don't want to be here Friday night, the tour guide would say. Nothing to do. Not even restaurants open.

As if on cue, a charter bus rumbles past him down the hill on its way out of town. Blank faces at the windows, some in those perky cotton hats, faux kibbutz, given free with the tour agency's shoulder bags. Too quiet to be Americans. Probably some guilty Europeans— Danish, Swiss, the ever-present Germans. He catches a woman's eye, knows what she sees: the oversized kippa, the tzitzit fringes dangling, exposed, near his belt, though the hair is too long to be really religious, really Orthodox. But she probably doesn't know that. *Young Jews reclaiming their heritage,* she's thinking. *Isn't that nice.* The bus rounds a curve and disappears, he hears the bounce of the shocks. He sees them all over the country, his parents' age, born after the war, sincere, prosperous-looking people—the old ones, he thinks, wouldn't dare come, or want to. But even these he finds offensive, as if they're atoning; as if boating on the Kinneret or buying ceramic candlesticks for their friends back home were atonement. He's been watching tourists in this country for five months now and likes the Japanese best because he can't understand their language, not a single syllable, and because they seem so game. Jews? What are Jews? Interesting. Let's go see. They seem to know little, unlike the Europeans who know too much. The Japanese women are always wearing the wrong kinds of shoes, high heels or flimsy ladies' sandals, and the men wear formal, pressed pants. They don't know how to dress for the climate or the terrain. Watching them at a war memorial full of rubble or at a dig with its treacherous potholes and insufficiently roped-off areas, he wonders if somehow they got to this country by mistake; if they hadn't meant instead to go to Rome or Madrid or some more civilized place, better paved, but got on the wrong plane.

A dumpster juts onto the sidewalk—overflowing plastic bags, a moldy rug—and he steps around it, catches a streak of gray, the wide whine of a cat. The hostel, he's been told, is at the bottom of one of these hilly streets, a ten-minute walk to the synagogue he wants to find. He heard about the synagogue from Aryeh, one of his teachers. A plum piece of intelligence. Not listed in the guidebooks, the tourists don't know about it. *The real thing, sometimes they still do secret ceremonies, anointing initiates, those who've learned The Way. They study for years, practice, they're not young.* In truth, he knows almost nothing about the mystics, the Seven Sefirot, the Infinite Ein-Sof, the migration of souls, they're only phrases he's read; knows almost nothing about the religion altogether, a juvenile Hebrew School education, a couple of courses in college. But he knows this is where he belongs, in Safed, at this synagogue. He wants to drink from this well, and Aryeh saw it, recognized it, told only him.

At the corner he checks his directions, then shifts the pack and turns right, leaving Arlozorov Street. Behind a cracking stone archway, off a tiny building practically buried in weeds, a man all in white is standing on a porch, eyes closed, silently rocking. A meditation. A flock of birds squawks overhead, and the man opens his eyes. He hurries on. There are probably dozens, maybe hundreds of people concentrating like that at this very moment, right here, the highest elevation in the country, the closest point to heaven. He turns down a side street, passes a florist, its metal shutters pulled closed. He should be on that porch, too, he's wasting his time in Jerusalem.

The street narrows, and it is mazelike where he's walking, winding streets within winding streets. And quiet. Too quiet. Where is the hustle and bustle, the children coming home from school early, the women rushing back from the markets to cook? He passes silent doorways, a few toys left out against the cement buildings—a tricycle, a child's battered wagon—then checks his watch, a fleeting worry he's lost track. Two o'clock. He lifts his wrist to his ear, hears it ticking, squints anyway at a clock through a window in a partially shuttered candy store and confirms the time again: only two. Maybe this is the influence of the Kabbalists, Shabbat brought in with silence and contemplation, even the streets paying attention to their breath.

And now he is there, where the hostel is supposed to be. Malachim Street. Street of the Angels. He looks to the top. Arlozorov is at the other end, he has been walking in a circle. There is no number 35. He looks again at the slip of paper, at Aryeh's scrawly handwriting, a crude map of the hostel and the synagogue, a dark circle colored in at each. The synagogue location was from Aryeh but the hostel was in the guidebook: 35 Malachim.

He finds 14, 27, 48, 63, walking the length of it, a short street with mismatched numbers. A car appears at the top, a dusty white Peugeot; he edges up against a building just in time to let it speed past. He combs the street again, looking for a sign—hostel, hotel, pension—spots a battered metal Coca-Cola placard hanging off a single nail, another one for Strauss Ice Cream. But the buildings are shuttered, whatever they are—restaurants, groceries, kiosks—closed. The whole block looks vacated, an aura of having been fled. But Safed is not a city to be fled, not like the towns on the northern border, Kiryat Shmona, or Metulla, whose residents routinely go underground.

He has exhausted the little street and also himself. He sits heavily on a stoop, puts his backpack by his feet. His boots are covered in dust, he could write his name across the leather. *Neal Fox*. He wants to change it, Naftali or Natan. Maybe Nachum, after the great seer of Bratslav, if he can work up the nerve. He flexes his shoulders, rotates his arms. The pack is too heavy, he could lose the second bottle of water, the camera—what was he thinking? it's Shabbat—his three books. Across from him the Coca-Cola sign flutters on its nail. This is not the first time something like this has gone wrong, it happens all the time in this country: buses regularly off schedule, businesses out of business, addresses listed wrong. No one is ever surprised. *Y'hiyeh b'seder*. It'll be all right. He has two hours before sundown. He's twenty-one and strong. There's a hostel somewhere in this city, he just has to find it. The next car, the next passerby—he'll ask.

Meanwhile, he pulls one of the water bottles from his pack and drinks. Waits. No cars come. The sky is deepening pink. He knows it's close to three. Shabbat begins at four-thirty.

SHE APPEARS AT the top of the street, at Arlozorov, blond, a Day-Glo orange ski jacket, a pack almost identical to his, only smaller. She's wearing a skirt and knee socks like his sister Carly when Carly was in eighth grade. Only this person is not fourteen.

"Excuse me, can you help me?" she says in Hebrew, an accent he can't place. "Do you know where is the hostel?"

Her Hebrew, he is certain even from this little bit, is better than his—the speed, the pronunciation, his gut sense that whatever her native tongue, she doesn't want to use it—and to show her he knows she's only a tourist, why is she trying Hebrew, he answers in English, "Do you speak English?"

"Oh. Sorry," she says. "I am looking for the youth hostel." She says *looking* like *loooking*, that extra *ooh*, and he finds it appealing. The fine blond hair, the pretty blue eyes, the earnest face, the accent, the knee socks: she is like Heidi, like the cast from *The Sound of Music*, like Gretel in an opera he once saw on TV. Like a German.

"Yeah, well, me too," he says, picking up his bottle.

She glances around, confused. "It's not here?"

"Doesn't seem to be." He takes another swig, puts the bottle away. He's seen these tourists, too. Young Europeans traveling alone, crisscrossing the world in six months or a year with a single small backpack. A girl from Finland once showed him the contents of hers. A quarter of a washcloth, neatly cut, a hand towel, one skirt, one pair of pants, one sweater, one shirt, one undershirt, two pairs of thin socks, two pairs of underpants, a half-sized toothbrush, and two tampons—enough until you get somewhere to buy, she said, oddly the only thing she commented on. Often he meets them on the way back from Turkey or Egypt or Iran, Israel a modern relief.

"Perhaps the guidebook had it wrong," she says, looking up to Arlozorov. "Perhaps it's not Malachim but HaPalmach or Rimonim, the next ones over," she says, turning, scanning, her street pronunciations polished, studied, expert.

"Perhaps." He folds his hands, looks past the hem of her skirt, which is eye level from where he's sitting, and wonders about the socks. Is it for comfort? Or did someone on the bus tell her to put on a skirt, slip it on over her pants, then take the pants off, the rules of modesty, in religious sections Jewish women don't wear pants. She would respect local customs. A seasoned traveler, no doubt, like the Finn.

"Aren't you going to look?" she says.

He hadn't gotten that far. But now that she's here, so efficient, he feels compelled to justify his inertia. "I was considering the situation," he says. "Thinking it through."

She makes a little *Oh* with her lips, then goes to the bottom of Malachim. Something makes him leave his pack and follow her, and they comb five streets. He knows where she got her Hebrew, has seen people like her in the ulpan studying with the new immigrants and Jewish students like him. They're good with languages, already know English and French in addition to German, and are pleasant to everyone, the Russian women want to bring them home and feed them. Some of them are Christians, there to proselytize, to get the Jews to join them so they can have their Second Coming, the Jews are holding it up. But you don't find that out for weeks, even months.

They walk through open gates, knock at unmarked doors. A lone pedestrian crosses the street and ignores them when they try to ask. Back at Malachim they compare slips of paper. Hers is also in English; she copied it from the same guidebook.

"So the guidebook is mistaken," she declares, studying her paper. Her pack seems feather-light; she has not yet put it down, while his remains on the stoop.

"Evidently." He makes a show of looking at his watch, pulling back his jacket cuff, wiping off the face. "If you hurry you can catch a bus to Tiberias, stay there instead."

She looks up. "What good will that do me?"

"It's a place to stay. There are two or three hostels there." He makes a sweeping gesture. "Unlike here."

"I will find."

He shrugs and goes toward his pack.

"And you?" she says, behind him.

He hoists the straps. "I guess I will find, too."

"Where do you need to be? Where are you going in Safed?"

He will not tell her. He wants his synagogue to be his own discovery; wants to be, for once, in a place unsullied by outsiders, by spectators there to gawk and paste the experience into some mental scrapbook. *Look how pious, how devoted*. He knows of course that he's an outsider, too, but he will do his best to fit in, be inconspicuous. "I want to be near one of the synagogues," he says, shifting the pack. It feels like there are bricks inside, extra weight accumulated since he'd first set it down, as if the cement of the building has seeped in through the canvas.

"Me, too."

"Yeah, well, good luck," he says, and starts to walk away.

"Which one?" she calls. "Which synagogue?"

He stops, thinks quickly, and turns around. Her hair has fanned out with the wind, a yellow curtain against the deepening rose of the sky. "You want to know which one to visit? Go to the Joseph Caro or the Ari, they're famous, everyone goes there. They're in all the guidebooks." He points to the top of the street, to Arlozorov. "Go to any of the shops, they'll tell you where."

She stares a moment longer. He has finessed her, that's not what she meant. She wanted to know where he was going.

But she knows she's been dismissed. She's well brought up, or perhaps more timid than he thought. She straightens up, her backpack almost floating, as if filled with air, gives a small comradely wave, starts up Malachim. He moves off in the other direction, then turns. In her orange jacket, her back to him, she looks like a frail bird.

AT THE ONLY grocery still open the proprietor tells him of a woman who takes in guests, Mrs. Baghdadi at 36 Montefiore. He loves these surnames, Baghdadi, heavy with place and history, while what does he have to show for himself? Fox, whatever gave it life, Folkshtein, Foxman, Feuerstein, long since chopped off at the root.

He buys a small jar of peanut butter, the three rolls left in the bin, the last two borekas, a liter of apple juice, a container of cottage cheese. Somewhere in his pack he hopes there's a spoon and a plastic knife. He was told the hostel served breakfast and would provide a cold supper Friday night if given enough notice, but now he's on his own. He thanks the proprietor excessively, grateful the store is still open this close to candlelighting, and the man gives a lengthy reply. Neal's Hebrew isn't good enough to fully understand, though he suspects it is the story of the man's life—he picks up something about Yemen, a wife, nine children—and he waits for a pause while the man collects his thoughts, then nods vigorously and says a too-loud Shabbat shalom and heads out.

It's turned cold, a chilly damp that feels like rain. Two men hurry past, their heads down, hair wet, and he sees then the tiny sign on a low stone building. *Mikveh*. For men. He's just recently found out about such a thing, men immersing themselves before holy days. For the truly devout, every week. He should do this, why hadn't he heard of it before? An old man is closing up, locking the gate, and Neal turns left, berates himself. Next time. Next time he'll come earlier, be smarter, better prepared. At 36 Montefiore there's a gate opening onto a thorny courtyard. He picks his way over broken stones and dead geranium petals, the bright red decayed to black along the edges, as if burned, and finds the door, knocks.

The woman who answers is like from a lithograph: shrunken, kerchiefed, wizened. He asks for Mrs. Baghdadi and the old lady shakes her head. Not here? Wrong name? Did he misunderstand? Immediately she begins talking in rapid-fire Hebrew. He can't understand a word and pain is pulling across his shoulders from the weight of his pack.

"One hundred shekels," the woman says, interrupting herself and holding out her hand.

"One hundred?" The hostel cost thirty-five, about nine dollars.

"One hundred," she repeats. When he hesitates she says, her Hebrew louder as if he were deaf instead of American, "All of Shabbat. Tonight, tomorrow, you can stay until after dark, or the next morning. Room is clean."

What choice does he have? He gives her the money, follows her to a room at the end of a long hall, the dense smell of cumin and cinnamon hovering above them. Inside are four bare beds cramped together, two of them perpendicular so that someone's feet would be up against someone else's head. He takes the one closest to the wall in case she's still doing business later, guaranteeing privacy at least on one side.

The woman appears with a sheet and a pillow. The word for blanket has suddenly evaporated from his already rudimentary vocabulary.

"More?" he manages, smoothing the top of the bed. She shakes her head, obviously annoyed. What could he want, more what?

He puts his arms around himself and pretends to shiver. "Something for cold," he says.

She leaves, returns with a rubber thing shaped like a kidney. A hot water bottle, he presumes. He sinks onto the bed. The springs creak like an old song. There is always his jacket.

THE SYNAGOGUE IS dark. He was not expecting floodlights, but he knows before even trying the door that no one is there.

Yet it is a synagogue, the synagogue. It's got the two lion heads on the gate that Aryeh told him about, the broken arch at the street, the two Stars of David carved over the door, one above the other. Even the address is right: 18 Eliyahu HaNavi. *Do you know who is Eliyahu?* Aryeh said, eyes flaming, drawing the little map. *Carried to heaven on a fiery chariot, his horse went through the sun, better than Icarus!* When Aryeh told him this, Neal felt himself shaking: this is what he wants, to fly into the center and merge with that heat, with that sun. Isn't that why he came, not just to Safed but to the country altogether, to find something true, a way? His Jewish friends at home were doing yoga, Buddhism; one was considering becoming a priest. Because what was there in America if you were Jewish? Temples with health clubs? Fundraisers? Rabbis like at his parents' synagogue, Rabbi Shore, preoccupied with building campaigns, numbers, membership rolls? Or, on the other side, rules, fetishistic rules, a black and white orthodoxy. But for the soul, what was there?

He tries the door one more time, then walks around the low building, looks in through two small windows. Prayerbooks stacked up, a table in the middle, next to it a wooden ark, chairs in a disorganized semicircle. And books, papers, lamps, stray articles of clothing cluttering the corners.

Perhaps he is early. He thinks not, he has passed several synagogues on his way and they've all started. But perhaps here they begin later, do it differently. At the Ari and Joseph Caro they have to toe the line, be routine, otherwise they lose their guidebook listings and, with them, American dollars. Ones and fives dropped into the shammes's wooden bowl on the way out after the tours on weekdays, loose change if the tourists are feeling cheap or unsatisfied. He's heard about these shammeses, toothless old men who don't wash, shuffle in and out. Ancients who wanted to be disciples, initiates, who are still hoping. They sweep and clean the toilets, and when the tourists come they give the men little cardboard hats like pyramids, the women bits of lace, and suffer with the wooden bowl for donations, murmuring, head down, from Psalms.

He glances around the courtyard, then to the neighboring buildings, shadows and candles in the windows, music, a female singer, Ofra Haza on someone's CD. There is no place to sit. He leans with his back to the building, then slides down, hunches up against the concrete. The ground is rocky and damp. He takes off his jacket, sits on it, hugs himself for warmth.

But this, too, is cold. He puts the jacket back on, searches his pockets for something to put between himself and the ground—a hat, gloves, a map, anything, where is his backpack when he needs it?—and, empty-handed, leans back, shuts his eyes, and tells himself to concentrate on his breath, on the drifting music, on the descending blanket of dusk. To allow contentment to spread within, that he is where he wants to be, not in Jerusalem for a noisy Shabbat with his roommates and the girls they met from the School for Overséas Students, the pickup scene they will all flock to later, downtown. And not in Boston, where he wouldn't be having Shabbat at all.

He is hungry. His breath is not holding his attention. He tastes the bland cottage cheese and the doughy roll he managed to down before walking over, wishes he had a candy bar. And then there is the German girl with her blue eyes and expert Hebrew wanting to know where he was going, probably doing penance for her SS grandparents, or a proselytizer wanting to convert him. Interlopers, they can't leave the Jews alone, even in their own country. As if the Crusades and the Inquisition weren't enough. And the old lady at Mrs. Baghdadi's. He was ripped off, should have bargained, when will he learn that in this country everything is open to negotiation?

He opens his eyes. His pants are damp. The courtyard is a bluish black. At the edge of the property is a bench sitting amid tangled vines. How could he have missed it?

He dries the seat of his pants as best he can and walks to the bench. It's stone, and cold, the vines reaching as if trying to touch it, but it's better than the ground. The sky is turning to night. From where he sits the synagogue is disappearing into darkness.

IN HIS DREAM the men are singing *L'cha Dodi*. There are fifteen or twenty of them, all old, sitting in the semicircle of chairs. When, at the last stanza, they stand and turn to the door to bow and welcome the Sabbath Bride, she comes in, still in her knee socks and skirt and the orange jacket. Her yellow hair gives off a shimmering light, and she smiles, radiant—Meira, they call her, *radiance*—and while they sing, she moves to the center, next to the ark, and takes off her clothes. First the jacket, then the skirt, then a pair of pants hidden beneath, then the sweater, the shirt, the undershirt, the two pairs of underpants, the knee socks, a second set inside them, and last, slipping out of her, the two tampons, pristine and smooth and white. At that, the men finish the song and move en masse, graceful and slow, as if in a ballet, and surround her, their eyes closed, their faces turned upward, and inhale slowly and deeply. She is a vapor, a white wind, a genie uncorked, floating inside the circle, and the men stand, enraptured, breathing in again and again until they have taken in all there is, and all that's left of her are the clothes lying in an orange heap on the floor.

He opens his eyes. The courtyard is black. He is horrified. The European—what European? the German!—as the Sabbath Bride! What is she doing in his dream, in his Shabbat, in the most unsullied synagogue in Safed! She has no right. The Nazi, the Jew-killer, masquerading as the messenger of Shabbat! She has polluted his mind; worse, she is standing naked before the most pious of men, men who'd sooner die than have to look at an unclothed woman.

His hands are numb, and he rubs them together, then runs them over his face. And there, again, he sees, under his palms, the heap of clothes, the naked girl—soft, white, blond. The dream is continuing but now is no longer a dream but a living thing, and he cannot stop watching. The men are smiling now at the girl, who is not vapor but flesh. She begins to dance, a slow undulating movement in the center of the circle, revealing herself, parting her legs, and the men stare, breathless, then begin to touch themselves through their clothes, their hands moving up and down, up and down, preparing to enter her.

He is appalled; he has to stop the dream, stop the reel! He gets up from the bench and shakes his head violently from side to side, then his hands, as if he might shake the girl loose, send her flying, then makes for the gate, groping along spindly vines, a thin tree, trips once, twice, hits something hard with his foot. A stone wall. He feels his way, finds the entrance, pushes himself out onto the path leading to the street.

Light. He stops, catches his breath. Shadows move in the windows of the buildings. He has no idea what time it is. Under a street lamp he checks his watch, four-forty, not possible, the time he arrived at the synagogue, listens for ticking. Silence. He hurries back to Mrs. Baghdadi's. The front door is unlocked. In the hall he smells not cinnamon and cumin but roasted meat, sweet peppers, apples. He is famished. But whoever ate and whenever the meal was, it is now long since over because the apartment is dark. If he is alone in his room he will eat another roll or one of the borekas, it will help him sleep.

But he is not alone. Two of the other beds are taken. They have been pushed together, the blankets spread across both—two men, two women, one of each, he has no idea, because it is too dark to tell. He goes out, finds his way to the toilet. There is no light. He does his business, washes his hands and face, returns and, in his clothes, lies down on his bed. Something cushiony meets his face. A blanket. He takes off his shoes, his jacket, his pants, shoves them under the bed with his backpack, and covers himself. After a few minutes he feels himself growing calmer, beginning to drift off, his terrible dream receding. Though all night he is stirred out of sleep again and again by the murmuring of coupling, unidentifiable sounds neither high nor low, three, four, five times, rising from the other side of the room.

THEY ARE GONE. And so is his backpack.

In the bright light of morning he finds his pants under his bed, checks the pockets. His wallet is there, the contents intact. His apartment key is safe, mixed in with his change.

He is hungry. In his jacket pocket he finds a package of peanuts and eats them quickly, washes away the dryness with water cupped in his hand at the bathroom sink. He smoothes back his hair, searches for toothpaste, finds none, and rinses his mouth again.

Outside, the sky is winter white, and it's late; everywhere, the morning services have already begun. He checks his watch, then remembers, hurries off in the direction of the Joseph Caro and the Ari. The trip needn't be a total loss, surely they are fine places, who is he to judge. But as he nears the street he should turn down, he finds himself walking in another direction, toward Eliyahu. He'll just check; maybe they don't meet Friday night, have only a morning minyan. *Hidden, obscure,* Aryeh whispered.

He takes the last part of the street in a run, can see into the courtyard and through the windows, and yes! there is movement inside. He is so lucky! Everything is going as it should, even his backpack. He is released from its burden, and isn't that a sign, the material world weighing him down? Confirmation that he's doing what he must, that in Safed he is on the right path.

Outside the synagogue he catches his breath, straightens his jacket, then softly opens the door so as not to disturb. The men are standing in a tight semicircle in front of the chairs, twelve, fifteen of them, their white tallises over their heads. Perhaps it is the silent Amidah. The prayerbooks are up front. He waits to see the men moving, rocking with their prayers, murmuring, but the men are still, so close together their tallises form a giant curtain.

A rustling, a soft shuffling. There is movement on the other side, someone inside the circle. It is the ceremony, there is an initiate. He can't believe his good fortune, can't wait to tell Aryeh. He was so right to come back.

He tiptoes to the ring of huddled men. One moves a hand, and he glimpses between the curtain of cloth into the opening.

It is she, the girl. She is standing in the middle, a huge tallis over her shoulders reaching all the way to the floor, her eyes closed.

"She is a German!" he shouts. "A child of Nazis!"

The men turn, and he sees her fully now, the skirt, those socks, the orange jacket visible through the white cloth, absurd, preposterous. Even more preposterous than the socks. "How can she be one of them? One of you! You have to be old, you have to be Jewish! She's a proselytizer, a usurper! She took our lives, our histories, now she wants our Path, our Way! She cannot have it!"

"Anyone can have it!" the men shout. "It is open to all! All with a pure heart, all who cleave unto heaven with humility and awe!"

"But she wants to destroy us!"

"Yes!" There are thirty, fifty, a hundred men, with ancient faces and modern faces, bearded and clean-shaven, forty years old and sixty years old and two hundred years old, all merging and blending. "She is your enemy, your hatred! She is everything you despise and judge and fear!"

The floor is shaking, the room loosening from its foundations. It is dark, and the center is spinning. It is the girl, she is transforming, melting, whirling before him. Now she is Mrs. Baghdadi, now the Yemenite proprietor, now an SS man, a Crusader on a white horse swinging a giant cross. She is his parents, Rabbi Shore, Aryeh, the other Americans at the institute. "You must merge with *all* worlds!"

the voices thunder. "*This* is the unity of Oneness! Not with God but with your enemy. Not with some old man in heaven but with your judgment. With all that you despise and demean and diminish and pity! You must merge with the All That Divides You!"

The girl melts, re-forms, melts again. She is a lion, an eagle, a cyclone whirling red, orange, yellow. The center is a blinding, scorching light. Neal buries his face in his arms. He will be burned and his eyes will be seared.

"Neal! Neal!"

A thin reed amid the thunder. It is she, that accent, that voice. She knows his name and is calling him. She wants to save him.

"Neal! Neal!"

He lifts his head, looks. She is a pillar of flame hurling toward him, a giant furnace. She will take him to the sun—she *is* the sun—and will leave him there.

"Neal!" he hears again, and understands. *Kneel!* She is commanding him to get down.

It is the fury of heaven, and he scrambles to the floor and presses his face into the stone, squeezes his eyes shut, and cries into the foundations for mercy, prays he will not be consumed.

THERE ARE NOISES. Buses, car radios. He is on the floor, his skin sticky with dried sweat. A wave of Led Zeppelin floats by. He pulls himself up, looks at the window. Night. Saturday night, the restaurants open, the shops, people selling CDs and silver jewelry from folding tables.

He runs a hand over his hair, then over his face. Stubble, as if days, not hours, have passed. His jacket is torn and his shoes are missing. A bus exhaust belches loudly, there is the powerful squeal of brakes. A charter has parked in front of the courtyard. A large man in a baseball cap motions a parade of middle-aged people down the bus steps and into a line, then leads them up the path and through the gate to the synagogue door.

"Allo? Allo?"

Neal stands in shadow in a corner. The tour guide adjusts his cap, flicks on a light, and motions in his charges. They file in, wait in a cluster in the middle.

"Everyone inside?" the guide booms, his English thick with an Israeli accent. "Come, Mrs. Feld, join us in the center." The door closes, heels clicking on the floor. "Now, this is the oldest synagogue in Safed, built in the 1490s, recently renovated and open to tourists. Most of it was destroyed in the great earthquake of 1837 but parts survived." Someone's flash goes off. A man takes out a handkerchief, blows his nose. The guide glances at the domed ceiling, at the intricate woodwork, and Neal pushes himself farther into the shadow. "The Kabbalists founded this one, too," the guide says, his voice echoing in the cavernous room, "just like the others we passed. You see how the ark faces south rather than east? And this one also has the special Chair of Elijah—you see, back there?" Murmurs, more flashes. "Watch out—if you sit there you'll have a baby within a year."

They laugh, make jokes. *What do they put in there, Viagra? Who wants to go first?* They disperse, pick up prayerbooks, examine the carved doors of the ark, and look at the decorations on the walls, elaborate framed writings, calligraphed letters snaking up the sides and along the bottoms. Neal tries to shrink into the corner. "It was near here, in a cave in Meron, that Shimon Bar Yochai wrote *The Zohar,*" the guide says. He's standing by the ark, the doors now open, two ancient Torahs watching. "Thirteen years it took him. The most famous book of mystical teachings, they study it still. Sit, contemplate, study. Union with God, that's what they wanted."

"Sounds like my son who went to India," one woman says, wandering over to the ark. "Last summer." She runs a hand over the velvet covering of one of the scrolls. Neal flinches as if she were touching him. "Now he meditates all day while on our money he's flunking out of NYU."

"*Nu?* Shammes!" calls the guide, looking around. "Where's the shammes?" He pivots, then lights on Neal, strides over and snaps something in Hebrew, waves at his baseball cap.

Neal sees on a low shelf near the prayerbooks the box with the cardboard pyramids and lace snippets, goes over and picks it up, hands it to the guide.

"Not me, you fool—to them!" the guide whispers in Hebrew. "Don't you want them to tip?"

Neal shuffles to the Americans and offers the box, his head down. A few take. One woman brushes past him. "Dov," she says, loud, to the guide, "can you ask the janitor where's the bathroom?"

Neal looks at her. The guide barks something to him, and Neal points to the back, a guess, though he is certain he is right. The woman bumps him with her pocketbook on the way; he smells a trail of cigarette smoke.

"How much longer, Dov?" the man with the handkerchief calls. "We're starving." Neal goes back to his corner. He is cold, especially his feet. He looks down. His socks are thinner than he'd thought, and there are holes.

"A few more minutes," the guide says. "As soon as Mrs. Goodman comes out of the bathroom."

"Oh, that Lynn," someone says from the back. "Everywhere we go, a pit stop."

"You think maybe she's pregnant?" someone else calls out, and everyone laughs, maybe she's been here before, has already used the chair. They have all lost interest in the synagogue except one couple who has been studying the walls, looking at the framed texts. They are standing five or six feet from Neal.

"What do you think it is?" the woman says to her husband, pointing at the frame. "Hebrew? Aramaic?"

"I don't know." He shrugs and tips his head toward Neal. "Ask him."

"He doesn't speak English. And besides, he's just the janitor."

"Not a janitor," the man says. "The sexton, takes care of the place. Like at the shul your father used to go to. They always know."

The woman smiles quickly at Neal, embarrassed, then calls to the guide. "Dov, do you know what this is?" she says, pointing to the frame.

Dov walks over, looks, then beckons to Neal.

Neal doesn't move.

"Come look," the guide tells him in Hebrew. "Tell them what it is."

Neal opens his palms, shakes his head. He doesn't know and can't speak, not in his terrible Hebrew nor in his perfect English.

"Fool!" the guide whispers, coming closer. "Make busy, make it up! They'll tip! This is what they want. To feel they've been near something old, from the very religious! Something real, something true! You understand?"

Neal inches over to the couple. Behind them Mrs. Goodman closes the bathroom door, complains loudly that the light doesn't work.

The couple stand politely at the frame. Neal looks at it. He has no idea what it is. It's long, four, five paragraphs, and it could be anything. He is ignorant, a stupid Jew who knows nothing, understands nothing. He needs twenty, thirty, fifty years before he will understand a single letter.

"*Tefila*," he mutters. It's a prayer.

"*Tefilat ha-derech!*" the guide booms, making it up, covering for him. "Prayer for a safe journey. Very good choice, Mrs. Weiss, because now we will continue our journey. Everyone ready?"

They line up like schoolchildren, make jokes about the crazy Israeli drivers, they should all pray good and hard for such a journey. A few talk about dinner, what are they having, Dov—fish? Italian? Someone heard in Safed there's now even Chinese.

Dov goes to the door, to the head of the line. "Shammes!" he calls, and Neal understands that it's for him. He walks over, spots the wooden bowl, picks it up. The guide nods. Neal stands by the door with his head bowed, eyes lowered, as the visitors file out, the bills floating down and landing softly on the bottom, the silence punctuated now and then by the clinking of falling coins.

HENNY'S WEDDING

SHIRLEY ROBINS'S SISTER, Henny, was going to have a small wedding, a little parlor party. What else could they do in the middle of the war, 1943 and half the men away or being shipped out any day, even Henny's intended, Nathan Silverman, holding orders to report a week after the wedding? They were keeping the whole thing modest, Shirley's mother told her from in front of the sink in the tiny apartment kitchen. It was just as well for Henny and Nathan to save their celebrating for better times and instead ready themselves for Nathan's departure, Fort Bragg, North Carolina.

"Separated from him one week after the wedding," Shirley said, drying each plate as fast as her mother handed it to her, stacking them up on the table, the good set plus some unmatched dishes she had never seen before. From her *bubbe's bubbe's* time, her mother had said, lifting them out of the box one at a time, blowing off the dust. After six weeks of basic, Nathan would be transferred, and then Henny would join him. Shirley ran the dish towel along the rim of an unfamiliar platter, a spray of faded little flowers in the center where generations of herring and smoked fish had held court. "And for so long."

Her mother ran the water over a stemmed cake plate and shrugged. "My uncle Louis didn't see his wife for nine years until she finally came from Russia, she wouldn't leave her mother." She handed Shirley the dripping porcelain. Thick, white, the kind Henny would get for a wedding present, as if overnight she would suddenly become hostesslike, having the relatives over for coffee and dessert. "You think everything's supposed to go like in a magazine?"

Half an hour later Shirley lay on her bed, flipping through *Vogue*. The smell of cabbage soup drifted in from the hallway; they would eat when Henny got home from work. Nathan was all right, an accountant, reliable, he'd be a good provider, perfect for someone who'd want nothing more than a new two-bedroom up in Yonkers and maybe a trip to Florida now and then. Not her type. Not even Henny's, if anyone asked her opinion—Henny, who could have had her pick of a hundred boys. Shirley's mother used to watch from the window while every day half a dozen of them would slavishly follow her through the courtyard, hoping for a backward glance. *A heartbreaker, that one,* her mother would say, shaking her head.

She turned the page—a woman in a Dior suit was posing in front of the Plaza, a hundred dollars at least—and considered Nathan's looks. On the short side but handsome. So maybe. Still, her type would have more pizzazz, a risk-taker with a yen for excitement. She rolled onto her back and stared at the ceiling. She wanted someone different, someone not so Bronx. Someone who'd come and sweep her along. So what if it was a Clark Gable type, she couldn't help it.

"Wake up, Shirley. Something terrible." Her mother was standing by Henny's bed, urgent in her coat and hat, the hallway behind her dark. "Henny, she's at Montefiore."

"What happened?" Shirley said, buttoning her coat against the cold as they hurried down Bainbridge Avenue to the hospital. Rush hour, six o'clock, and already dark, the sidewalks crowded. It felt like snow.

"An ambulance brought her, she collapsed at work."

"And?"

"And nothing."

Shirley waited. Her mother was impossible, Shirley couldn't get a word out of her. Though she was better than some of the other women in the building. Mrs. Ringwald downstairs would have been shrieking so loud by now they'd have heard it all the way to the Grand Concourse.

A knot of boys in uniform, in heavy loden overcoats, was coming their way, Harry Sobel from the next building, and Benny Green, both of them stationed in the city and still living at home. Shirley hunched into her collar, hoping they wouldn't see. Mrs. Green had been after her mother all year. *Shirley in college and Benny saving up for law school, what could be bad?* The boys briskly passed, she heard Harry's cocky laugh—he'd once gone for Henny but she wouldn't give him the time of day; now Shirley heard he was engaged to a rich girl from Staten Island—and Shirley turned to her mother. She was concentrating, focused like a four-star general on the next block, Gun Hill Road where the hospital was, as if by thinking about it hard enough she could will the two of them to fly over the crowds and land at the hospital door.

"Well, did you call Rhoda?" Shirley asked finally. Rhoda, the responsible daughter, the married daughter. The one her mother always called.

"No answer."

How could Rhoda not be home at this hour? Saul would be home any minute and the baby would have needed to eat. Shirley followed her mother to the hospital entrance, her mother gripping the railing as if she were seventy instead of fifty-five. "You know,

Mama, Saul's not going to kill her if she gets a phone call about her sister in the emergency room. Even if it's dinnertime."

At the door her mother turned, mouth set like a schoolmistress, or a female prison warden from the movies. "I'll call her if I need her." She wheeled around and pulled the enormous handle. Shirley reached over and helped her. She hadn't called Rhoda, her impossible notions about not intruding on a married woman, even her own daughter. Inside the overheated entry her mother abruptly stopped and turned around. "Meantime, her husband comes first."

THE WAITING ROOM was jammed. Crying babies, expectant fathers and grandmothers going back and forth to the phones; one whole family was fingering rosary beads. Shirley found a spot for them by the grimy windows and scanned the room in vain to find her mother a seat. Wooden stretchers lined the walls, straps and sharp metal clasps dangling off the slats, the smell of ammonia competing with stale cigarette smoke and burnt coffee. Where was Henny?

"Mrs. Robins?" A woman rustled over in a crisp uniform, loud enough for the whole waiting room to look up and listen. "Your daughter is Henrietta?"

Her mother grabbed Shirley's hand. "Yes, and this is my youngest, Shirley." Her voice wavered. Shirley looked at her. What was wrong with her? The nurse was not interested in the family tree.

"Come with me," ordered the nurse, and led them down a corridor to a bench next to a door marked *No Admittance*. "Wait here," she barked, and pushed open the door and disappeared inside.

Shirley's mother sat and immediately opened her pocketbook and took out a white handkerchief. Was she going to cry? Shirley had never seen her cry, not even at their father's funeral. *Stonewall Jackson*, Henny had called her that day, whispering to Shirley in their first-row seats in the cold chapel. Even Rhoda, after telling Henny to be quiet, admitted the name fit. Her mother dabbed at her eyes and tucked away the handkerchief. You had to keep up a good face, a good face to all things.

"Mrs. Robins?" The *No Admittance* door swung closed. "I'm Dr. Bell. Your daughter's going to be fine."

Her mother stood, clutched the pocketbook. The doctor towered over her, gray hair, white coat, stethoscope dangling. "What is it? What's she got?"

"Well, she was bleeding pretty heavily, but what she's got is either a boy or a girl, and she's still got it."

Her mother gave a loud gasp and covered her mouth with her hand. Shirley caught her by the elbow. "Sit down, Mama," she said, guiding her back onto the bench. Her mother fumbled for the handkerchief.

"I understand the husband's away in the service?"

Shirley looked up. Henny lied? Bleeding, passing out, she managed to lie? Shirley glanced at her mother, whose face was pressed into the white cloth. Was she hearing any of this? "That's right," Shirley said quickly. "Fort Bragg, North Carolina." She scanned the doctor's face. "Though obviously he's had a leave recently."

"Obviously," the doctor said, not blinking.

"A few weeks ago, I believe."

"About six."

"Six, that sounds right."

"And what's the patient's married name?" the doctor said, taking a pad and pen from his pocket.

"Silverman. Mrs. Nathan Silverman."

"All right." He scribbled something on his pad. "Now, Miss Robins, I'm awfully backlogged here at the hospital, sometimes I don't get to filling out these medical reports for days. Just how many days would you think?"

Shirley stared at him. "A week would be fine. Ten days even better."

"Ten days it is," he said, writing on his pad. "Now, you tell your mother," he said, looking at her mother, who was patting her forehead with the handkerchief, "Henrietta's fine, she's sleeping now, but she's going to need to rest up at home." Her mother looked up, as if this were the first she'd heard. "And you tell her she's going to make a fine grandmother."

THEY TOOK HENNY home in a taxi the next morning. Shirley brought her tea and toast in bed.

"She won't talk about it," Henny said as Shirley placed the tray over the bedspread, the plate of toast sliding on the wood.

"What do you expect? She should play trumpets from the roof because you can conceive? You're lucky she even took you back. Remember Frances Miller?"

Henny bit into the toast. "She'd never do that, Frances Miller didn't have a boyfriend. That's the difference. Mama wouldn't want to lose Nathan."

Shirley sat on the edge of her bed and watched Henny eat. She was still beautiful, even in her pasty state. A shaft of light was making shimmering lines on the white chenille spread. "So, did you tell him?" Shirley said.

"Nathan? Are you crazy?"

"You're not going to be able to hide this," Shirley said, gesturing at Henny's middle. "Think of what you'll look like in four weeks." Henny tipped her head, made a helpless smile. "What are you going to do when he figures it out?"

Henny picked up her tea. "Say we miscalculated?"

THEIR MOTHER WAS clattering around in the kitchen pulling out baking pans and bowls.

"Aren't you going to talk to her?" Shirley said, wandering over to a tray of marble mandelbrot cooling by the window. Her mother carried a stack of pans to the table, then began opening bags of flour and sugar and salt. "Well, will you talk to me, at least?" Shirley said, exasperated.

"To you, yes. To her, no." Her mother cracked eggs into a bowl, dropped in uneven cupfuls of flour. Whistles and hoots rose up from the courtyard: the marble games breaking up. "Stay away from that mandelbrot."

"He's just as much to blame as she is," Shirley said, picking up a pan and buttering it. "Maybe if she told him about it he would take some of the responsibility, and you could stop blaming Henny so much."

Her mother glared at her. "Not a word to anyone, you understand? No one. Anyone asks, you tell them it's nerves, wedding fright."

She understood. A *shanda*, something to be ashamed of. Her mother was probably blaming herself as it was, telling herself it wouldn't have happened if their father had still been alive. As if he could have held the two of them, Henny and her, the ones who weren't married, in check. She passed her mother the greased pan. As if her mother had had the power to prevent her father from dying. "Well, did you call Rhoda?" Shirley said.

"No." Her mother poured batter into the pans. "It's no one's business. Not even Rhoda's." She brought the mixing bowl to the sink, turned on the faucet. "The only reason you know is that you were here."

Shirley took the sponge and wiped off the table. You didn't spread your shame around the street. Unless maybe you were Mrs. Ringwald or Mrs. Cooper—the whole neighborhood knew within five minutes when Milton Cooper was arrested for shoplifting. But not if you were Sophie Robins's daughters. "I'll go get Henny's tray," Shirley said, returning the sponge to the sink.

"Wait." Her mother turned, handed her a plate of mandelbrot. "Make sure she eats."

EVERYONE WHO WAS supposed to come came, except Nathan's frail grandmother, Mrs. Berlin, from Rochambeau Avenue. "Maybe you'll bring her a plate after," her mother told Shirley when the ceremony was over. Their uncle Julius, their mother's brother, gave Henny away. Henny would have preferred Sam, their father's handsome younger brother, but their mother refused, he looked too much like their father, bad enough the wedding was almost exactly like Rhoda's, same dress, same food, they didn't have to invoke their father's ghost.

"Wonderful cake," Mrs. Lipshitz from upstairs said to Shirley over the din, taking a napkin and another slice of her mother's poppyseed cake, fifty people squeezed into the overheated living room. Shirley had been up half the night with her mother cleaning, wrapping, checking that the cream cheese at the windows hadn't frozen, while Henny threw up three times in the bathroom. Shirley had to put on the radio so the neighbors wouldn't hear. She smiled at Mrs. Lipshitz over the noise and put the platter on the coffee table, then weaved through the crowd, nodding at the aunts and second cousins until she got to the empty hallway.

"Henny, it's me. Shirley." She knocked softly on the bedroom door, opened it, and peeked in. Henny lay face down on her bed, Rhoda's puffy white dress bunched up in whipped-cream mounds around her, her feet dangling off the side, her shoes on.

"You've got to get out there," Shirley said, closing the door behind her. "People are beginning to ask, even Nathan wanted to know where you were."

Henny rolled onto her back and put a hand to her forehead, the dress twisting around her. "I'm so sick," she mumbled. "I should have done something about this."

"What something?" Shirley said, suspicious, sitting next to her.

Henny stared at the ceiling. "You know."

"Yeah, with a coat hanger and a bottle of apricot brandy, like Sylvia Fishman's cousin who almost bled to death." Shirley leaned over and propped Henny up against the headboard. "You look awful," she said, and went to her dresser.

"In a few months it'll just be you and Mama," Henny said. "You going to be all right without me?"

Shirley came back with a bottle of rouge and a couple of lipsticks. "There's Pop's insurance until I go to work." She twirled open the lipsticks and examined them.

"That's not how I mean."

Shirley looked at her. Henny was the one who most looked like their father, the broad open face, the soft brown eyes, while she and Rhoda had inherited their mother's steely hazel. What was there to say? He was gone and soon Henny would go, too. Could she jump onto some giant clock and stop the hands? "Hold these," she said, handing Henny the lipsticks, "and stay still."

"What did you do to Henny?" Rhoda said after Shirley walked Henny back to the party and delivered her to Nathan. Rhoda's two little ones, in matching sailor suits, were crawling around Rhoda's feet, chasing each other and giggling and hanging on to her legs; any minute Rhoda would summon Saul to collect them and take them home. "She's got enough face paint on to play Cleopatra."

Shirley glanced at her sister. Rhoda should only know. Henny had felt so sick sitting upright that Shirley had to apply the makeup to her lying down. She'd felt like she was embalming a corpse. "I just helped her freshen up, that's all," she said, gazing around, pretending to be checking for dirty glasses.

"How far along is she?" Rhoda said casually.

Shirley whipped around. "How did you know?"

"You think I was born yesterday? She's in bed for a week with so-called nerves, Mama's seething, and today she's made up like Frankenstein's bride." Rhoda shrugged. "Don't you think there's a tip-off somewhere in there?"

"Can everyone tell?" Shirley whispered, looking around the room.

"Nah," said Rhoda, looking with her, then reaching down and scooping up a tangle of pudgy arms and legs. "Only the women."

A tapping on glass. Nathan's brother Jack was up on a stepstool proposing a toast. Shirley took two champagne glasses from a tray going around, gave one to Rhoda, and watched him. She'd met him only once, tall, wavy hair, perfect smile. You wouldn't know he and Nathan were related.

"To my little brother Nathan," Jack said, holding up his champagne, "who always manages to do everything before me. Even this." Nathan looked off into a corner, embarrassed, while Jack pulled something from his pocket and waved it around. His orders, Shirley heard, from the Navy. In three weeks he'd be in California, the last stop before the Pacific. Everyone drank their champagne, and Jack laughed and got off the stool and patted Nathan on the back, and all the Silvermans nervously laughed, Mrs. Silverman, Mr. Silverman, Nathan's sister Bea, probably thinking about both boys in the service plus all the things Nathan had accomplished—finish college, find a steady job, get married—that Jack, though smart enough and certainly good-looking—there was no shortage of interested girls, Shirley had heard—still hadn't done.

Next, Nathan climbed up and made a short toast—*To my beautiful bride*—looking at Henny, who smiled, her face a little cakey but not terrible, Shirley had seen worse. Then came Uncle Julius— *L'chaim!*—then Sam, who in his good suit and tie looked more like their father than ever, lifting his glass and speaking in that hushed way—soft, reassuring—as if it was their father right there in the room with them. Shirley finished off her champagne, then Rhoda's, too, after Rhoda went off to find Saul, then collected glasses and carried them into the kitchen, where she filled the sink with suds and tried to remember the sound of her father's voice.

"May I dry?"

She turned: Jack, holding her mother's dish towel, his big dark eyes fixed onto hers. She stared at him, momentarily lost, then picked up a faint musky smell, though it was not unpleasant. "Are you sure you haven't had too much to drink?" she said.

"Oh no, I'm quite in control." He moved closer, his sleeves rolled up, his forearms muscular, like a swimmer or a wrestler. Shirley handed him a dripping glass, felt a charge, a quick current. "I hadn't noticed you last time," he said, drying the glass gently, easing the towel lightly over the rounded bowl and then slowly drawing it up and down the delicate stem. "Did you leave early then?"

"No." The champagne was hitting her. Tea at the Silvermans', Mrs. Silverman's chocolate chip loaf, Jack staying for five minutes, just long enough to be introduced. "It was you who left early."

"Did I? Well, then, my loss." Shirley searched the suds for another glass. He was a smooth talker, she'd be crazy to fall for him, just the type her mother would warn her about. Her mother looked over their young men the way she scrutinized a garment, a pin in her mouth, checking every seam, every hem, no detail unnoticed. Shirley would get a look—pursed lips, raised eyebrows—and some terse words: *Watch that boy, he's a lot older than you.* "I must have confused you with your other sister," Jack said. "The sergeant."

Shirley let out a laugh. Rhoda, a sergeant. How did he know? "Am I right?" he said, obviously pleased. "She's the sergeant and you and Henny just go along?"

Shirley smiled and handed him another glass. Henny had said he'd broken a few hearts. She could see it. He had a way of bearing right into her, paying attention, talking about her instead of, like all the other boys, talking about himself. "I hear you're the one with the brains in the family," he said. Shirley's cheeks flushed. "Beauty and brains, it's an irresistible combination."

She pushed herself away from the sink and went to the refrigerator. The smoke, the champagne, the dense scent of him—she was light-headed, her legs a little too loose. "You're a smooth talker," she said, pulling out a platter of fruit.

He took the platter from her. "Maybe," he said, smiling. "But I always tell the truth."

The crowd was beginning to thin out, the Brooklyn cousins worrying about a two-hour ride on the subway, the neighbors not wanting to overstay their welcome; someone said it was starting to snow. By the end, only the immediate relatives were left. Mrs. Silverman and Shirley's mother were in the kitchen, Mrs. Silverman insisting she help and her mother refusing. Jack sat on the couch with Henny and Nathan, adding up their checks. Shirley emptied ashtrays and folded chairs.

"Shirley," her mother said, emerging from the kitchen with a plate covered with waxed paper. "Would you take this to Mrs. Berlin over on Rochambeau Avenue, a little something from the wedding?"

Shirley placed the last folding chair against the wall and looked at the plate. She was exhausted. "Isn't it a little late? I could do it tomorrow."

"Here, Jack will walk you," Mrs. Silverman said, coming out of the kitchen wearing one of her mother's aprons. Jack looked up. "You'll walk Shirley here to Nana's, won't you?"

Jack smiled. "My pleasure."

The crisp cold, the velvety dark, a sliver of moon: the snow dotted Shirley's shoes, open-toed, borrowed from Henny. "Isn't this lucky?" Jack said. "A chance to take a walk with you, and I didn't even have to ask."

Shirley kept her gaze ahead and walked fast, holding the plate.

Overhead, the streetlights winked. *Watch that boy.* "You, on the other hand," Jack went on, working to keep pace, "are a little uncertain. Here you are with someone you hardly know, your brother-in-law's brother, of all people, and you're probably wondering about him, heard a few things from Henny." Two couples hurried past, arm in arm, laughing, giddy and loud, the women's lips colored a fiery red. "You're thinking he's forward and brash and has a lot of nerve," Jack said, inching closer. "Especially now with him suggesting you have, let's say, a little affair."

"Affair?" She turned to him. The waxed paper flew off the plate. "I don't even know you, and I'm going to go to bed with you? You're not just brash, you're crazy."

"It'll eventually come to that, don't you see?" Jack said, retrieving the waxed paper and following her. "A few dates, a few drinks, and then, bam, there we'll be. Why not call a spade a spade? We don't have forever, you know."

Outside an apartment building a party was breaking up; she smelled cigars, strong perfume. Jack caught up with her and fitted the paper over the plate while one of the women, glittering earrings, too much rouge, smiled at her, a half nod, half wink. "You're pretty sure of yourself, aren't you?" Shirley said, hurrying on. "You think you can just go and talk to me like that and I'll go right along with it. Well, personally, I'd like to believe I have a shot at romance."

"Ah, a romantic. You mean you want to be courted and cajoled and pleaded with, you want to be flattered, and lied to, and bought."

They were in front of Mrs. Berlin's building. A street lamp spilled a pool of white light onto the snow-covered walk. "There are other things to romance," she said, turning to him, impatient.

He studied her, his eyes roaming from her forehead to her cheeks to her chin, then finally to her mouth, where he placed a finger on her lips and slowly traced their outline, as if painting them on her face. She held her breath, a statue, bits of snow falling on her hair, her nose, his finger. "You're right," he murmured, and leaned in and kissed her.

No movement, no sound. She had never been kissed like that, her whole being hovering at her mouth. Suddenly it seemed as if all the boys and dates and groping caresses of the past belonged to some-one else's childhood. The wet plate of little cakes shook in her hand. She opened her eyes. "Ring your grandmother's bell," she whispered.

A small woman in slippers was waiting in the doorway. Aunt Gert, Jack said. She took their coats, then led them to a tiny living room where an old woman sat in a wing chair, her eyes closed.

"Nana," Jack said, taking the plate from Shirley and lightly kiss-ing his grandmother on the head. "I brought you some cake. From Nathan's wedding."

Mrs. Berlin's eyes fluttered open. Shirley could see she was nearly blind. "Who is this—Jack?" She reached up and touched his face, ran her hand along his cheek.

"Some cake from Nathan's wedding, Nana. I'll put it on the table."

"Who's that?" Mrs. Berlin said, lifting her chin in Shirley's direc-tion. "Bea? Did Bea come with you?"

Jack pulled up a hassock next to her and sat. "No, this is the bride's sister. Shirley." Shirley had clasped her hands in front of her, lost without the plate. Should she wave? Go up closer?

"You going to marry her, Jack?"

Shirley's cheeks burned. Jack turned around and smiled. "I don't know, Nana. We just met."

Shirley stared at him. *I don't know, Nana. We just met.* "Well, maybe you ought to," Mrs. Berlin said. "That way I could get more cake."

Jack smiled again, turned to his grandmother. Shirley stood fixed to the carpet. Who was this man? What had she fallen into? "Nathan came yesterday," Mrs. Berlin said. "Introduced me to the girl again. What was her name?"

"Henny," Jack said. "For Henrietta."

Mrs. Berlin nodded. "And this one?" She gestured with her chin. Shirley's cheeks flushed again.

"Shirley."

Gert padded in with a tray of tea, put it on the coffee table, and gently directed Shirley to a chair. "Did he go yet, did Nathan go?" Mrs. Berlin said suddenly.

"In a week, Mother," Gert said softly, pouring.

"Twenty years they had to serve when it was the Czar," Mrs. Berlin said, waving a bony forefinger. "Mendel and Nunya, they never came back." Jack ran a finger along the hassock, making little lines in the fabric. "They told me Papa died of consumption, but it was grief. Mendel and Nunya, they never came back."

"That was a long time ago, Mother," Gert said, handing Shirley a cup, then Jack. "It's not like that anymore."

"Oh, it is, they never come back. You'll see, in this one, too, all the boys won't come back."

Gert carefully held out a cup for the old woman, whose hands fluttered near the porcelain like lost birds until they found the handle and the saucer. "Don't say those things, Mother," Gert said, and turned away. "Tell us about the wedding, Jack."

They drank their tea and left. At the corner of Rochambeau

Shirley hooked her arm through Jack's and pulled him close, the snow coming down in thick wet flakes. Neither of them spoke, everything around them hushed. Shirley's eyes teared from the cold, and if someone were to see them, they would think something was wrong, that something terrible was happening to them. But maybe it was terrible—the wedding over, Henny gone with Nathan in a borrowed car for their honeymoon in Pennsylvania, Nathan leaving soon for Fort Bragg. And then, a few weeks later, Jack. And who knew when either of them would be back?

They were at her building. Quickly she led Jack around the side, out of range of the streetlights, and pressed up against him, his back to the brick. He pulled her to him, one hand around her waist, the other under her damp hair, and kissed her, hard, urgent. Impatient, she unbuttoned her coat and pushed it open, letting his hands travel over the soft folds of her dress, over her breasts, her belly, her thighs, until finally, after ten minutes, fifteen, she had no idea, she forced herself away. "I have to go in," she whispered. "They'll be wondering. My mother, your parents."

He walked her upstairs, his mouth brushing her ear as he breathed *Call you* at the door. The apartment was still. Her mother lay stretched out on the couch, the living room vacuumed and put back in order. Shirley sank into the easy chair and closed her eyes. The taste of his breath, the heat of his hands, the nubby texture of his coat.

"Well, it's over," her mother said.

Shirley opened her eyes. Over? She meant the wedding. Her mother put her hand on her forehead and sighed. "Now we have to worry from Henny's baby. I don't know what's going to be with her."

Shirley lay her head against the seat back. Henny seemed a long time ago. "Don't worry, Mama. She'll be fine." It was, after all, the middle of a war, people did a lot of things they might not otherwise do.

Her mother turned to her. "I wonder what your father would have thought. She looked all right, though, Henny. She kept up a good face, didn't she?"

Shirley nodded. "Well, that's what counts," her mother said, and closed her eyes, and after a minute her breathing became deep and even, the lines in her forehead softening. Shirley watched the rise and fall of her breath. If her father had lived, would he have danced in the living room that afternoon, as he had for Rhoda even though their mother had clucked her tongue and told him to stop, it was too much strain, a breathless Bulgar or, arms folded, a Russian Sher, a father's privilege, he'd announced to everyone then, to dance at his daughter's wedding?

Her mother was asleep, a faint rhythmic whistling coming from her nose. Softly, Shirley pulled herself out of the chair and went to the hall closet, took down the afghan, and gently spread it over her mother's sleeping form.

THREE DAYS LATER Henny returned, the honeymoon cut short. The baby wasn't Nathan's. There was no possibility. Nathan would go to Fort Bragg and think things over, decide if Henny should join him. If not, it was finished between them.

Shirley sat on the edge of the couch, Henny lying beside her, the late afternoon shadows stretching across the carpet. Their mother wasn't home. Nathan was driving around, Henny said, trying to make sense of his life.

"Who did I get involved with?" Henny said, staring at the ceiling.

Circles ringed her eyes. She'd been crying for three days; Nathan had figured it out in the first fifty miles after Henny made him pull over four times to be sick. "The worst in the book, a married man. It went on for months, I couldn't help myself. Finally I gave him up and started seeing Nathan. But then I panicked and couldn't stay away, went to see him one last time." She waved at her middle. "And this is what I get for it."

Shirley glanced at Henny's midriff, no rounder, really, than it had been three days before, as if that very minute it might begin to betray Henny's terrible mistake, an unstoppable advertisement to the world of her foolishness. Is that what being swept up did to you? Took away your sense and made you helpless against its demands? Because if that were so, she, Shirley, would be its next willing partner. What was the choice? A life with another Nathan? Benny Green? Anyway, it was too late for that. She was on a moving train, and she wasn't getting off.

Henny turned to Shirley. "The sad part is that I was beginning to think I could really love Nathan. How, once I was with him for good, it might actually turn out fine." Her eyes welled up, big and brown, their father's eyes, the saddest eyes in the world. "But now I don't think that can ever happen. Even if he takes me back I don't know if he'll ever get over this."

Shirley brushed a few damp strands off Henny's cheek. Poor beautiful Henny. "Maybe he will," she said, but Henny was probably right. Who could pretend such a thing didn't matter, that it didn't change things forever? Nathan loved Henny, she had no doubt about that, but how much could he delude himself?

"There are some men . . ." Henny said, looking away, her voice trailing off. "I hope you never meet someone like that." She seemed to be talking more to the ceiling than to Shirley. "I don't know how to describe it. It's like a moth to a flame. I couldn't stay away." She shook her head, as if the ceiling had sighed in sympathy. "Can you imagine such a thing?"

Shirley turned, the last bits of sun retreating softly across the carpet, her mother's footsteps just outside the door, the rustling of paper bags. Beside her Henny said, "Like a moth to a flame, Shirley. Can you ever imagine?"

ACCOUNTING

SOLOMON HIRSCH HAD always been an honest man, so it came as no small shock, the registered letter from the state tax authority saying he owed thousands—forty? fifty? he could hardly look—and which, if true, meant other letters, federal, the SSA, the city, were not far behind.

He stood in the hallway of the apartment holding the letter in one hand, the torn envelope in the other, Ruth in the bedroom in the back, asleep. He had answered the door on the first buzz, the mailman silent, grim, having had to trek up two flights, the elevator temporarily out of order, stiffly holding out the little slip for Solomon to sign and looking at him accusingly, as if he had already been found guilty. What would you know? Solomon had wanted to spit out at the mailman, at his poker face. Do you also have such a son, a son who makes you go overnight from decent to criminal, who smiles at you so you melt and then breaks your heart?

Because, of course, this was Eliot's doing, and Solomon knew it even before he opened the envelope. Eliot, who must be running Solomon's business like it was his own personal stash. Solomon had been expecting something for months, though he hadn't realized it until that moment, the letter burning a hole in his hand merely a confirmation. Although it was bigger, worse, than anything he might have predicted: Dear Solomon Hirsch, It has come to our attention that taxes have not been paid by the entity known as Hirsch Payroll Service, possible fraud, triple penalties, criminal action.

He looked at the ripped envelope, its pink registered-letter stripe screaming *Important! Look what's happened to your business! Your family! Your life!* running down the side like dried blood. He didn't have to read the dates, could have told the tax people himself the quarters, months, weeks exactly, starting from the day Eliot came to work for him fourteen months before, Solomon eventually letting him handle the day-to-day so he could cut back, take it a little easy, start to think about retiring.

He walked to the narrow kitchen, crumpled up the offending envelope, and threw it in the trash, then sat down at the dining room table where his tea was, now cold. It was half past four in the afternoon, the hour when he'd recently taken to having tea, when Ruth napped. It was their routine: leave the apartment midmorning, he to the office, she with friends or to visit the little twins, Eliot's children, home with his ex-wife, Pam. By three-thirty they were back, and at four, regular as clocks, Ruth would rest and he would make his tea.

He looked at the cup, Earl Gray from a fancy tin, untouched, the pot a gift from Eliot, a sturdy blue stoneware thing imported from England, where, Eliot said, they really knew how to make tea. It was an indulgence of his newfound leisure, the tea; he had been strictly a coffee man his whole life. Who had time to linger over tea, steeping the leaves or putting them in a little silver holder or even waiting for a bag, when you were running a business? When you ran a business you drank bitter coffee from thick styrofoam cups lightened with powder that left the taste of chalk. You would never prepare, savor, the way you did with tea sipped from a porcelain cup. Tea was contemplative, thoughtful. You couldn't rush it even if you wanted to.

But now the tea was cold and useless to console, and he pushed it away along with a half-eaten cookie on the saucer, a little round fluted thing with a dab of chocolate in the center, and lay the letter on the table, the lower third flipping up like the legs of an insect on its back. He smoothed down the paper and put the saucer on the bottom to weight it.

Fifty-six thousand dollars.

Employee withholding, workers' comp, sales tax, unemployment, quarterly estimated, interest, penalties, the works. Never one to play favorites, the boy who made sure every kid on the block was picked for a team, even the skinny ones who couldn't throw and the slow kid who went to a special school, Eliot hadn't discriminated: every tax for an entire quarter, and he hadn't paid any of it. But the books balanced, Solomon had written the checks himself, and the money was gone. How could he have thought he'd get away with it?

He scanned the rest of the page, the bottom saying this was the fifth such notice. That the first four had been received by the taxpayer, the dates right there, from two months ago to last week, and that there'd been no response. And that there would not be another. Next would be a notice of lien, attachment of taxpayer's property, garnishment of wages, commencement of criminal proceedings.

He sat back and stared at the cookie. An ambulance sounded in the distance. It would go from bad to worse. Of course this would be a final notice. Of course the first four would have been signed for by Eliot, who would have written in Solomon's name for the ones delivered to the office and somehow managed to intercept the others, the ones addressed to the apartment, at the post office.

Or maybe those last had been signed for by Ruth, for the complicated house of cards she had been constructing over Eliot his entire life in order to save him, shield him, from himself. Solomon could just hear the way it would have gone, the conversation between the two of them, that complicity no one ever talked about: *Anything comes from the tax people, Mom, just pass it on to me, I'll take care of it.*

Then that big smile of his, and Ruth thinking, *Maybe this will be nothing, maybe he's changed.*

IT WOULD NOT have been the first time they'd hoped for change. Two years before, Eliot had run off, fled to Europe, leaving his job, Pam, and twin baby daughters in a newly built condo in which their things were not even unpacked. Forty-one years old with a respectable salary from a brokerage firm in the city, he couldn't stand the pressure, he told them, crying on the phone from London three days after disappearing. The marriage was bad, work was killing him, he had to get away. He loved them. He was sorry. He would stay in touch.

They called Pam. Eliot had cleaned out the bank account, had even taken the silver from their wedding, still in boxes from the move, and Pam's few pieces of good jewelry. Solomon listened on the extension in the bedroom, a faint nausea beginning to churn in his gut. It was happening again, signs of Eliot's shadow self that had been dormant long enough for them to have been lulled into believing it was gone bubbling up and seeping into his life, threatening, like always, to destroy everything.

"We're so terribly sorry, dear," Ruth said from the kitchen phone. "You know we'll do everything we can to help."

Pam was trying not to cry. Solomon could hear Ruth breathing. "I can't ask my mother for anything," Pam said, her voice breaking.

"Of course not, the poor thing," Ruth said. Solomon stared at the clock radio on the night table. For once, Pam's mother was lucky, her mind gone from Alzheimer's, her body bereft in a nursing home somewhere in New Jersey, spared the truth about her son-in-law. Unlike the rest of them.

"But I don't understand what he'd want with the silver or the jewelry," Pam said, fearful, as if she knew this was going to be bad, would uncover something deeper, more terrible than she'd ever imagined. "Unless he's in some kind of trouble."

The digital numbers on the clock suddenly changed, a big mocking zero bobbing up to replace a nine, appearing like a doomsday-face before him, commanding: *Now is the time! Speak!* The nausea rose and lodged in the back of his throat. "Who knows why?" Ruth said. "Maybe he panicked, maybe he lost his senses." Her tone turned soothing. "But that's not important now. What's important is you, what you need, you and the babies."

He stared at the zero-face. It knew Ruth was lying. Of course Eliot was in trouble, and Ruth knew it, he knew it, only Pam didn't know it. Should they have told her before she married him, their handsome, compassionate son with whom she was so blissfully in love? Disclosed things they'd heard about Eliot over the years, though never from him? Gambling, drugs, prostitutes, God knew what else. Ruth was calmly asking about bills, when the next mortgage was due, whether Pam had money for food, diapers, gas; he could hear her pulling in her chair at the dining room table and telling Pam to cancel the credit cards—did Pam have the numbers? old bills?—before charges could be run up by their son.

The zero was looking at him, accusing. What—did it really think warning Pam would have spared anyone any pain? That she would have listened? Two people in love, thirty, thirty-five, a chance for something good? Who were they to deny anyone that? Ruth asked about the car, whether it was in both names. He heard Pam's voice crumble. And who was to say back then that Eliot wouldn't change? He had so many good sides—loving, supportive, funny, the potential to be a great father. Could they have predicted with such certainty, fortune-tellers, that they should have had to choose between protecting Pam and hoping for everyone a little bit of happiness?

Pam was checking on the time for her next doctor's appointment, a follow-up with her obstetrician. Ruth would babysit. Disgusted, the zero floated off the screen, a one anchoring itself in its place. Solomon took a breath, forced the bile taste back down his throat.

"Pam," he said. "I know this sounds bad, but while you're there, at the doctor's, get an AIDS test."

The one glowed, approving, on the screen. On the extension Ruth took a sharp breath, seethed, "Solomon!"

"It's just a precaution," he said. "But you have to check. You have to be sure."

RUTH WAS MOVING around in the bedroom, Solomon could hear the door to the bathroom open, the water running. She was up from her nap but he was not ready for her, not ready to ask how much did she know, and when, and how.

He took his cup and saucer, put them on the kitchen counter, then folded the letter and put it in his pocket. He scribbled a note— *Went for a walk, be back by six*—took his coat and left the apartment.

It had turned cool, the little hint of spring he'd felt earlier in the day having vanished along with any tranquillity. The shrill of the rush hour a block away carried to the entrance of his building. He put on his coat and walked through the courtyard to the street, cars and buses jamming the roads, their exhausts roaring, people squeezing out, depleted. He watched the dizzying traffic, then turned left out of habit. Before cutting back his hours he had never walked the streets of Queens; if he wanted air or scenery, like everyone else they knew they took a drive. Upstate to Bear Mountain, or out to Montauk. Ruth would pack a picnic and sometimes, when Eliot was young, they'd find an amusement park along the way. But now, the last few months, he walked home from work every afternoon, two, two-thirty, and found he liked it. What had started for the exercise had become more than that, a little window in his mind clearing of some built-over obstruction, a chance to see things he'd not noticed before.

He turned down a side street. By a low stucco building a lone dogwood was sprouting its first buds. An apartment dweller his whole life, never interested in cultivating a single blade of grass, lately he'd begun to pay attention to the trees. White birches. Flowering cherries. The magnolia a woman the week before was carefully uncovering in her front yard, telling him all about frost dates while she removed the burlap.

He moved up the street. A pair of stone cherubs smiled at him from above a church door, chubby, with curly stone hair, fluttery stone wings. Trees, yes, but also stone carvings, he saw them everywhere. An eagle on a bank facade. Heads of Plato and Aristotle by the steps of an elementary school. And the strangest of all: the seven deadly sins above the doorway of the library that was now a senior center across the street from his office. Sloth and Gluttony and Envy on the left, Anger and Lechery and Pride on the right, and above them all, Avarice, as if, in addition to wanting everything that was

beautiful and good in the world, it craved even that which was per-
verse and depraved, unable, in its terrible greed, to know the difference. A couple of months before, he'd gone in and inquired at the
desk: Why, he wondered, hadn't they removed the grotesque faces?
Surely the current clientele had more spiritual concerns, did not
need to be exhorted so chillingly against such ferocious appetites.

The young woman had leaned forward and, in a hushed voice,
told him they couldn't get a work crew that was willing. That everyone was afraid to tamper with them lest the dreaded spirits behind
the masks be set free, turned loose on the innocent city streets.

A school bus stopped beside him, the squeal of brakes, the
cough of the exhaust. Half a dozen children spilled out and ran past,
fanning out to the buildings. He hadn't been able to tell if the woman
at the senior center was mocking him or actually believed she was
telling the truth. Though now he wondered: Perhaps there had been
some seepage after all. Some bit of Greed or Lust snaking its way
down the wall and under the street, through the pipes, and into his
building, drawn to his son like a parasite to a susceptible host.

The bus rumbled away, and he walked on. Though there had
been no stone sins on the new condo with Pam, only Pam's remark-
able grace. After Eliot had fled, after that terrible first phone call, the
AIDS test negative, thank God, Pam had let them help. Had let
them pay for everything, let Ruth shop, cook, babysit.

They were grateful. Cleaning up after Eliot had become for
them not only an act of penitence but an attempt to correct the balance, an effort to ensure that the world did not suffer a net loss on
account of their son. For every debit inflicted by him they were
obliged to provide, in the other column, a credit.

He stopped, a cold wind at his neck, and pulled up his collar.

But now what credit could he possibly provide in his own column? Who would right the balance for his own suffering?

He was at the corner near his office. He walked another block, then sat on a low cement wall, the screaming traffic in front of him, Avarice and Pride behind him, their stone mouths fixed in a permanent sneer. He and Ruth had tried everything to right the balance after Eliot's misdeeds except the one thing Solomon had ever believed might have done any good: make Eliot have to stanch the damage himself.

But that, Ruth was not prepared to do. *You know he'll do nothing if it doesn't come from us. What good would it do to hold him accountable now except hurt the others more?*

The cold blew against his back. For it was not guilt at Ruth's core, the belief that Eliot's deeds were, at bottom, their fault, a flaw in his upbringing, something in his genes. To Ruth, absorbing Eliot's failures had become simply an extension of their obligations as parents. A burden they were required to shoulder just as surely as if their son had been born deaf or blind, or crippled by polio or mental retardation.

And what about him? What had he come to in his forty-three years as a father? Only this: that it was not the sins of the father that were visited upon the innocent son but the weaknesses of the son that came back and haunted the father, visiting themselves upon him over and over, an insistent cry calling out each time with new force: *Look what has become of him! Open your eyes and look!*

ACROSS THE STREET, above his building, the first hint of a moon hung in the pale gray sky. In the fourth-floor windows, in the same office where he'd started Hirsch Payroll Service thirty years before, Eliot's light was on. Once, Solomon had tried to hold back. Force

Eliot into taking responsibility. Eliot had been back from Europe for two months, living in their spare bedroom that doubled as a den, leaving the apartment each morning for interviews, to network. It was going nowhere. No one would take a chance on a forty-two-year-old broker who one day had just upped and disappeared.

They were eating breakfast, Solomon and Ruth finishing their coffee in the dining room. Eliot, holding his overcoat and a briefcase, a list of headhunters from the *Times* in his hand, had just persuaded Ruth to let him make dinner. He hated being a freeloader, at least they could let him cook. He would pick up some fish at the market near Solomon's office on the way home, he'd be there anyway to use the copier or one of their printers. Solomon didn't mind, he knew Eliot needed to be with people.

Eliot kissed each of them on the top of the head and went out the door. Solomon looked back at the paper.

"I think you should take him into the business," Ruth said.

He had been expecting this. He put down his coffee. " I'm not doing that, Ruth. Eliot has to find his own job. We can't bail him out anymore."

Ruth's eyes began to well up. "But what if he can't find anything? You heard the judge." She imitated him, stern, her voice a mocking baritone. " 'I don't care what your parents do, Mr. Hirsch. You fail to make those payments and you don't see your children.' " She leaned toward Solomon. "He's making the payments now, but we don't know how much he has, when he'll run out."

He nodded. "That's right. Did he send a dime while he was gone? A penny for those babies?"

Ruth waved a hand. "But he knew we were taking care of them, that they'd be all right."

"Exactly! Because we were taking care of them he did nothing."
He could feel his cheeks getting hot, his whole face burning up.
Months of anger spilling out, erupting, as if it had been sitting there
on the top of his head, waiting for the first possible trigger. "I'm glad
the judge said that. Someone had to, and God knows it wasn't going
to be one of us."

Ruth looked away. He would not let her ignore him. He raised
his voice. "And what do we say to him when he comes back from six
months doing who knows what in Europe, completely out of touch,
a couple of phone calls so we know he's alive?" he demanded, waving
at the door. "Do we ask him, How could you have done this, run off
and left your children, your wife, with nothing? Stolen from them,
even?" He flicked his wrist as if he were shooing away a fly, or a little
fairy, a Tinkerbell sprinkled with magic dust. "No! We tiptoe around
him, afraid he'll run away again. We say, Don't worry, get your life
back together, get a job, we'll help you."

"And what should we have said?" Ruth said, whipping back.
"You're a failure, a miserable human being, a terrible father?"

"Maybe! Yes! Maybe for once we should say it! Tell him, and stop
protecting him from the truth of who he is!"

"Which is what? A damaged person who doesn't function very
well, who can't hold it together? Who has problems none of us
understands, not me, not you, not him! Who's been screwing up his
whole life and knows it, knows it in spades!"

"Because you wouldn't make him face anything, force him to
change!" he shouted. "You've been coddling him his entire life! And
you made me do the same!"

Furious, he looked away, glared at a philodendron in the corner.

It seemed to change size in front of him, he couldn't tell how big it was, there was no scale, just a plant on a stand by itself. It was a ridiculous place to put a plant. They had been over this a hundred times, a thousand.

He turned back to Ruth. She was staring at the table, rubbing her forehead. They had been arguing over Eliot for thirty years. What kind of marriage might they have had if they'd had a different son?

"He's trying so hard," Ruth said. She looked worn, aged. All those months helping Pam, caring for two infants, sixty-six years old. It hadn't been easy. "He makes those payments to Pam like clockwork. And he's so good with the babies, you've seen it when he brings them here. They love him."

He sat back, exhausted. It was painful to watch, painful to see his son capable of so much tenderness, feeding them, playing on the floor with them, sitting with them while they fell asleep on Solomon and Ruth's bed. The same son who could disappear—had disappeared—and walk out on those babies like they were so much furniture. Leaving with less regard for them than most people had for a kitten or a pet bird.

Slowly, like an old woman, Ruth began stacking the dishes. Now all they could do was try and buy those babies some time, some memories of Eliot that were going to have to carry them for when he messed up again. Which he would, sooner or later.

"All right," he said. "He can start next week."

Another time Ruth might have run over and hugged him, thrilled he'd seen it her way. This time she only nodded. "Maybe something good will come of this for you, too, Sol. Maybe you can take it a little easy."

He looked away.

"What will you have him do?"

"There are things, I'll find something."

PEOPLE WERE FILING out of his building. Weary, he pushed himself off the wall, dusk descending fast around him, and made his way across the traffic, the headlights glaring at him, blurring his vision. Eliot had worked hard, updating the computer system, coming up with new services. Everyone liked him; he was a good manager, concerned with the employees' problems, their families.

He pulled open the heavy glass door and stepped into the lobby. He had allowed himself to be pulled along by the conscientious engine that seemed to be Eliot. Eliot, who found a one-bedroom for himself nearby, big enough so the twins could eventually sleep over; who was making his payments to Pam religiously; who brought the twins over every Sunday, along with something for them—danish, a fresh bread, or, for Solomon, a fancy tea. The Eliot who was coming to work each day, arriving promptly at eight and not leaving until the work was done. Solomon gave him more responsibility, started to think about retiring, of having Eliot take over.

He pressed the elevator button, the floor indicator light on four. His floor. He put his hand in his pocket, felt the letter. Now Eliot's life had begun to unravel again, though why, Solomon would never know. In that way Eliot was strangely considerate. Just as Ruth had worked so hard to shield Eliot from the consequences of his acts, so Eliot had tried to spare them from having to see those acts too closely, instead leaving only traces, tracks, debris.

The floor light was still on four. He would, of course, pay the taxes, go to the bank the next day and get a cashier's check. He would find the money, cash in his retirement if he had to.

Then, when he was done with that, maybe he would close up the business. Sell off the furniture, transfer his clients. He was tired, had had enough. He wasn't one of those men who would be at a loss, nothing to do without a job.

The elevator wasn't moving, out of order like the one at home. An elevator epidemic. Closing up wouldn't be difficult, he had to do an audit anyway, figure out how Eliot had done it. It wouldn't have been hard: tear up the tax checks right after Solomon had cut them, enter them in the book as void, then skim the equivalent with phony invoices slipped into the bookkeeper's, Marianne's, pile, using a dummy name, a post office box.

There was noise on the stairs, a chorus of familiar voices. Marianne, some of the data entry people. And over them all, a cheerful, masculine voice.

Eliot.

They were all talking at once, the sounds of a friendly office, people who liked working together, having coffee, doing a day's work, then going home satisfied.

The footsteps were louder. He stepped away from the elevator and ducked into a corner under the stairwell, out of sight of the stairs. The voices seemed giddy, high, wild, the footsteps resonating like a stampede. He heard his son, then laughter, maybe a joke, a funny remark.

He huddled under the steps, the street outside the glass door dark, punctuated by the lights of the shrieking traffic. He would not sell his business. He would not stop working, would work until the day he died. Because someone had to take into account those babies. He would climb the four flights, call Ruth to say he was working late, then stay, reconstructing the records, piecing together what had happened in order to balance it, set it straight.

They spilled down into the lobby, laughing, loud, a cluster of young people in raincoats and light jackets, and there, in the middle, like a phoenix, rose Eliot, a head taller than any of the others, with his big smile and dark, wavy hair—movie star looks, Ruth used to say, in more hopeful times—the magnet around which they all so innocently circled. One of them opened the door, a great gust of cold air blowing in and wrapping itself around Solomon's legs and pinning him into place, and the circle of people seemed to spin, almost dancing, into the black night.

He waited a moment, then came out from under the stairs. He glanced once more at the frozen elevator, then looked up the long stairway. He would climb them, work all night, and then, the next day, after everyone was gone, he would show Eliot the letter, listen to his tearful confession. Then he would go home in the dark and hope that Eliot returned to work in the morning.

THE DIVINERS OF DESIRE: A MODERN FABLE

WHEN HER DAUGHTER wasn't looking, Tru Borenstein slipped a snippet of lace from the hem of her musty ivory wedding dress into the powder-blue suitcase. Because you never knew when the desire to marry might overcome a young woman, even timid Shoshana.

Yet why now? Was it something in Shoshana's freckled face? Her red-haired Shoshana, formerly Susan, twenty-two and newly religious, leaving New York after a ten-day visit home and returning to Jerusalem to finish out her year teaching English at the Harriet Gertelsman School for Girls? Tru couldn't be certain. But surely she saw something, something that caused her to reach back into her own dustily Jewish past for an appropriate and transportable custom. Hence the snippet. A carryover, the idea was, from one successful union to another.

Not that Tru hadn't considered packing the entire dress altogether. But that, she reasoned, would be rushing things. There was, for instance, the small matter of a groom. Though that, Tru thought as she laid in Shoshana's prim blouses, her neatly ironed skirts, then nestled into the corners socks, stockings, a pair of new shoes, would be the easy part. Take the Number 15 bus to Me'a Shearim, go to one Leibel Frehn, the butcher on the corner of Yafo and Strauss that Shoshana had told her about and, when she had the nerve, ask him for the name of a shadchan. A matchmaker. Tru would never suggest this directly to her daughter, but surely this Leibel Frehn had such information in his great store of local wisdom. Hadn't he, with his fluent English and kindly manner, directed Shoshana's new acquaintances to doctors, dentists, compassionate landlords, the Turkish baths, and even a podiatrist for an ingrown toenail? Matchmakers were all over the city. Surely he would know of someone sympathetic to the likes of Shoshana, American girls not raised religious, barely raised Jewish, but trying. For the matchmakers it would be a mitzvah, a double mitzvah, Tru presumed, carefully tucking in a slip, a soft nightgown, and a bra. Extra bountiful holiness earned by bringing one more floundering soul into the bosom of right living.

Because if they didn't take on such girls, the logic ought to go, Tru thought, working in bath powder, a hair dryer, a mini sewing kit, and a little gift box containing a delicate pendant Shoshana might like, might not such girls be tempted to chuck the whole Jewish enterprise entirely, get on a plane, and go back to America? And then who could predict what would happen?

WHICH INDEED WAS, from time to time as the occasion arose, the reasoning of Mrs. Ruti Shtarr, the esteemed Madame Shtarr, who, about the time Shoshana's plane was landing at Ben Gurion, was thinking of retiring. Turning in her matchmaking badge, as she liked to joke to her son Yossi, a little slow but in truth the one she loved best, the only one of her sons with a sense of humor. She liked her work, and helping those American girls had its special rewards, but maybe it was time to take it easy, yes, Yossi? Loll on the beach in Netanya or maybe go topless in Eilat. At that, she and Yossi doubled over and howled with laughter, the other boys mortified over their Gemarahs in the next room. Oh, she was tired, Yossi, and besides, maybe it was time for a new career. She'd been at this for twenty-one years already, since she was a precocious thirty-year-old with six children, able to sniff out a perfect match the instant she saw one and veto on the spot those she knew would be doomed. Ruti Shtarr's track record was legend in Me'a Shearim—what Me'a Shearim? all of Jerusalem!—and she was justifiably proud. Humble, too, of course, always humble, because such gifts don't grow on trees, nor do they spring from within. The source is always You-Know-Who, and Ruti Shtarr made a point of thanking Him every day for her good eye, good ear, good reputation, and good fortune. Because all those blissfully correct unions had yielded Ruti one of the largest flats on Strauss Street, six rooms, virtually unheard of, and a good thing, too, since Yakov, her husband, wasn't much on the earnings side. Expenses yes, but revenue—forget it.

Not that he was extravagant or spendthrift. Not like, say, Hinda Katz upstairs, who collected Judaica and owned more etrog cases and megilla holders than you could count on the fingers and toes of her nine unruly children. *Rescued, thank God!* Hinda breathed over her display cabinet whenever Ruti found herself sipping tea in the overstuffed Katz living room. *Saved from the ruins of Europe, so much that didn't survive!* Only partly true, Ruti thought, stirring in another sugar. Judaica was floating around Jerusalem like crows over a wheat field after the war; there were more kiddush cups than eggs, and half the population of the city lived for years off the proceeds of their salvaged candelabra and silver challah plates. The buyers, Ruti wanted to tell Hinda but politely refrained, were of course the snooty German Jews from whom Hinda was descended, coreligionists who'd simply gotten there first and who struck some pretty unmerciful bargains with their suffering brethren.

But Ruti's Yakov was not interested in acquisitions. Old Dutch haggadahs, filigreed spice boxes, two-tiered brass menorahs: these were not his love. Rounding out his days translating the ancient Slovenian mystic Yosef ben Berli into Hebrew, a project that had been going on for ten years and for which Yakov received a miserly monthly stipend from a devoted group of disciples in Belgrade, was Yakov's true, and fairly recent, passion: Americans. Specifically, American Jews. More specifically, young American Jews who found themselves stumbling into the Holy City. They were the same ages as his children, and it mystified him. Why had they come here? Yakov wanted to know. Sure, he knew about Jewish longing, the search for roots, the cleaving toward Zion, but it didn't seem to add up. What kinds of lives did they come from that they should schlep so far and for so long from their families, twelve hours on El Al from New York, and that was nonstop? The questions burned at him and bored a little hole in his brain.

And so it became Yakov's project, self-designed. An independent scholar, Ruti mused about her man, who'd had a respectable yeshiva education like everyone else, but nothing out there, in the secular world. These Americans fascinated him. You think maybe I have some American blood in me? Yakov asked her, and Ruti rolled her eyes. Yakov, it's the other way around. The Americans are looking for Yerushalmi roots, a bit of your black hat and beard in them, not the other way.

I don't know, I don't know, said Yakov, drifting off, taking his umbrella, just in case, and leaving the flat to go about his research. Which he conducted watching, listening, eavesdropping, on the street.

WHICH IS HOW Yakov Shtarr came to hear about Shoshana Borenstein. Because a chief source of Yakov's research was none other than Leibel Frehn, the butcher.

"Hello, my friend," Yakov called, the door closing jauntily behind him. Leibel had recently hung a strap of bells on the frame, a gift from a former customer now in Cincinnati. "What's fresh today?" Yakov asked.

Leibel bypassed the obvious answer, letting Yakov look at the display of briskets, chicken parts, and livers himself, and went directly to the heart of things. "There's a girl comes poking around now, once, twice a week, especially on Thursdays. Red hair, freckles, shy, *nebbach*, timid almost."

"Yes?" said Yakov. "What's she looking for?"

Leibel shrugged. "Chicken wings. Sometimes a few franks."

Yakov nodded. "Anything else?"

Leibel sighed pensively and wiped his hands on his bloody apron. Over the months he'd catalogued an array of vaguely expressed desires for Yakov, diffuse longings he'd divined from these healthy-looking souls in their hiking shoes, even in summer, and heavy backpacks, even the girls. Usually they were looking for—dare he say it?—meaning, belonging, truth, and consolation. Sometimes an anchor, a bridge, a life preserver. With each visitor Leibel smiled, listened, exchanged a few words, eventually heard the story of a life, and sent them out with half a chicken cut into eighths.

"This one," Leibel said, raising a finger in the air, "is different. She, I think, is looking for a husband."

"A husband?" Yakov said, widening his eyes. This was new. In all his research, remarkably, he hadn't come up against this one. Maybe because he seemed to be specializing in the younger ones, nineteen, twenty, who weren't looking so much to plant their feet on the ground as to fly upward. "A husband," he repeated, intrigued.

"A husband, what can I say?" Leibel said, waving his big hand. "*Nu*, business for your wife."

"But did the girl say as much?" Yakov said, leaning close to the display case. The smell of garlic turkey rose up and greeted him like an old friend. Maybe he'd buy a quarter kilo on the way out, Ruti's favorite, which they rarely allowed themselves, the garlic lingering on their breaths for days, a definite impediment in both their lines of work.

"Not quite," Leibel said. "I'm not sure she herself knows. But I can see it in her face." He nodded sagely. "One more order of chicken wings, maybe a small steak, and she'll probably bring it up."

Yakov nodded. A new phase for his research, possibly a turning point. He was most indebted to Leibel, most indebted.

"Fascinating," Yakov said, and turned his gaze to the case. He pointed to the suffering turkey breast, the curved garlic ends visible through the cheek of tender whiteness, and ordered a quarter kilo, no, make that a half.

THE DOOR OPENED. The strap of bells jangled like December on Forty-second Street, the jolly sound of Santa and the Salvation Army, and Shoshana was seized with a wave of homesickness so great it almost sent her running the other way. She was having second thoughts about her life, her decisions, even her cuisine. What was she doing here, Shoshana asked herself every day, and couldn't remember the answer. Maybe she should have stayed in New York, not come back after her visit home, and let her roommates finish off her junior-sized jars of peanut butter and mayonnaise without her.

She closed the door carefully, muting the strap, and tiptoed to the meat counter in case the door sang in response to movement, like the lighted motion sensor over her parents' faraway garage.

"Ah, Miss Chicken Wings, how do you do?" Leibel said, a broad smile. "I haven't seen you in a couple of weeks. Everything all right?"

"Fine, thank you," Shoshana said, nervous, though in fact she was slightly nauseated at the moment. She'd been a vegetarian until recently but had, in this arena, as in everything else since coming to Jerusalem, radically changed her ways. A paradigm shift: nothing less was required. At times she felt the ground sliding away from her, and some weeks ago had found in herself a craving for meat. Hot dogs, steak, lamb chops. The old Shoshana was gone—Susan, to be exact—and a new carnivorous one had taken her place.

Still, she found the butcher's meatily aromatic shop a difficult place in which to linger. She mustered her courage and looked up at the butcher's kindly eyes, bypassing the red-stained apron.

"A piece of beef stew, please," she said. "If you have. Small, very small."

"Beef stew?" Leibel's eyebrows went up. "There is no such thing as a piece of beef stew."

"There isn't?" But she had planned, she said; she had a recipe from her mother. Carrots, potatoes, onions. She really didn't know how to cook, she said. Her only seasonings were a little pepper and salt.

"Ah, miss. To make a beef stew you buy flanken meat, or chuck. Shoulder or brisket or bottom round. From that you can make a nice dish."

"Oh," said Shoshana, patting her neck as if needing to recover from distressing news.

Leibel leaned forward. She was a slip of a thing and, with those freckles and red hair that seemed to belong in pigtails, could be easily mistaken for sixteen. They looked so young, these Americans, whereas his beloved Chava, only thirty, looked forty—five children and a life in the sun. "You need some help? Advice on the recipe?"

Shoshana fished in her pocket, pulled out a piece of paper, and handed it to him.

Leibel squinted. He had learned his English the year his father filled in as chief rabbi of Newcastle. Leibel ran loose, played with the coal miners' children, twelve years old, such a wild ox his parents came rushing back before his bar mitzvah, afraid they'd lose him for good if they stayed a minute longer.

"A fine recipe, you just need some nice cubes of meat," he said, handing the paper back. He reached into the case and pulled out a hunk of something red while Shoshana lowered her eyes.

"So you're cooking a nice meal," Leibel said, his back to her, slicing deftly and handling the cubes with care. "How much did you say? How many people?"

"Two," she said, looking up, surprising herself. Two? Where did that come from?

"Ah, two," he said, dropping the chunks onto brown paper and putting them on the scale. "Big eaters? Little eaters?"

She cleared her throat; it seemed to him she was blushing. "I don't really know."

"First time your guest is having dinner with you?"

Her voice had a small catch. "First time."

He brought the order to the register, wrapped it into a little packet, and tied it with string. "Will be delicious, I'm sure," he said, handing it over with a smile. "Anything else?"

She stared at him, her mouth partly open. "Actually, there is."

"Yes? Don't be shy."

A long pause, the mouth still open. "Two chicken wings?"

He moved, reluctant, to the case. Two wings were like two bites. Who could eat only two wings? Why even bother to take out a pan, sauté an onion, turn on the gas? A person wanting two wings was like a bird herself, an angel who required no sustenance other than air. He took two wings from the case, first searching for the largest, wrapped them, then said to her over the glass, "Anything else?"

"Well," she said, turning and glancing at the bells, the clock behind Leibel's head, the doorway to the back where Leibel's silvery new walk-in refrigerator hummed happily. It had just now come to her, and she had to ask. "I do have a question," she said, inching forward, whispering, as if the half cow dangling behind the Magic-Seal metal door might overhear them and laugh.

DID RUTI SHTARR really want to do this? Oh, Yossi, I'm wearing out. A nice girl, maybe, but timid, shy—it would be a lot of work. Not every boy in the world is suited, you have to look hard, keep digging. Yossi smiled, bounced a rubber ball, and went outside to toss it at the laundry lines.

Yakov pleaded with her, cajoled with Leibel's magnificent turkey. For his research; couldn't she do just one more for his research? The other Americans she'd handled, that Lynn from California and Maureen from Boston—an Irish name, yet, you think it was easy?—he wasn't paying attention, was too busy with his Slovenian. But now: How could he let such an opportunity go by? What brought her here, Ruti? You have to ask.

What brought her here, Yakov? What do you suppose brought her? Ruti said, spooning out the compote. The garlic would stay with her into the night and bring her good dreams. The Garden of Eden. Manna from heaven. Didn't they all yield clusters of fulsome garlic? Who could live happily without it, a garlicless life? You might as well eat farina all day, or vanilla ice cream, another phenomenon Ruti didn't understand. She's looking for a man, Yakov. A nice young man.

Yes, but why here? Plenty of Jewish boys in America, don't tell me this is the only place on the planet to find your bashert.

Ruti shrugged, a piece of cooked plum on her spoon like a shimmering jewel. Maybe she's looking for adventure, someone exotic. Like our Yossi.

Yossi? Exotic? A ball tapped out a rhythm on the sidewalk—rum-ta-dum, rum-ta-dum—then soared, angelic, into the sky. A pair of socks rained gently down. But Yossi is not normal, Ruti. Yossi's different, not a boy for a match.

Ruti tipped her head. It was just for an example, Yakov. But a sense of humor, like Yossi's—it wouldn't hurt.

A SENSE Of humor, it turned out, was the least of Ruti's worries. The girl, it seemed, had allergies. Many allergies. To cats. Dogs. Shellfish (not a problem). Also room fresheners, dishwashing soap, detergents. She could wear cotton but not polyester. Silk but not rayon. Linen but not a mix. If she handled such items she broke out in a rash that took months to heal. Rubber gloves sometimes helped but only the surgical kind from dentists and gynecologists. Forget the thick ones from the supermarket, they contained lanolin. A killer that made little buds grow on her wrists and palms until they bloomed into flowery red sores.

"Anything else?" Ruti said, a polite smile, her hands folded on the Formica. The cuckoo clock was about to spring two, quitting time for Ruti, who badly needed a bubble bath and a healthy dusting of lavender talc. Then came her afternoon nap until the stores reopened and business resumed at four.

The girl looked miserably into her cup of tea. Yakov's research was not going to be substantially enhanced by this one. What made her come here? Perhaps she thought it was less allergenic here than in America. Or maybe she went from place to place, following her nose. In any case, it was not likely Ruti would extract the girl's motives for coming here any more than she would learn about her kashrut practices, desired number of children, or whether she wanted the fellow to be bearded or clean-shaven. It was pulling teeth all the way.

"Yes?" Ruti prodded, leaning down to meet the girl halfway. "Don't be reluctant. Everyone has some preferences."

"There is, I suppose, one more thing," the girl said.

"Yes?" Ruti said, glancing quickly at the clock. It was late. Had the cuckoo fallen asleep?

"I'd like someone who is kind and considerate," the girl said, concentrating on the table. "Someone open-minded and compassionate. Free-thinking but not without principles. Someone serious and pure and good, who cares about the world."

Ruti nodded, her chin resting on her palm. A simple request: a combination of Ghandi and the Mashiach. But fragrance-free. A departure from the usual list specifying height, looks, occupation, and family background.

The clock made a ticking noise, and all at once the wooden door flew open and out came the little bird, its spring wobbling. It sounded its blissful shriek: *Cuckoo! Cuckoo!* Startled, Shoshana looked up just as the clock rained down a cascade of fake pinewood shavings ground up by the failing spring.

"Oh, I'm so sorry!" Ruti said, bouncing out of her chair and sweeping the shavings off Shoshana's arms, which had flown up, elbows bent, like a Kewpie doll's. Ruti brushed, then swept the Formica with a towel which, she only then noticed, smelled strongly of her most perfumed imported Tide.

"I think that's probably enough for now," Ruti said, fluffing the towel behind her. She had everything she needed; actually, more than she needed. This one was going to be a stretch. But Yakov had begged.

She walked the girl to the door and wished her a pleasant afternoon. On the sidewalk Yossi sorted ladies' underpants into brightly colored piles.

HE CAME INTO the shop at a little past two, the bells ringing merrily behind him. Leibel saw him from the back where he was once more checking his beloved refrigerator. He ran a hand over the smooth cool surface, then strode to the front of the store.

"May I help you?" Leibel offered, a big smile. The young fellow had the backpack, the hiking shoes, the jeans. Leibel guessed a city, not New York. Maybe St. Louis, Milwaukee, Chicago.

"How do you do, I'm Steven Epstein, new in the neighborhood," the young man said, and thrust out a big hand.

Leibel wiped his own on his apron, then shook. A firm grip and a friendly face. He liked this one. "You're looking for some cuts of meat, some chicken?" he said.

The young man held up the hand. "In a moment, if that's okay. I came in for some advice. I hear you might be able to help me in my search."

Search, search. They were all searching. Leibel smiled. "And what might that be?" he said.

"Well, I'm studying the Jews, my Ph.D.," Epstein said. "That sounds ridiculous. What I mean is, young Jews like me. Americans. I want to know what made them decide to come here. I hear you meet a lot of them in your shop and thought you might be able to help me."

Help? He could more than help. A matchmaker deluxe. Forget Ruti Shtarr, now there was Leibel Frehn.

"In fact I can," Leibel said. "I have a friend who studies the same phenomenon."

"Really? Can I meet him?"

"Certainly. I'll write you his name and address."

"Wow, this is a lucky break," the young man said while Leibel scribbled Yakov's vitals onto a shred of brown paper. "I don't know how to thank you. Perhaps you have a suggestion for a suitable house gift for your friend?"

WOULD RUTI SHTARR let him get past her living room on the way to Yakov's study without an interview? Do I know my business, Yossi? Ruti smiled at the young fellow, a cloud of lavender talc billowing around her before she thought to put the canister down with an aromatic puff on the coffee table. Off the hall, the tub sweetly filled, burble burble.

So, from where? Ruti asked pleasantly. Chicago. How interesting. A student. And the family—a doctor? Skin? Important work. Oh yes, her husband was indeed home, he'll be delighted, a compatriot, let me get him right away, a book from the ancient Yugoslavian. Whoosh, whoosh, my son is an airplane in the kitchen. You're here long? This garlic turkey, what a treat. Call me Ruti. And here we are. Yakov, Yakov.

A soup, a stew, a potion simmering in Ruti Shtarr's brain, and she wondered: what about him with the girl? The tub was full, the bubbles a blanket of glistening foam. Ping. Pop. She dipped in a tentative toe. No one else had come to mind, though she'd tried, really she had. Even while the girl sat with her at the kitchen table the day before, and then after that, in yesterday's shvitz, Ruti, immersed, had run through her prospects and come up dry. This one too old, that one too religious, another one too loud. And who would like her? That was even harder. Timid, freckled, foreign. For Lynn from California she had found Hersch from Wisconsin, and for the Irish Maureen there was Sean. Miriam and Shmuel, they were now, sending her baby announcements and yontif greetings once a year from the New Age moshav by the airport.

But for this one? Ruti put in one foot, then the other, the temperature not too hot, not too cold, but, like for Goldilocks, just right. She glided down, stretched herself out. Pop. Ping. Bip. Pop. This boy in Yakov's study, with his Ph.D. and Mount McKinley boots and a father in a convenient medical specialty: was it a fit?

Steam rose by her feet, a twinkle of toenail visible through the shimmer. She would watch the bubbles for information. Yes? Bip. No? Ping. Bip. Pop. Ping. Bip. Yes no yes no. Finally, nah. It was not a match. He was too—what? Cheerful? Too bubbly himself? And not interested. If there was one thing Ruti could spot, it was a young man not ready, and this one was as unready as they came. He planned to sow his oats, play the field, and do all those other agricultural things that meant he was taking his time.

She slid deeper under the foam and closed her eyes. Shwoo shwoo! Whoosh whoosh! In the kitchen Yossi took off, flew, landed.

LEIBEL WAS WORRIED. The beef stew chunks would go bad if she didn't cook them soon, and already two days had passed. But what could he do? Dinner for two had to happen quickly but Ruti Shtarr was the matchmaker, not him. He was only the butcher. But food, food, didn't it always start with food? Look at Eve with the apple, Abraham cooking for the angels, Jacob making Esau's lentils and winning his poor blind father's heart. Didn't love always start with food?

He tapped the counter, glanced at the clock. Three-ten. Business was slow, everyone sleeping. Why he stayed open during the hafsaka when everyone napped, he didn't know. Chava told him: open at three. The women will come, they hate the crowds. But they didn't come, and every day he twiddled away the hour until four with nothing to do.

He marched to the back, pulled out a pot, an onion, a clove of garlic, a clump of rosemary, a sprig of sage, and began cutting. The girl needed help. How would she get a man with six cubes of meat and two chicken wings? Two chicken wings and a canister of salt.

YAKOV SHTARR COULD not believe his good luck. A fellow traveler. This Steven, this Epstein—related to the Zvi Epsteins? the Binny Epsteins?—eager to record Yakov's stories, take down his observations, share his burning questions. It was a mystery, they agreed. What sent these Americans here? A conundrum, a modern dilemma, an ancient quandary. Who could penetrate the innermost reaches of the human heart? They'll try anyway.

They made surveys, questionnaires, and left them at the colleges, yeshivas, Leibel's butcher shop. Also the pizza place, the record store, the cafés on Ben Yehuda, the Burger King in the Malha Mall.

And, miracle of miracles, they got answers.

More than answers, they got tomes. Overnight, they found in the boxes memoirs, autobiographies, plays in three acts. Act 1, I was born. Act 2, I was confused. Act 3, I came here. Sonnets, poems, stories, epics. Yakov and Epstein were inundated with paper, bloated with prose, swamped with explanations: Freud, Heschel, Timothy Leary, Anne Frank. You name it, the pages quoted it.

"It's a lot to read," Yakov said, lugging a box to the door, Epstein behind him carrying two. Cartons with life stories spilling out like foam off a thousand glasses of beer.

"A treasure trove of insight," Epstein said, excited, but maybe not, Yakov thought. Maybe a drowning pool of confusion. Would he be grateful when this was over so he could go back to his Slovenian, who'd waited thirty-four years to see the number two surface on his window one day and know therefrom the meaning of existence? There could be great satisfaction in such a simple conclusion. Maybe he should try it one day, draw a big two with his finger on the foggy bathroom glass when Ruti took her daily soak.

He and Epstein plunked the boxes down, sat, opened, read. Epstein took notes. Yakov took aspirin. So many broken hearts and fractured souls. So many meaningless seders and incompatible roommates and cotton-headed parents and trips to the therapist. Who could survive an American youth?

Behind the wall Yossi blew into a broken harmonica.

DEPARTING FROM A routine of fifteen years, Leibel Frehn left the store, putting Avshalom, the kid from the candy shop across the street, in charge. Ten minutes, Leibel said. Tell the ladies to wait. Give out free slices of salami.

How did he know where the girl lived? How! With his intuition! His insight! His newfound penetration into the workings of the human soul! Also with his not-so-bad English, because it was written on the slip of paper with the recipe, a little address on top like a business card. The same building where his brother-in-law Shmulik lived for ten years before trading up to a four-room in Ramot.

Holding the still-warm pot with two sturdy oven mitts, he climbed the three flights and rang the buzzer. It was brazen, but he was a man on a mission. Who could fall in love without food, without hot, tasty food? Okay, Eve only had an apple. But that was then, this was now.

He waited, the stew so fragrant he could fall in love himself. Not with the girl, heaven forbid, Chava he adored with all his heart, but with his own cooking. Oh, Leibel, Leibeleh, you are so gifted! So talented with the garlic, the onion, the clove!

A shuffling of shoes. The door opened. She looked at him, then at the pot, astonished. "Mr. Frehn, what's this?"

"Don't ask!" he said, handing over the pot, covered handles first. He held up a palm, turned, and ran down the steps. "Return the pot by Friday!"

A MESSAGE FOR the girl, Ruti told Yakov, glum and sweaty from the bath. I can't do it on the phone, it's too hard. I have to give her the news in writing.

So urgent? Yakov said. It must go now?

It's not fair to make her wait. I racked my brains through two baths already. Ruti shook her head. Yakov tipped his in sympathy. It hurt his wife as much as her clients when she couldn't imagine a match; when the bubbles yielded up nothing but the ping! of emptiness. Ah Ruti, Ruti, a heart like a wheel, as big as the sun.

Take a little walk, Yakov. Ruti gave him an envelope and gestured with her chin, a bit of bubble stuck to it. It was endearing, and Yakov watched it pop, then captured the liquid silkiness between two fingers. Go with the young fellow, Ruti sighed. He'll walk with you, and you can continue with your research after. Please, Yakov. I did for you, now you do for me.

Yakov and Epstein left the flat, Yakov secretly relieved. He couldn't bear to read any more. Hundreds of stories pouring out, sentence after sentence, grasping at straw after straw. A bad childhood, a wonderful childhood. A love of tradition, a hunger for the new. A worship of the sun, a tendency to burn. Yakov's head was spinning. But to the zealous Epstein he'd promised they'd return immediately after their errand and continue to mull, collate, compile. Epstein was welcome to stay for supper, Ruti's compote was not from this world.

Epstein, invigorated, agreed. At this rate, he figured, he'd have the whole thing mapped out in days. Then ship everything back to Chicago, be home in a week, his dissertation guaranteed. So what if the stories told no one thing, strayed all over the field, pointed at a thousand reasons, ten thousand? Myriad causes, he'd conclude. Didn't everything spring from myriad causes? And if they formed no particular pattern and resulted in no comprehensible conclusions, what did anyone expect? This was social science! Academia! Dissertations!

Thus buoyed, Epstein emerged onto the street, Yakov trundling behind him. Strauss was alive, people strolling, shopping, wheeling baby carriages. Was it the first day of spring? Who would have known? Epstein was practically flying. His successful research, borne of coincidence giving birth to coincidence: his aunt's neighbor in New York, a Mrs. Trudy Borenstein, passing on to Sandra Epstein the name of the butcher Frehn, who led him to Shtarr, who led him to a gold mine of writerly American youth. The very air of the city was uplifting. Truth was, he'd never been here before, marooned in the double diaspora of the Midwest. He'd never felt the desire.

But now there was this beautiful sunny afternoon, these delightfully colorful streets. They took a right onto Yafo. The scent of cumin floated past, and Epstein turned, tried to follow it with his nose, lost the trail. Where did it go? They walked past an open-air market, a rainbow of ripening peach, plum, and apricot above them. He stifled the impulse to reach up and try to grab it.

"So, Mr. Epstein," Yakov said, the umbrella swinging foolishly at his side. It was time to retire it until next winter. "You like our fair city?"

"Oh yes, yes," Epstein said, pulling his face out of the rainbow sky with effort. Though his nose was still up there. "Everyone's so friendly, so nice."

Yakov nodded. "That's good," he said. "You plan to stay awhile?"

"Oh no. A week at most. I have things at home."

"Mmm," Yakov said. "A wife?"

"No, no, Mr. Shtarr," Epstein said. Where was his nose? Busy, over there, by the halvah stand, investigating the sesame candy. And now, over there, by the chocolate macaroons. He forced himself to yank his face back and talk to the kindly gentleman beside him. "I'm too young for marriage, Mr. Shtarr. In America we wait. Twenty-eight, twenty-nine, thirty, that's plenty of time."

"Mmm," Yakov said. "Here we rush. Twenty, twenty-one, it's time already."

They passed now Miller's Candy, Avshalom jumping in the window. Yakov took a second glance. A lunatic, that boy. He was holding a piece of—what? Licorice? Yakov squinted. Salami. He made a mental note to stop in on the way back to buy his Yosseleh a chocolate bar and maybe something for Ruti to cheer her up. At that, he checked his pocket for Ruti's note. It crinkled forlornly, and he took out his hand.

They continued down Yafo, Epstein riveted by the surroundings. It was hard to keep the young man's attention; he seemed to Yakov preoccupied. A toothless soul was selling strawberries from a jumble of crates, and they bought a half kilo to nosh. Epstein was intent on sniffing them. Yakov let him. Spring. Now that Epstein was leaving, their research nearly finished, did Yakov have any answers? Not really. He'd waded through hundreds of scribbles and found only what he'd already guessed: that they were led here by instinct. Not by philosophy or dogma or intention but instinct. But wasn't that the case with everything? In the end, it was an unknowable thing, a vague urgency that pushed one here or there. What made him go left instead of right, choose coffee instead of tea, take the long way and not the shortcut? It was all a mystery. Who knew why they did anything except in the exact moment of its doing? Once it was done it was past, the flash of certainty vanished; any attempt afterward to explain was a pale guess, nostalgia. But in that first moment, in that one sparkling instant, like ben Berli's two in the window, it was the Truth.

They passed Fishman's Shoes, Bergelson's Jewelry. Outside Steinman's Gifts and Judaica, Hinda Katz looked mournfully at the glass.

"Just window-shopping, Mrs. Katz?" Yakov called.

"Ah, Mr. Shtarr," Hinda said, shaking her head. "Such treasures." She pointed at an etrog box like a mother wanting to adopt just one more child. "If only I could save them."

They reached the building. Yakov smelled it from the entry. They followed the scent, Epstein instantly wrinkling his nose, up the first flight, the second, the third, sniff sniff sniff, as though he'd never sniffed a single thing in his life. All the way to the girl's door, where his nose was moving so fast Yakov feared it might fall off.

Yakov pushed the buzzer. The girl opened the door, looked first at Yakov, then at Epstein, who gazed at her, then at the room behind her, which unfolded before them like Eden. Green and fragrant, alive with all the trees and birds and animals and fruits of the natural world, all waiting to be touched and smelled and tasted.

"Oh my," Epstein said to the girl, flustered, transfixed. He seemed to be swallowing air. "I'm Steven. Epstein. Why haven't we met before?"

She stared at Epstein, a delicate pink blush blooming across her face like a soothing flower. In his pocket, Yakov crushed his wife's envelope. The scent from Leibel's stew rose up from behind and sheltered them like a wedding canopy.

AN HOUR
IN PARADISE

Joan Leegant

AN HOUR
IN PARADISE

Joan Leegant

A NOTE FROM THE AUTHOR

The stories in *An Hour in Paradise* were written mostly over a five-year period, from 1997 to 2002. However, several of the stories reach back almost twenty years to my experience in Jerusalem where I lived for three years in my late twenties and where I became intrigued by—and partly immersed in—the varieties of Jewish religious life. Still, when I began to write fiction I didn't write immediately about Israel or Jewish life; that took another six or seven years. Looking back, I think that I first needed to master more of the craft of fiction writing, and do my apprenticeship, so to speak, before I could delve into material that was so close to the bone.

One of the most joyful aspects of writing these stories is that they are not autobiographical. I was totally free to invent. This is what I find so exhilarating about writing fiction: uncovering and inhabiting another reality that seems as real as my own. This is the fun part, even with all the hard work, and even when a story is dark and disturbing. I love imagining other people's lives. I used to do it all the time in restaurants or on the commuter train, but then you're limited to whoever is at the table next to you or in the seat across the aisle. In fiction, you can conjure anyone, anywhere. My impulse is not to judge or even to understand (which I don't think one can ever really do in life); it's to illuminate. In real life, we're seldom privy to the truth about anyone, even those we're closest to. That's what fiction can give us: a look inside, so that we feel less lonely, less isolated, and sometimes more compassionate.

DISCUSSION QUESTIONS

1. Several of the stories suggest possible visitations by characters who fall outside the bounds of ordinary human experience, such as the mysterious conjoined twins in "The Tenth," and the sister Miri in "The Lament of the Rabbi's Daughters." Do you think such visitations definitely occurred, or are the stories open-ended on this question? How do the meanings of these stories change depending on how the reader answers the preceding question?

2. In "How to Comfort the Sick and Dying," why does Reuven go back to the hospital at the very end? What has happened to him while he was sitting by the expressway? Who might the drunks be, especially the one who hovers closest to him? And what is the role of the italicized sayings sprinkled throughout the story—what voice or wisdom do those sayings reflect?

3. Several of the stories turn on relationships between strangers or cordial (or not so cordial) neighbors: Reuven and Mr. Ash in "How to Comfort the Sick and Dying," Boaz Deri and Rachel Locke in "The Seventh Year," Koenigsman and Mezivosky in "Mezivosky." Consider how each of these relationships works in each story. Who is helping whom, and how? What might these stories be suggesting about the transformative power of such relationships?

4. Mothers and their grown daughters appear in "Lucky in Love" and "Henny's Wedding." How are those mother-daughter relationships portrayed in each of the stories? A mother and adult son are portrayed in "Accounting," filtered through the lens of the father. How do the mothers in each of these stories come across? How do they compare to the fathers in these stories?

5. Why is the last story titled "a modern fable" ("The Diviners of Desire: A Modern Fable")? How is it like a fable versus a straight fiction? What are the elements that make it more fable-like?

6. Speaking of story titles, what are the multiple layers of meaning of the title "Accounting" in that story? What about "Lucky in Love"—were those characters lucky or not?

7. Several of the stories feature storytelling within the story: the bizarre tales Reuven makes up in "How to Comfort the Sick and Dying," and Blanche's stories in "Lucky in Love" about what Solly did on the day each of Blanche's children were born. How do these bits of storytelling function in each piece of fiction—what do they accomplish in terms of illuminating character, mood, tone? What do they suggest about the role of storytelling in relationships?

8. At the end of "Seekers in the Holy Land," the main character, Neal, is left standing, head bowed, holding a wooden bowl for donations. What has happened to him, and why? Consider how the longing to experience the divine runs through other stories in the collection ("The Tenth," "Lament of the Rabbi's Daughters"). What are all these stories suggesting about this longing—and about the possibility of it being satisfied?

9. In "The Seventh Year," Boaz tells his friend Chaim not to be so hard on himself for leaving the early State of Israel and adds, "Believe me, Chaim, you didn't miss anything by leaving." Elsewhere, Boaz recalls his adult son, upon spending a year in Australia, observing that with a computer, a modem, and a phone, he could be living anywhere. Later Boaz recalls Chaim saying in 1959 that "it was a delusion to believe in belonging. What did anyone think they belonged to—a particular piece of ground, call it a homestead, a village, a country. Hadn't they learned that lesson already?" What might this story be saying about the idea of attachment to any one place, especially for Jews after the Holocaust? What do the Biblical passages in the story suggest about the meaning of belonging? Does Boaz "belong" anywhere in particular? Do any of us?

10. Several of the stories make some critical—some might even say harsh—observations about the state of American Jewish life ("Seekers in the Holy Land," "The Lament of the Rabbi's Daughters," "The Seventh Year," "The Diviners of Desire: A Modern Fable"). What are these observations? Do you agree with them?

11. Minor, or secondary, characters often carry more heft than their simple weight in stories. Consider the roles these minor characters

play in their stories—what they add to each story in terms of the meaning or themes: Ellie in "The Tenth"; Noah in "The Seventh Year"; Dov, the tour guide, in "Seekers in the Holy Land"; Yossi in "The Diviners of Desire: A Modern Fable"; the dog in "Mezivosky."

12. In "Accounting," why does Solomon, at the end, "hope that Eliot returned to work in the morning"? What are Solomon's choices at that point? Likewise, at the end of "Henny's Wedding," why does Shirley, knowing her choices, cast her lot with Jack? What do you think of their choices? Do you agree with the characters' assessments that it's too late for them to make different choices?

13. Why do you think Rachel Locke became pregnant by the end of "The Seventh Year"? Was it chance, or had something shifted for her or within the story to allow that to happen? Had Boaz changed in the course of the story? How?

14. One critic described reading these stories as akin to "watching a procession of modern-day Jewish pilgrims in a medieval tapestry: seekers captured in the act of seeking." How does that description fit these stories? What are the people in these tales seeking?

15. The book's title comes from the Yiddish proverb, "Even an hour in paradise is worthwhile." How do you interpret the title in light of these stories?

MORE NORTON BOOKS WITH READING
GROUP GUIDES AVAILABLE

Diana Abu-Jaber, *Arabian Jazz*
Rabih Alameddine, *I, the Divine*
Robert Alter, *Genesis**
Christine Balint, *The Salt Letters**
Brad Barkley, *Money, Love*
Andrea Barrett, *Servants of the Map*
        Ship Fever
        The Voyage of the Narwhal
Charles Baxter, *Shadow Play*
Frederick Busch, *Harry and Catherine*
Abigail De Witt, *Lili*
Jared Diamond, *Guns, Germs, and Steel*
Jack Driscoll, *Lucky Man, Lucky Woman*
Paula Fox, *The Widow's Children*
Judith Freeman, *The Chinchilla Farm*
Betty Friedan, *The Feminine Mystique*
Helon Habila, *Waiting for an Angel*
Sara Hall, *Drawn to the Rhythm*
Patricia Highsmith, *Stranger on a Train*
        Suspension of Mercy
Hannah Hinchman, *A Trail Through Leaves**
Linda Hogan, *Power*
Dara Horn, *In the Image*
Janette Turner Hospital, *The Last Magician*
Helen Humphreys, *The Lost Garden*
Erica Jong, *Fanny*
        Shylock's Daughter
James Lasdun, *The Horned Man*
Don Lee, *Yellow*
Lisa Michaels, *Grand Ambition*
Lydia Minatoya, *The Strangeness of Beauty*
Patrick O'Brian, *The Yellow Admiral**
Jean Rhys, *Wide Sargasso Sea*
Josh Russell, *Yellow Jack*
Kerri Sakamoto, *The Electrical Field*
May Sarton, *Journal of a Solitude**

Susan Fromberg Schaeffer, *Anya*
Buffalo Afternoon
Frances Sherwood, *The Book of Splendor*
Vindication
Gustaf Sobin, *The Fly-Truffler*
In Pursuit of a Vanishing Star
Ted Solotaroff, *Truth Comes in Blows*
Jean Christopher Spaugh, *Something Blue*
Mark Strand and Eavan Boland, *The Making of a Poem*
Barry Unsworth, *Losing Nelson*
Morality Play
Sacred Hunger
Brad Watson, *The Heaven of Mercury*

*Available only on the Norton Web site:
www.wwnorton.com/guides